"It's your grandchild."

"What?" Susan whispered, sinking to the floor.

"Your daughter and my son left it with me yesterday so they could follow some guru to California." Andrew knelt beside Susan. "Hey, are you okay?"

Her nod lacked conviction. "Lisa went to California and left her baby with you?"

"That about sums it up."

"Is it a boy or a girl?"

"A boy." That much Andrew knew. He'd had to change a few diapers in the last forty-eight hours. "Look, Mrs. Montgomery, I work for an oil company and I'm gone for weeks at a time. I can't take care of it. It would be better off with you. Women are much better suited for this kind of thing."

Dear Reader,

We're wrapping up the holiday season for you with four romantic delights!

Our final Women Who Dare title for 1993 is by **Sharon Brondos**. In *Doc Wyoming,* Dr. Dixie Sheldon is enthusiastic about opening her new medical office in the small community of Seaside, Wyoming... until she meets the taciturn local sheriff, Hal Blane. Blane seems determined to prevent her from doing her job. And he especially doesn't want Dixie treating his mother, for fear she'll unearth family secrets he'd prefer to keep buried.

Longtime favorite author **Margaret Chittenden** has penned a charming tale of a haunted house and a friendly spirit in *When the Spirit is Willing.* Laura Daniels, needing to start over after the death of her husband, moves to picturesque Port Dudley to raise her daughter in peace. But peace eludes her when she discovers that her new home is haunted, and the resident ghost appears to be an aggressive matchmaker!

Two of our December Superromance titles will evoke the sort of emotions the holidays are all about. The moving *Angels in the Light,* by **Margot Dalton**, focuses on Abby Malone, who is decidedly unenthusiastic about her latest story assignment. She absolutely does not believe in near-death experiences. But she has no idea how to explain the new Brad Carmichael. He is no longer the selfish, immature boy who'd simply taken off when she'd needed him most, but a sensitive, gentle man who wants Abby to believe anything is possible.

New author **Maggie Simpson** will charm you with *Baby Bonus.* Susan Montgomery's life is turned upside down from the moment Andrew Bradley knocks on her door to inform her that she has a grandson to care for—courtesy of her runaway daughter and his irresponsible son. Even worse, Andrew is determined to stick around to make sure the baby is raised according to the Andrew Bradley School of Grandparenting!

In January, Lynn Erickson, Peg Sutherland, Judith Arnold and Risa Kirk will take you to the Caribbean, North Carolina, Boston and Rodeo Drive! Be sure to come along for the ride!

Holiday Greetings!

Marsha Zinberg,
Senior Editor

Baby Bonus

Maggie Simpson

Harlequin Books

TORONTO • NEW YORK • LONDON
AMSTERDAM • PARIS • SYDNEY • HAMBURG
STOCKHOLM • ATHENS • TOKYO • MILAN
MADRID • WARSAW • BUDAPEST • AUCKLAND

ISBN 0-373-70577-8

BABY BONUS

Copyright © 1993 by Margaret Masten and Saundra Pool.

ABOUT THE AUTHOR

Margaret Masten and Saundra Pool, writing together as Maggie Simpson, are new to the Superromance team of authors. In addition to collaborating on their first book, the two are professional colleagues at an elementary school in Morton, Texas. They have a second Superromance novel under way.

Baby Bonus was a finalist in the 1991 Romance Writers of America unpublished writers' contest.

Along the beaches of Texas lie the fragile remains of sand dollars. Legend links them to the story of Christmas. An image of the star of Bethlehem graces the front of the shell and the Christmas poinsettia is etched on the back. When broken, the shell reveals five tiny doves—symbols of goodwill and peace.

PROLOGUE

IT HAD BEEN a while since anything exciting had happened on Palm Dale Drive. Well, mercy, I'd say it must've been eight years, at least. That's when Milly Adams got caught in her backyard with a city councilman. And they weren't mowing the lawn, either. But after Susan Montgomery moved in across the street and Andrew Bradley showed up with his surprise, things hadn't been the same in our quiet neighborhood.

That surprise made me the center of attention at my bimonthly meeting of the Corpus Christi Senior Citizens' Quilting Club. With only four regulars in attendance, our conversation at most meetings was about who ached where, how badly, and which doctor prescribed the newest medication. As much as I hate to admit it, Bertha Clark always seemed to be able to come up with the most bizarre ailment and the most expensive cure.

It was a warm winter morning when the four of us gathered around the Lone Star quilt top down at the Senior Citizens' Center and took out our needles and thread. As we got settled I knew they were all dying to hear what had been going on across the street from my house, but I wanted to let the suspense build so I sat

*quietly threading my needle. Besides, it had gotten so
I could concentrate on only one task at a time.*

*Out of the corner of my eye, I could see Bertha
fidgeting, until apparently she'd contained herself as
long as she could. "What do you think will ever become of the baby?" she asked, breaking my train of
thought.*

*"Oh, I don't know," I replied, giving my needle an
assertive push through the batting. "It really isn't any
of my business."*

*"I declare, Agnes Johnson! You hem and haw
about it every chance you get. And, it is, too, your
business." Bertha tried unsuccessfully to tuck a white
strand of hair back into the bun at the nape of her
neck. "After all, you've helped with that baby for
weeks."*

*"What baby?" asked Era Sullivan, another mem-
ber of our group. "I knew I shouldn't have gone on
that tour. Every time I leave, I miss something."*

Tour, my eye, *I thought, but that's Era for you. At
my age, I have a little trouble seeing close work, so I
adjusted my bifocals. Then I turned to Era who would
have missed everything even if she hadn't gone to Eu-
rope for three months to visit relatives. On a clear day
she stays lost in her own house. And it's small. "I'll fill
you in just as soon as I get this knot out of my
thread." It only took me a minute. "I've never seen
two more unlikely parents in my life," I began, "or
two people more suited for each other than Susan
Montgomery and Andrew Bradley. I have a feeling
about those two."*

Totally confused by now, Era asked, "Who's Susan Montgomery?"

Bertha interjected, "Oh, you know who she is, Era. She's that young schoolteacher who moved across the street from Agnes. The one who looks sixteen but is supposed to be thirty-six."

I wasn't about to let Bertha Clark steal my thunder so I picked up the description from there. "She's kind of quiet and reserved. Been there several days before I got a chance to meet her. Betsy—you know my granddaughter Betsy, the assistant principal at Hodges Elementary School—she's the one who told Susan about the house for rent across from mine. I can't remember the name of the town Susan came from, but it's up on the Plains somewhere. She moved here . . . July, I think it was, because it had gotten really hot and muggy. Anyway, she came to try and find her grown daughter."

"She has a grown daughter?" Era wrinkled her brow in bewilderment. "She's not old enough to have a grown daughter if she's only sixteen."

Bertha rolled her eyes. "She just looks sixteen, Era," she corrected.

"From what I can gather," I continued, "the daughter's in her late teens. She just took off and ran away more than a year ago. Susan searched the whole state until she finally tracked her down here."

"What happened to Susan's husband?" Era inquired.

"She hasn't said, and I haven't asked. But I've got a feeling there's a story there."

The fourth member of our quilting group, Virginia Black, had been sitting quietly taking it all in. With the exception of myself, Virginia was the best quilter in Corpus Christi. She broke a thread apart with her teeth before she asked, "Now how did Susan learn about the baby?"

Bertha stopped massaging her wrist and jumped right in. "Virginia, I swear, you're getting senile. Agnes told us about that last time."

"That's been two weeks ago and I had to leave early for my beauty-shop appointment, so I missed part of the story," Virginia reminded her. "Indulge me. Besides, Era hasn't heard the whole story, either."

Leaving a wake of lilac in the air, Bertha stood up and circled the frame to inspect our quilting before she gave a hhmmph and settled back to work. She didn't like having her feathers ruffled by Virginia, primarily because Virginia lived on exclusive Ocean Drive and could keep her mouth shut. I suspect it gave Bertha an inferiority complex.

I knew Virginia was a little skeptical of the whole affair with the baby, so my feelings weren't hurt when she inquired, "How would you know what went on, Agnes?"

"I'm not sure about all the little bitty details," I confessed, "but from what I can piece together from what Betsy, Susan and Andrew told me later, I have a pretty good idea. And I saw a lot of it myself. I well remember that Sunday afternoon in late October when Mr. Bradley pulled into the driveway across the street. He's a most attractive man."

*Leaning forward to emphasize my words, I re-
peated,* "Most attractive. In his early forties, I'd say—
when men begin to look their best." *The ladies nodded in agreement.* "He's on the tall side and carries
himself well. One of those men who takes charge. A
lot like my James used to be." *I paused, thinking
about the similarities to my recently departed husband.* "Hair's a different color though, kind of light
brown." *I stopped to rethread my needle... and for
effect.*

Era clapped her hands in front of her breasts. "Oh,
this is better than my soap opera. Do go on."

"I was in the yard, down on my hands and knees
pulling the weeds out from around those yellow chrysanthemums I set out three years ago. I saw the whole
thing. I had on that feed sack bonnet like we all made
for Pioneer Day and a pair of old—"

"Agnes, for Pete's sake, we don't care what you
were wearing. What happened?" *Bertha interrupted.*

*I had their attention now, so I settled back in my
chair to begin the latest installment of the story I knew
they were impatient to hear.* "I'll just start at the beginning for Era's benefit. It was pretty obvious Andrew was flustered when he got out of that little red
automobile."

CHAPTER ONE

HE WOULD HAVE LIKED to kick Chris's irresponsible butt. Of all the dumb, fool stunts his nineteen-year-old son had pulled over the years, this one had hit the hardest—like a class-four hurricane. He was still reeling from the impact. A baby! His grandchild!

Clutching the steering wheel of his sports car, Andrew Bradley double-checked the faded number stenciled on the curb of Palm Dale Drive before pulling into the narrow, shell-covered driveway. In a few minutes, the knots in the back of his neck would dissolve. He'd be able to relax. Just as soon as he found Susan Montgomery.

He swung cramped legs out of the car and stood up. The sweltering coastal heat surrounded him like an unwelcome blanket as he turned to study the tiny bundle sleeping peacefully in its car seat. "Why couldn't you have done that hours ago?" he mumbled.

The drive from Houston to Corpus Christi had been a nightmare. The baby had cried until it saw the skyline of the city silhouetted in the hazy southern distance. Then it dropped off in a blissful slumber, its tiny lips sucking on an imaginary nipple. He wondered if he should risk waking it or wait to see if Mrs.

Montgomery was home first? He'd called before leaving Houston, but when a woman's voice answered, he'd hung up. He sure didn't want to risk warning her he was coming. It might be a case of like mother, like daughter.

Deciding to leave the baby in the car, he left the air conditioner running, hurried up the narrow path through the tall grass and took the wooden steps to the white porch in one bound. His index finger glued to the doorbell of the Victorian-style house, he studied his surroundings.

Nail heads protruded from the rails lining the front of her porch and grayed wood lay revealed beneath the curls of white paint. Hurricane shutters framing the long multipaned windows were only a faded reminder of the deep forest green that had once trimmed the house. But the neighborhood looked peaceful rather than run-down.

Across the street, a plump older woman sat on a short stool in the middle of a bed of yellow chrysanthemums. At least he guessed she was older because of her slow movements as she pulled at stray weeds. Andrew couldn't tell much else about her because she had on a bright turquoise flowered bonnet that kept turning toward him. The neighborhood busybody, he supposed, turning back toward the door when he heard the knob rattle.

The screen opened, and a young woman with long dark hair stared at him with impatient brown eyes. "May I help you?" she inquired with a soft, Southwestern accent—the same accent he'd heard earlier on the phone before he'd hung up without a word.

He was momentarily speechless. The woman standing before him couldn't have been the baby's grandmother. She wasn't at all what he'd expected, neither old nor wrinkled. Her silky skin was marked only by a tiny scar on her lower right cheek. For some reason, he'd expected her to have gray hair pulled back into a bun. Instead, it seemed to float around her head like a curly crown. She didn't have a big lap covered by an apron. In fact, he'd bet a hundred-dollar bill she wore no underwear beneath her purple gauze dress. This wasn't the right woman.

"May I help you?" she repeated when he didn't answer.

He thought of several ways she could help him. But today he didn't have the time to pursue this woman, no matter how desirable she looked with the light behind her outlining her barely hidden curves. Today he had a different mission. "I'm looking for a Susan Montgomery."

Glancing up at him with an exasperated expression, the woman pushed away a long curl that had fallen over her eye. "So you said."

"Is this the correct address? For Susan Montgomery, I mean."

"Yes, it is."

"Then would you please tell her Andrew Bradley is here to see her." He stressed the "please" out of irritation rather than courtesy.

She studied him curiously for several seconds before she spoke. "Is the name Andrew Bradley supposed to be significant?"

"Only that it's my name, and I need to see her. Lady, would you mind getting her?" He didn't like repeating himself on a good day and that was the last thing he was having at present. He was dead tired. Too tired for the niceties of pleasant conversation.

"There's no need for me to go anywhere," she said. "I'm Mrs. Montgomery."

"You can't be," Andrew blurted out. "You aren't old enough."

"You must think I'm deaf as well as old." Susan indicated his finger which was still pressing the doorbell.

Considering the squalling he had been subjected to for the past several hours, he had been oblivious to the ringing noise coming from inside the house and didn't really feel like apologizing for it. Instead, he jerked his finger off the tiny button and got right to the point. "Are you Lisa's mother?"

The woman's face underwent a change as Andrew watched. Her tired eyes flashed with something that resembled disbelief, then hope. Her small chin tilted up as she reached out and grasped his arm. "Lisa? Have you seen Lisa?" she pleaded. "Is she okay?"

He disengaged his arm from her slender but strong fingers. "Yes, yester—"

"Where is she?" the woman demanded.

"As far as I know, she's on her way to California with my son."

"To California?" A puzzled look wrinkled her forehead. "But I thought she was here in—"

"It's hot out here. May I come in?" he interrupted, impatient to get this over with and be on his way.

"Oh, I'm sorry, I wasn't thinking. Come on in. What about Lisa? I've searched for her with no luck. You're the first person I've talked to who's seen her in the past three months." Leading the way into what had once been a parlor, she continued to talk as she tiptoed barefoot around cardboard cutouts, poster board, stencils and piles of paraphernalia that he couldn't identify.

Andrew followed her into the room. He was so busy gawking at the clutter on every available surface that he slipped on a piece of wax paper he hadn't noticed lying on the floor. Catching himself by grabbing the corner of a table, he exclaimed, "What in the...?" Instinctively, he stepped sideways without looking at the floor and crushed a red colored marker, sending shards of plastic in all directions.

The woman glanced over her shoulder at him and, seeing his predicament, shook her head and sighed. "You have to watch out for the mess," she said, grabbing a roll of paper towels before kneeling on the polished oak floor. Picking up the pieces of the marker and moving other things out of his way, she explained, "I'm preparing for class tomorrow." She dropped the pieces in a bowl of odds and ends sitting on the tabletop.

A terminal neat freak himself, he shook his head at the disarray. "I take it that organization and neatness aren't the main topics." Immediately, he regretted his rudeness. Just because he was having to mop up after one more of Christopher's mess-ups was no excuse for his nasty comment. Besides, the woman probably didn't know about the baby.

The baby! "Damn!" Andrew burst out of the house, the screen door crashing behind him, sprinted across the lawn, jerked open the car door and peered into the interior. The baby was still fast asleep. He breathed a sigh of relief before unbuckling the infant seat and switching off the engine. Even though he bumped the door handle with the seat, the baby stayed fast asleep, blissfully unaware as Andrew jockeyed it and the blue diaper bag into position. How women managed to carry all of that stuff was beyond his comprehension. In just a few hours on Friday, he had reconfirmed his suspicion that he wasn't any good at this parenting stuff. That's why he'd decided to do the decent thing and bring it to its grandmother. Grandmothers were supposed to be good with babies.

But he had his doubts about the grandmother waiting on the porch with an amazed expression as he walked up the path, balancing his slumbering cargo in one hand and swinging the large quilted bag in the other. This grandmother was young, beautiful and under any other circumstances he would have found her very desirable.

"What do you have?" she asked.

"A baby."

"I can see that," she said with an edge in her voice. She held the front door open for him, peeping inside the blanket as he walked by. "Is it yours?"

"No!" He replied curtly as he maneuvered his laden frame through the doorway.

"Baby-sitting?"

"Absolutely not."

"Then whose baby is it?"

Inside the house, he turned and thrust the baby toward her. "It's yours now." In just a minute he would have accomplished what he'd set out to do and be out of this place and headed back home. He didn't have time for a baby, he reasoned, and wouldn't know what to do with one even if he had the time. When he left Corpus Christi, he intended to do it alone.

Alone.

In peace and quiet.

"What do you mean, it's mine?" she asked, cocking her head to one side in confusion while she clasped the handle to keep the car seat with its precious cargo from falling on the rug.

"It's your grandchild."

She stared at him in disbelief. "My what?"

"You heard me."

"I may have heard, but that doesn't mean I understand." Big brown eyes dared him to repeat his assertion.

Realizing she didn't comprehend the situation, he drew a breath, and, weary of the whole mess, resolved to put an end to her confusion. "It's your grandchild, courtesy of my son Chris and your daughter Lisa."

He felt like an actor in a bad soap opera as he stood in the center of the parlor and watched myriad emotions play across Susan's face as if they were ripples on a pond. Finally she whispered, "What?" and sank to the floor with the baby.

"They left it with me yesterday so they could follow some guru off to California to expand their consciousness, or some such bull." He knelt on one knee beside her and studied her expressive face. "Hey, are you okay?"

Her nod lacked conviction as she studied the sleeping baby. "Lisa went to California and left her baby with you?"

"That about sums it up."

She turned back the thin cotton blanket covering the baby. "Is it a boy or girl?" The soft scent of baby powder floated from the tiny bundle filling the narrow space between them.

"A boy." He knew *that* for a fact. He'd had to change a few diapers in the past forty-eight hours and discovered that when a diaper was folded back, the baby thought it was a signal from nature. After being sprayed twice and turning a diaper backward only to ruin the sticky tapes when he tried to correct his error, Andrew had learned to be more careful with the diapering. It was something he'd seldom had to do for Chris, and his expertise had evidently not improved with the years.

"What's his name?" She gingerly traced the outline of his jaw with her finger.

"Cory, Calten, ah, I . . . let me look." He stood up and dug into the pocket of his pale blue-and-white knit golf shirt. Finding nothing, he reached into the back pocket of his slacks and retrieved his wallet. He thumbed through his credit cards until he found what he was looking for. "I wrote it down," he assured her.

"You can't remember his name?" She looked at him in disbelief. "And he's your grandson?"

Ignoring her comment, he triumphantly produced a folded scrap of yellow legal pad. "Here it is. Its name is Colton Andrew Bradley. Born July fourth," he read, before tossing the paper on one of the few clear areas of the coffee table.

"Colton," Susan whispered to the sleeping baby as she trailed a finger down its soft cheek. She unbuckled the harness strap that confined the baby and lifted it over his down-covered head. "He's darling."

Andrew thought that was a matter of opinion, having been kept on the run by the "little darling" for the past three days. He had scrambled in his efforts to keep the baby dry, keep it fed and keep it quiet only to find he had to repeat the process again and again. He couldn't believe people actually got something else done, like sleep, when a baby was around.

Susan still looked slightly dazed as she picked up the baby and stood up to confront Andrew. "You're sure Lisa is his mother?"

He'd never considered she would doubt him. "Of course, I'm sure." Andrew unzipped the side pocket of the diaper bag and produced an official-looking document that he'd found when he'd stopped at a roadside park and rummaged through the compartments trying to find a miracle to stop the crying. He didn't find the miracle, but he pulled out what he did find. "Here's a hospital record. Read it."

Cuddling the baby with one arm, Susan reached for the certificate he offered. She bit her bottom lip as she read the scanty information.

Andrew shifted his weight. Emotional women made him uncomfortable. He could see the tears gathered in her eyes as she silently handed the document back to him. He felt sorry for her. This whole affair must have been a surprise, but he didn't know what to say or do to make her feel better.

Not wanting her to think he was some kind of an ogre, he started to explain his position, as much to himself as to her. "Look, Mrs. Montgomery, I work for an oil company offshore in the Gulf of Mexico. I'm gone for a week at a time so I can't take care of a baby. It would be better off with you. Women are meant for this kind of thing."

Visibly, her spine stiffened and her eyebrows raised, daring him to continue. Indifferent to her body language, he went on, afraid that if he paused, he'd weaken and do something he'd regret later. "Of course, you had some problems the first time around with your daughter. No girl who was raised half-right would abandon her baby and go halfway across the continent looking for some mystic experience."

Susan glared back at him with cool eyes that only moments before had melted with warmth when they swept over the baby. "The same could be said for your son, Mr. Bradley. No man who was reared half-right would leave his baby, either."

Andrew flinched. He hadn't meant for his words to indict her. It's just that he felt victimized. Still, he was glad she had a little life in her. She'd need it to take care of a baby, he thought. For the record, he stated, "I didn't raise Chris. His mother gets the credit for that."

"Oh. Do you mean you skipped out on your son, or did you dump everything on your wife, since women are meant for that kind of thing?"

Maybe she had a little too much life in her, he decided. He didn't feel like explaining his personal situation to a virtual stranger, so he settled for the simpler, "I'm divorced." He intended to stay that way, too. "Marriage is a mistake I don't intend to repeat."

"I'm sure womankind will regret the loss," Susan mumbled under her breath.

"Look, I don't have time to stand around and trade insults. I've got a long drive ahead of me." He had already stayed longer than he'd intended. "Here's my card, if you need to get in touch with me." He dropped the card on an end table and started for the door.

"Wait, Mr. Bradley, I'm sorry. This is all so overwhelming—this finding out I'm a grandmother. Lisa had a baby and I wasn't even there. I didn't even know anything about it." She laid her hand on his arm to prevent him from leaving. "Tell me about Chris and Lisa before you go. Please, tell me everything you know."

The pleading look awash in brimming tears drew him up short. He guessed they probably weren't the first tears she had shed for the irresponsible Lisa. Surprised to find he wanted to wipe them away for her, to erase the pain from her dark brown eyes, he found the emotion so unsettling that he shoved it to the back of his mind, the way he did all the other feelings he didn't want to deal with, and turned to look out the window. "There's not much to tell. I only see Chris a few times a year. Usually when he's in trouble or needs some money."

Susan nodded and sank down in a large oak rocker. Her eyes begged him to continue as she settled the baby against her breast.

"Back last year he told me about this girl he was seeing, but I didn't know anything about a baby until the day before yesterday." He ran his fingers through his well-combed hair when he recalled how overwhelmed he'd felt when he came in, tired, ready to shower and fall into his oversize bed only to find his house occupied by his son and new family. "Chris and Lisa were waiting on me when I came in from a week offshore." The quiet that followed his explanation was punctuated by the creak of straining wood and the muffled thud of rockers against the oak floor.

"What happened?" she prompted when he paused to study the disturbing picture she and the baby made as they rocked.

"Chris said they had been staying with friends, but it hadn't worked out. He didn't tell me in so many words, but I suspect the friends got tired of the bumming."

Susan interrupted. "Why didn't he go to his mother's, since she was the one who reared him?"

"She remarried and moved to North Carolina last year." Andrew remembered the relief he'd felt when she moved. "Anyway, Chris pulled out his usual bull and told me he was ready to settle down. He just needed to find a job and a place to stay."

Andrew stopped, not wanting to expose any more feelings of anger and betrayal.

"What about Lisa?" Susan traced Colton's chubby cheeks with her fingertip.

"What about her?"

"Is she okay? Is she happy? How does she look?"

"I guess she's okay. She looked all right." Andrew realized that he had hardly talked to the girl, so he couldn't tell her mother much of anything. "She really didn't say much, just held the baby and..."

Susan glanced up at him from beneath thick, dark lashes clumped together with tears. The lost, forlorn look caused a renewed stirring deep inside him that he couldn't identify. It wasn't sexual desire. At forty-two he'd had enough experience he could recognize that. This was more elusive. In fact, he'd probably only imagined it. He hadn't had lunch. That was it.

She interrupted his thoughts. "Why did you let them go off and leave Colton with you?"

"Let them? You must be out of your mind." With renewed fervor, the mysterious feeling forgotten, he paced back and forth in front of the rocker. "Early the next morning, Chris said he'd found a job possibility listed in the paper." Andrew's eyes hardened.

Susan nodded attentively.

"Of course, he didn't have a car—he'd wrecked his—so he borrowed mine. Lisa said she needed to get a few things for the baby, and would I mind keeping him while she went with Chris. Hell, yes, I minded. I didn't know what to do with a baby."

"You were trapped."

"I knew Chris was broke—he always is—so I gave him a hundred dollars." Andrew sighed. It seemed that he was constantly giving Chris things and money, but the boy had never shown an ounce of appreciation in his nineteen years. "They were supposed to be gone a couple of hours. The baby woke up screaming while they were backing out of the driveway."

Susan frowned sympathetically. "I think I'm beginning to get the picture."

"About noon I got a telegram, and it sure wasn't the singing kind. It said they had left my car at the bus station."

"At the bus station? What did you do?"

Andrew continued. "I got busy. A neighbor kept him—" Andrew nodded toward Colton "—while a friend took me to the station to get my car. When I read the note Chris had left in the seat, I knew I was in trouble. They had gone to California. I checked to find out which bus they'd taken and where it was going, because I planned to haul them right back to Houston and their baby."

His temples throbbed as he recalled his initial anger and disbelief. A look of resignation settled over his face as he continued his story. "Not one damn ticket had been purchased in their names, or to anyone who remotely fitted their description, so I couldn't put out a trace to find them. I checked the airport. Nothing! They're not missing, so the police won't get involved."

"So you don't really know where Lisa is?" Susan's voice faded.

"No, I'm afraid not. I'm not even sure they're in California. That's what the note said, but for all I know, they might have been trying to mislead me."

"I see. And how did you find me?"

"I finally remembered the name of the town where Lisa said she grew up. I called the county sheriff to see if he had any information about you."

"And?"

"I would've had better luck trying to get a steak from a starving dog."

Susan smiled. "Sonny was just trying to protect me. You know how a small town can be."

"No, but I found out. I was so desperate that I called an old friend in the police department. He got me your address and phone number here within half an hour."

"I moved to Corpus Christi because this was where Lisa was the last time I heard from her. She sent a postcard in June telling me she was okay and for me not to worry."

"Well, you just missed her. She and Chris came to Houston in July after the baby was born."

"That figures. It seems like I've been just days behind her for the past year. The police haven't been a lot of help because she's eighteen now and left home of her own free will," she said matter-of-factly, nudging Colton's tiny hand until it gripped her little finger. "He's so helpless. How could they just up and leave him?" she asked incredulously.

"Who knows? Of course, it hasn't had much of a life as it is, living like they were. A baby needs stability, a mother to take care of it and a father to support it. Chris can't support himself, much less a baby."

"Where did they get the money for the trip to California, or wherever they went? Your hundred dollars couldn't get them very far."

"Chris doesn't have a pot to pee in, so I know he didn't pay for it." Andrew instantly regretted his crudeness. At least he'd toned down the expression, he thought. "He probably conned someone into loaning him the money, or hitched a ride with someone. Who knows?"

Susan's eyes narrowed. "You don't think they did anything illegal, do you?"

"I don't put much of anything past Christopher, but I don't think he'd stoop to something that low." Andrew turned and looked out the window at the woman working in her well-tended yard. She had moved to the flower bed on the opposite side of the walk and positioned her stool for a better view of Susan's house.

"What do we do now?" Susan inquired behind him.

CHAPTER TWO

"WE?" Andrew turned to face her. "I'm going back to Houston. I can't take care of it. In four days I have to be back at work offshore." He'd be glad to get there, too. The production platform conformed to a schedule. Unlike one baby he knew.

"In other words, you're saying that Colton is *my* responsibility now."

"Uh...yeah, I guess I am." He avoided her accusing eyes. "This is the best solution."

As if she had heard enough, Susan rose from the rocker and carried her sleeping bundle over to the sofa. "Don't you worry, precious, I'll take care of you."

Andrew felt like a jerk as he edged toward the door, gingerly stepping around and over the junk. It wasn't that he was unfeeling or that he didn't want to help, he was just out of his element. He had thought he was doing the best thing for it by bringing it here. Now, this woman was making it sound as if he was abandoning it. He tried again. "I don't think you understand about my job. This isn't a good time for me. I have to be at work Thursday."

"Good for you. I have to be at work in the morning." Cooing to Colton, Susan settled him onto the afghan-covered sofa. She plumped up overstuffed pillows and propped them around the baby before turning to Andrew. "I'm not prepared for this, either, you know."

The thought that she couldn't take care of the baby had never dawned on him. Not even when he'd called to make sure she was home before starting the long drive to Corpus Christi. "Can't you take some time off?"

"Now is hardly the time," she explained. "I'm being evaluated this week. Tomorrow, in fact."

Andrew moved away from the door. "What has that got to do with it?"

"This is my first year teaching here, and I have to do well on this evaluation. If I don't, I could be bumped from the career ladder and lose my extra stipend, or worse, lose my job if there are layoffs. Since I'm not independently wealthy, I can't afford either option."

Andrew wasn't sure if that was a cue, but he had planned to do his part. "If money's the problem, don't worry. I'll help with any expenses you incur."

"That would be appreciated, but right now, that isn't the point," Susan said. "The point is that before morning, I have to find someone to baby-sit Colton." She sat on the floor beside the sofa and thumbed through the pile of the Sunday paper until she found the classified section.

"What're you doing?" he asked.

"I'm looking for a day-care center or someone who will keep infants in their home." Susan spread the paper on her lap and trailed down the columns with her finger.

"You can't be serious." Andrew reached down and began stacking and folding the various sections of the newspaper, including the one Susan was holding.

She made a grab for the paper as he slid it from her lap. "I don't have a choice. Since I've only lived in this town for four months, I don't know any baby-sitters. This is the best I can do."

Andrew deposited the paper in a basket near the end of the sofa. While he was there, he slipped several of the wide-tipped markers into a plastic margarine container sitting on the end table.

"Mr. Bradley, I'm not through with those markers," Susan said as she dug the newspaper out of the wicker basket.

Andrew hadn't meant to offend her, but he didn't know how she could tolerate the clutter. He'd thought he was helping her.

Susan found a number and picked up the phone.

"No, you don't." Andrew reached out, took the receiver and replaced it. "You can't leave it with some strangers we know nothing about. I won't have it."

"You won't have it?" Susan asked rhetorically. "I thought Colton was my responsibility now. You said you didn't have time for him."

"I don't, but…" Andrew paused. "We can't let just anybody take care of it. We need references and—"

"Then what do you suggest?"

"I don't know. Don't you know some grandmotherly type who would keep it?"

"No, I don't."

"What about the lady across the street? The one who was working in her yard when I came in but seemed more interested in this one. She watched me like she was a paid detective."

"Agnes Johnson? She's a dear, but she could never keep Colton. I wouldn't dream of imposing on her that way. Besides, she has a job at the Senior Citizens' Center here in town."

Andrew had heard all kinds of things about day-care centers and their staffs. Not many of them were complimentary. He couldn't stand the thought of just anyone taking care of the baby. It was his grandson, after all—he had a responsibility. He was trapped. Again. He was beginning to recognize the feeling.

He looked down at the parquet floor without noticing its intricate design, then looked again at the baby sleeping peacefully on the sofa. Only an occasional soft moan floated through the silent room. This was Sunday. He didn't have to be at work for four days. "I can't believe I'm saying this..." he said, voicing his thoughts aloud.

Susan's expression turned to one of dismay as he continued, "I could come back in the morning and...sort of watch him while you're at work." He rushed on before he could change his mind. "I'll come up with something by then. I'll find a place to stay here in town, and I'll be back in the morning." He ran his fingers through his neatly trimmed hair. "What time do you leave to go to work?"

"Around seven-thirty, but—"

"I'll be here," he said, opening the door and closing it quickly before he could renege, as he suddenly felt like doing. What had possessed him in there?

On his way down the steps he halfheartedly waved to the lady across the street, then climbed into his oven-hot car and settled back. He didn't mind its heat. It was such a relief not to hear any sound for a change. Tomorrow was likely to be another day of crying.

He touched his fingers to his temples just at the thought. Why had he said he would come back?

It would only be for one day, he reminded himself. After a good night's sleep, he could handle it. He had always been able to handle whatever came along. This was no different.

As Andrew backed out of the driveway, he wondered why his son couldn't have been more like himself. But, no. Not Chris. Andrew had always given everything to his son, everything except responsibility. Maybe that was the problem. Chris had never seemed ready for responsibility. Now, Andrew had another big mess to handle.

And this one cried.

DECIDING SHE could no longer bargain with time, Susan crawled out of bed and, eyes swollen half-shut, felt her way to the bathroom. A shower would erase most of the signs left by the previous day's trauma. When Lisa had run away from home, Susan had thought she'd cried until there were no tears left. She'd been mistaken. Last night had proved that. It had been three o'clock before she'd finally fallen asleep with Colton tucked safely against her side.

The warm water made her feel better, but it also woke her up enough to recall the handsome guest of the afternoon before, and the fact he was coming back. He hadn't even given her a chance to say no, even though she'd really had no recourse.

That he was used to getting his way, or thought he should, was evident in his every gesture, every word— even the way he walked. After she found a baby-sitter, she would have no regrets if she never saw him again, she decided, pushing aside the floral curtains that surrounded the claw-footed tub and stepping onto a deep plush rug. It had been a long time since she had reacted as strongly to another person—positively or negatively. Mr. Bradley definitely evoked the latter reaction. If it weren't for his looks, she thought, the man would have very little going for him.

No doubt he thought women found his masculine assertiveness appealing, she decided as she wound her damp hair up on top of her head and out of her face while she applied her makeup. But his manner was irritating, to say the least.

She dressed quickly, then hurried downstairs and rushed about stacking schoolbooks and boxes on the kitchen table. She couldn't afford to forget anything today. The evaluation was too important.

Susan was already running late when tiny cries emanated from the upstairs bedroom. Sprinting back up before Colton could work himself off the bed, Susan promised herself she would get organized before tomorrow morning. By the time she paused to catch her breath and study the waking baby, he was again sleeping peacefully. "You little bluffer," she whispered.

Her heart swelled with love, bringing a lump to her throat as she observed his little rosebud mouth pursed in sucking movements beneath a tiny turned-up nose. Fine brown curls stuck to the side of his head where he had lain. He was beautiful. He reminded her of how Lisa had looked as a baby.

Lisa, the daughter she had not seen in eighteen months. The daughter who disappeared from her life without a word of explanation. Oh, there had been the arguments about college and the crowd Lisa was running around with—the usual teenage things. They shouldn't have been enough to cause Lisa to run away. No, there had to be something more. Every day, Susan faced the painful thought that her daughter had not trusted her enough to confide in her.

Susan figured she had been too permissive as a parent, but she had only been trying to be a balance for George, Lisa's father. Most of the time he wanted little to do with rearing his daughter, but occasionally, to make up for his neglect, he became the authoritarian parent—usually at the wrong time, in Susan's opinion.

Three postcards, all with different postmarks, had been her only contact with Lisa. Again, her daughter had gotten the upper hand. Susan didn't know what to make of this latest development.

The last postcard she'd received lay where she'd left it the previous night on the nightstand by the bed. She reached for its frayed edges, and once again scanned the meager words she'd committed to memory after four months of reading and rereading.

Mom,
I'm fine. Moved in with a wonderful guy and looking for a job. Will write more when I get my head straight. Don't worry.

Lisa

P.S. I've got a big surprise.

Leave it to Lisa to cut everything down to the bare bones. "Don't worry." Just what was she supposed to do? Grin and bear it? Well, that's what she'd done. Lisa probably wasn't even aware of the havoc she'd caused, first taking off without a goodbye, now abandoning her baby. Leaving home and moving in with a man she hardly knew was one thing. Susan could forgive her for that. But the baby! That was different. She wondered if Colton was the big surprise. Why hadn't Lisa let her know?

And where was she? She might or might not have gone to California. Regardless of where Lisa was, Susan couldn't very well pack her bags and head out there. She'd spent almost all of her savings moving to Corpus Christi, and besides, she had a teaching contract to fulfill. Teaching was one of her few successes in life—perhaps because she was rational about it. Not like her personal life, she thought wryly. Maybe she was getting another chance with Colton. Her grandson.

Goodness, she thought, as the impact of being a grandmother began to sink in. She was too young to be a grandmother. Mr. Bradley had been right about that.

She still felt like an adolescent, sometimes—barely capable of taking care of herself, much less another person. No, that's not true, she realized, remembering the years she'd taken care of Lisa's father, who had been more of a liability than a help while Lisa was growing up. Occasionally she indulged in the fantasy of having another person to share responsibilities. But that was all it was, a fantasy.

While she was lost in thought, Colton awoke and stared at her with big blue eyes. He had his grandfather Bradley's eyes, she decided. Velvet eyes, soft and deep. Those eyes were impossible to ignore. And Colton had them, too.

How could Lisa and—what had Mr. Bradley said his son's name was? Christopher? Chris?—how could they just leave this adorable little boy, Susan wondered as she changed his diaper. Despite Lisa's faults, she had been a delight as a child. What had caused her to be such an irresponsible teenager?

More puzzling was the fact that they left him with Mr. Bradley. Even though he was the baby's grandfather, he was obviously uncomfortable taking care of Colton. He didn't seem the type to tolerate the confusion and mess that came with a baby. Or markers on the floor.

That the baby was left with him rather than her hurt deeply. Why? Didn't Lisa trust her enough to care for her own grandchild? Maybe going to California had been a spur of the moment decision, she tried to reassure herself.

Picking up Colton, she kissed his soft cheek. "Yes, kid, you *are* better off with me," she told him as she carefully descended the stairs, yawning widely.

Last night, of all nights, she'd needed her sleep, and today, of all days, she needed to be able to concentrate on her work. That was going to be difficult, if not impossible, after the curve she had been thrown last evening.

In the kitchen, Susan balanced Colton in one arm as she sterilized and prepared his bottle. It felt good to hold a baby again, even if the circumstances weren't exactly of her own choosing. With the day's formula prepared and safely stored in the refrigerator, she glanced at the ceramic teapot clock that hung above the range. She wouldn't have time for breakfast.

The doorbell surprised her as she started to pour a cup of coffee, causing her to spill a few drops on the countertop. Ignoring the mess, she hurried to answer the door.

Trying to hold the baby bottle under her chin so Colton could continue to suck, she used her free hand to unlatch the door. Mr. Bradley's large grin greeted her. "Come on in."

"Good morning." He was even better looking than she'd remembered, but his sun-streaked hair and amused expression as he looked her up and down didn't make up for his words. "A rough night?"

Refusing to begin the day with a confrontation, she ignored the provocation. "You don't know the half of it. Here, would you mind feeding Colton while I drink my coffee?" She handed him the baby before heading back to the kitchen.

He dropped the baby blanket, then awkwardly re-wrapped Colton as he followed her into the country style kitchen, stopping before the round oak table. Hands full, he pulled a chair out with his foot and sat down.

Embarrassed about the clutter that was strewn over the tabletop, Susan decided to mention it before he did. "Let me move some of this out of your way." She piled the mail in a basket and dropped a few pencils in a cup before turning to face him.

He was wearing a different shirt than he'd worn the day before. More to cover her nervousness than because she cared, she nodded toward his clothes. "Did you go shopping last night?"

"No need to. I always carry a change of clothes and a shaving kit. In my line of work, I never know where I might end up," he explained.

"A Boy Scout, huh? Always prepared. Would you like a cup of coffee?"

"I can get it." Andrew consulted the kitchen clock. "You'd better get a move on or you'll be late."

Susan looked at the clock again. "Darn. Colton needs a bath, but not until he's had time for the milk to settle. You'll need to..."

"I can handle things," he said, walking over to the white cabinet and wiping up her spilled coffee. Pouring himself a cup, he added, "I'll see about getting a baby-sitter today."

"Okay, but..."

"I said, I can handle it."

"I heard you." Susan finished gathering up her teaching supplies and books and shoved them into a

large fabric bag. "If you need me for anything, the
name and phone number of the school where I teach
are on the chalkboard hanging above the phone. I'll
be back shortly after four."

Andrew stood in the doorway of the kitchen,
watching her. His gaze made her uncomfortable. Finally, she asked, "What's wrong?"

He nodded toward her hair. "Are you going to wear
your hair like that?"

Susan's hand flew to her head. Her hair was still
piled haphazardly on top of her head. "Uh, no. I..."
How could the man make her feel so incompetent with
just a question? In front of her antique mirror hanging over a washstand, she quickly unwound her hair
and ran her fingers through it. It would be dry and
fluffy by the time she got to school.

She picked up her bag and hurried from the house,
grateful to be out of his sight. She noticed that Andrew had parked on the street so she'd have no trouble getting her old blue Buick out of the driveway. She
wondered if the man ever made a mistake.

Even after weaving quickly through the morning
traffic, she was still five minutes late for work. That
was all she needed to start the week. She rushed to her
room and assembled all the items she required for
class.

She hoped Mr. Garcia, her principal, would come
to observe her before lunch. She wanted to get it over
with. She knew she was a good teacher, but still, it
made her nervous for someone to watch her every
move, evaluate her every word. Maybe that was what

bothered her about Andrew Bradley. He tied her stomach in knots, too. He was a born evaluator.

"Mrs. Montgomery! Mrs. Montgomery!" Students poured from the hallway into the classroom. "Billy's got a snake in his pocket."

"John said a bad word."

"I left my homework on the bus. Can I go get it?"

"My mom said for me to stay in at recess. I don't feel so good."

Susan was amused that she was being put to the test so early. Here, she felt in control. Here, she knew what to do. "I'm sorry you don't feel well, Jorge. Billy, bring me the snake. Yes, Misty, go get your homework." She chose to ignore John and the bad word as she started class.

THE AFTERNOON EVALUATION went well, but the last hour of the school day stretched her patience to the limit. She said goodbye to the last student and closed her lesson-plan book after scanning it to make sure she hadn't forgotten anything for tomorrow. She was eager to see Colton and find out how Mr. Bradley had fared.

Apparently okay, because they were rocking in the porch swing when she turned in to the drive. "I see you guys survived," she remarked, lugging her bag filled with books and papers up the steps.

"Barely. He just swilled down the last bottle, and there's only one diaper left. You need to go to the store."

"*I* need to go to the store?" Susan emphasized the word *I*. She wanted to remind him that she had been at work all day and was exhausted, but she didn't.

"Sure, men don't know what to get. I'll give you some money."

To keep from telling him that she didn't want his bloody money, she ignored him, set her things down and picked up Colton. "How was your day, sweetie pie?" she asked the baby. "You need some new diapers and clothes, don't you? Let's go to town and buy you those cute little diapers ... the new kind with the animals that appear when they get wet."

"Huh!" Andrew grunted. "Animals will be shining on his bo-hind all the time if that's the case."

Susan continued to talk to the baby. "And we'll buy you some little cotton sleepers."

"Sleepers? He's a boy. He needs pajamas."

"He's a baby. All babies wear sleepers. They're comfortable."

"Maybe I should go with you to the store."

"Suit yourself. Let me change first." Susan handed Colton back to him, picked up her things, and hurried in the house to put on a pair of jeans.

Like everything else she had done that day, this took longer than anticipated. Her favorite jeans were in the dirty-clothes hamper because she had forgotten to do the laundry the night before. It wasn't that she'd really forgotten, but she'd watched the baby every minute, afraid to take her eyes off him. Flinging socks to the side, she dug through her sock drawer until she found a pair that matched. Then it took another two or three minutes to locate a belt buried under shoes in the bottom of the closet.

Andrew was pacing the porch with Colton when she emerged from the house ten minutes later. He reminded her of a caged animal. Graceful, even handsome, yet definitely out of his element. His discomfort was evident in every stride of his long, powerful legs.

He didn't have to say a word as he checked his watch. Susan knew that he was displeased with her again. It was a good thing they didn't live together.

"Sorry it took so long, but I..." she started to apologize.

"It doesn't matter. Let's get this over with." He led the way down the steps to her car. "There isn't a back seat in my car," he explained as he pushed books out of the way to make a place to buckle in the infant seat. Bumping his head on the door frame as he backed out, he swore softly under his breath, then settled into the passenger side of the car after removing a candy wrapper from the seat.

"Where do you want to go?" Susan buckled her seat belt, then backed out of the drive.

"You decide. You know this town better than I do."

"How about the Sunrise Mall? It's on Padre Island Drive which isn't far from here. I've seen a baby shop there. They always have the cutest stuff displayed in their windows."

The parking lot was crowded for Monday, so she made several trips up and down the rows of cars while Andrew silently squirmed in his seat. Finally she found a parking space.

In order to avoid a replay of Andrew's scowling, Susan left the infant seat in its position in the back as she got Colton out. Nestling the baby against her body, she wove through the parking lot with Andrew following a few steps behind. She didn't have to look over her shoulder to know that he, like most men, would rather be anywhere than in a mall with her and a baby.

She tilted her chin and entered Little World with a brisk stride, doing her best to forget that she was being stalked by a pouting male. He was not going to ruin her fun, she decided as she thumbed through the tiny outfits displayed near the entrance of the store. "This is cute," she said, pulling out a blue sweat suit appliquéd with a baseball and laying it across the top of the clothes rack.

Andrew glanced at the tag. "They've got to be kidding. Forty dollars?" He looked at a few more price tags. "This is ridiculous."

Susan noticed the saleslady staring at them from across the room, and wanted to hide. The woman probably thought they were having a marital spat. She turned her back to the woman and whispered, "Do you want to go somewhere else?"

"I darn sure do. There's got to be a sensible store in this town."

Susan didn't say a word during the drive along the palm-tree-lined street to WalMart. Even though the prices had shocked her, too, his comments had dampened her excitement about her first shopping trip for Colton.

At the discount store, she pushed the basket through the crowded aisles, stopping only briefly to get formula, bottles, disposable diapers—the white generic kind—and a couple of sleepers. She certainly didn't want another scene like the one at the mall. She'd show him that she knew how to shop. "I guess that's about it."

Andrew twirled around a rack of infant wear. "I thought you wanted some of these." Holding up a sweat suit for her to see, he asked, "Isn't this a lot like that one over at the other place?"

"It's similar," Susan acknowledged. But it didn't have the baseball appliqué.

He looked at the price tag. "Why don't we get it a few of these. Is this about the right size?"

Exasperated with the man just a minute ago, Susan realized that he was trying to do the right thing by Colton. "They're all cute," she said, looking with chagrin at the eighteen-month-size Andrew now held toward her, "but he won't need too many of one size." Thumbing through the rack, she had a hard time making up her mind which sets to get. "Baby clothes are so precious," she explained. "It's hard to decide."

"Just pick three or four of them and let's go," Andrew suggested. "There are a few more things you probably need."

"Like what?"

"A baby bed."

Later, as they were standing in the checkout line with their basket bulging, Andrew picked up a book buried among the bestsellers and tabloids. After studying it a minute he tossed it into the pile of items being checked. ''This might come in handy.''

Susan reached for the book, accidentally brushing his fingers with hers. She couldn't help noticing that his hands were large and rough. The hands of a working man. The kind of hands that could make you feel secure, cherished.

She glanced at the front of the book, then forced a smile as she laid it back on the checkout counter, title upright. *Child Rearing Made Easy.*

CHAPTER THREE

"I OUGHT TO HAVE stock in that store," Andrew muttered a half hour later, after his third trip to the car to haul in their purchases. "Now, where do you want me to set up the baby bed?"

"In the spare room across from mine, I think." Susan briefly pictured the empty corner in her bedroom, but decided against it. As she started climbing the stairs to the second-story bedrooms, she looked back. "Do you need some help carrying that? It looks awfully bulky."

"No, I can manage." Andrew lugged the cardboard box that contained the pieces, which, when assembled, would become Colton's crib. Every other step he had to stop and reposition his unwieldy cargo to keep it from sliding back down the stairway.

Susan looked over her shoulder at the struggling man and offered again, "Are you sure you don't want me to carry one end?"

"No, I can handle it."

Then she'd just let him be bullheaded, she decided, taking the last few steps more quickly. Leaning against the spare-bedroom doorjamb, Susan studied the room arrangement. "I suppose it could go in either of the vacant corners. Take your pick."

Andrew didn't appear winded from the awkward climb as he steadied his heavy cargo against a wall and indicated the corner straight ahead. "This one. You can see it from your room across the hall."

"It's fine with me." Before he could protest, she took one end of the box and guided it to the corner he had indicated. "Do you need help putting it together . . . or anything else?"

"Don't believe so. I can get it from here," Andrew said as he tore into the large box. "I find women more of a distraction than a help," he added with a hint of a smile.

To keep from saying something she would later regret, Susan turned and left the confining room. The man just couldn't accept help. Fine. She'd let him put the "baby bed" together by himself. And she wouldn't tell him what most people called it.

She had just gotten Colton's new clothes in the laundry when Andrew appeared in the kitchen doorway. He leaned a shoulder against the door frame and studied first Colton, then her. "Look, I didn't mean to make you mad," he offered in apology.

"It's okay, Mr. Bradley," she lied, busying herself with imaginary kitchen tasks.

"And can't we drop the Mr. Bradley bit?"

"Okay."

He stood against the doorjamb for a moment longer before stating, "I need a screwdriver if you want me to put the bed together tonight."

She wanted to say, Thought you could handle it, but instead she said, "There's one in the bottom drawer over there." She nodded toward a section of cabinet next to the refrigerator. As he dug in the cluttered drawer through electrical cords, cookie cutters and old coasters, she added, "Don't say a word."

"I wouldn't dare." He held up a screwdriver and pliers. "Found them."

"Is that all you need?"

"I think so. I'll holler if I need anything else," he said as he headed back upstairs.

Under her breath, Susan whispered, "You just do that" at his departing back before she headed to the utility room to get Colton's clothes from the dryer. He could holler all he wanted to—she wasn't going to answer.

Andrew's take-charge manner didn't really lessen Susan's excitement about dressing Colton in his new clothes. It had been a long time since she had folded such soft, tiny garments. Just looking at them made her heart swell with love. Taking an animal-print cotton-knit sleeper in her hands, she rubbed it against her cheek, delighting in its delicate warmth.

"You look like little Tater in the comics," she cooed, putting the sleeper on the baby. While she carried him to the living room, a loud thump resounded from the bedroom overhead.

Colton smiled and gurgled with pleasure as she played patty cake with his feet, but in less than five minutes he wearied of the game and began to yawn and whimper. It was his bedtime. As she laid him on her shoulder and nuzzled his soft cheek, she realized there were rewards to being a grandmother.

Haltingly at first, then with more confidence, she began to sing an old lullaby she had sung to Lisa eighteen years earlier. Colton was just beginning to drift off to sleep when she heard a loud clang overhead and felt the walls shake. The dozing baby jerked and began to cry.

Frowning toward the ceiling and the unseen handyman it hid, Susan rocked Colton with renewed fervor. She was going to have to do something about that man or Colton was never going to get to sleep.

"Grandpa should have your bed ready anytime," she assured the sleepy baby as she carried him up the stairs to investigate. She knew, as she said the words, that they probably weren't true.

Susan glanced into the spare bedroom where Andrew was assembling the crib. Just as she'd suspected, it didn't look as if he had accomplished much more than emptying the parts from the box. She put Colton on her bed again, patting him a few moments to reassure herself that he was sound asleep.

She crossed the hallway to what was going to be the nursery and watched Andrew pick up pieces, try them, then discard them for another piece. After a few minutes she could stand it no longer. Now was the time to do something, even if he didn't want her help.

The assembly instructions lay on the cluttered floor, still encased in their original plastic bag. She edged over and removed the junk lying on top of them. Andrew didn't look up from his trial-and-error work.

She picked up the discarded instructions and scanned them for several minutes before studying the array of screws and rods assembled on the polished hardwood floor. Andrew was trying to hold an end and a side of the bed together at a ninety-degree angle while he threaded a metal rod through rings to connect them.

"Would you like me to hold that?" Susan asked with exaggerated sweetness.

Andrew's head snapped up as he noticed her for the first time. "No. I can handle it," he repeated, just before the side panel crashed to the floor.

"Maybe you can, but I can't. You'll wake Colton. Again." Susan crossed to the center of the room where Andrew was kneeling on one knee. Standing the panel on its end, she held it in place while Andrew connected the headboard.

"Thnnks..." he mumbled, turning to pick up the next piece.

"What?"

"I said, 'Thanks.'"

"You're welcome." Susan smiled at his discomfort. "That piece doesn't go next," she pointed out as he tried to wedge two pieces together.

"It'll work."

Susan stood silently while he fitted the two parts together, only to leave a gap where a spring should have gone.

Finally in exasperation, he said, "They sure looked like they fitted together. I don't know why these things aren't designed logically. I'll bet some hotshot engineer right out of grad school planned this thing."

"Sounds like you don't think much of engineers."

"No, that's not true. Most are okay, but occasionally I run across one who doesn't understand the practical applications of his designs." Andrew stood up and swung his lower leg back and forth to get the kink out of his knee. It popped a couple of times. Seemingly satisfied, he said, "A few months back we installed a large engine on the platform where I work. Space is at such a premium that the contractors followed the engineer's plan to a T, trusting that he knew what he was doing."

Susan stood quietly as he talked in a low, well-modulated voice. This was the first time Andrew had volunteered any information about himself or his work. The way his eyes lit up was fascinating. The man needed to relax more often, she decided.

He ran his fingers through his hair before continuing his story. "After it was completed we couldn't get to one side because it was hanging out over the ocean. Wouldn't have been so bad except that was the side with the hole to put in the oil. Engines don't run long without oil."

"What did you do? Lower someone from the deck above when it came time to change the oil?"

"Oh, no, you don't understand the oil industry," Andrew explained with a sarcastic edge to his voice. "We had to spend more money building a steel cat-walk around the outside of the engine." He looked at her with an embarrassed grin. "What I'm saying is that I don't want to have to build on to this room when I finish. I guess I could use your help. What do I do now?"

His smile was genuine, and that was as close to a peace offering as she was going to get. It was also to her advantage to get the bed together, so she picked up the instructions. "You put a spring between A and D."

"I'm sorry for what I said about women."

"Now, put that piece over there and screw the two of them together with these." She handed him a plastic package of long wooden screws.

"Did you hear me say I was sorry?"

"Yes, but you've said the same thing before, and then you go and insult me again."

"I'm sor—" he began, then caught himself. "How did you get to be so—" he indicated the confusing pile of screws and rods "—mechanical?"

"I'm a farm girl. Most farm kids are resourceful because they help out with things, summers and after school. Besides, I'm not really mechanical. I can read and follow instructions, though. That goes over there."

Andrew followed her directions silently for several minutes before he spoke. "Speaking of school, how did your evaluation go today?"

"Well. I think. I won't know the results for a couple of days. But there was no big surprise or disaster."

"How long have you been teaching?"

"This is my thirteenth year." She was proud that she enjoyed her profession. It wasn't just a job. It gave her personal satisfaction and a sense of purpose.

He paused and looked up from his task. "Thirteen years in the classroom. When are you going to move up to principal?"

Susan formed a fist around the panel she was holding. "I don't *want* to work in an office. I want to work directly with the children. *Their* moving up is my only concern."

"But isn't the pay a lot better in administration?"

"Some, but not enough to make up for what you have to put up with. There's mountains of paperwork and every child seems to have either no parents or parents, stepparents, grandparents and a dozen aunts who are unhappy about something."

Andrew nodded while he thought over what she'd said. "You couldn't pay some of the men I work with enough to take a promotion, either. They're satisfied with the status quo. They have no ambition, and they don't want any more responsibilities." He fitted two pieces together. "They've risen to their level of incompetence."

"Nothing was said about dodging responsibilities or lacking ambition or being incompetent."

"I didn't mean..."

"Then be more careful what you say." Susan looked him squarely in the eye. "There's more than one way to be ambitious. My own ambition is centered less on making money and more on helping kids learn, helping them survive." After a faint sigh, she continued, "Today, children need all the help they can get...from all of us."

Running his fingers through his hair, Andrew shifted from one foot to the other. "True, but being a principal doesn't mean you can't help. And you'd get a lot more pay. But if you're happy where you are, more power to you."

Susan didn't want to argue. All of her life, her headstrong parents had made their home a battleground. For that reason, she had vowed to avoid confrontation whenever possible, and for the most part had succeeded. But this man left her no choice. "Thanks for your permission."

"You don't have to get sarcastic. I'm sorry for what I said. I really do want to help. That's why I bought that book. It's for both of us. It's been a long time since you've cared for a baby, and I never have. I thought it might help."

When she didn't answer, he continued his explanation. "Look, it's this whole mess with the baby and Chris. I ... Would you hand me the screwdriver?"

She suddenly found herself wanting to ease his discomfort. "I think I understand," she said as she gave him the screwdriver.

"I'm glad you do, because I don't," he said, giving a screw a final turn.

After he checked the sturdiness of a connection, he turned to face her. His eyes danced with mischievousness as he deliberately positioned himself, feet wide apart and arms crossed over his chest. "I don't take back all of what I said in the kitchen."

Thinking she was not going to like what she was about to hear, she mimicked his stance and crossed her arms over her chest. Meeting his blue eyes with her brown ones, she raised one well-formed eyebrow in a questioning gesture.

He held her gaze for a long second before speaking. "You *are* a distraction."

A pink blush slowly spread over her cheeks at what she took to be a compliment. Turning to hide the discomfort his words had caused, she bowed her head to allow her hair to form a protective veil between herself and the disturbing man. His soft laugh echoed in her ears as she tried to position a pin in a very small hole.

He said, "Now, help me hook the springs in place."

Was he flirting with her? If he was, he could just forget it. Still, the gush of warmth she'd felt lingered in the pit of her stomach.

They worked until the crib stood assembled in the middle of the room. Helping Andrew drop the mattress in place, Susan finally thought of something to say. "You surprise me. As methodical as you seem to be, I would've expected you to read the directions and follow them explicitly."

"I do for complicated things. This was supposed to be simple." He stood back and surveyed their work.

"Obviously you haven't assembled many things meant for children. They can be very complicated. One Christmas Eve, I put a bicycle together for Lisa. Santa Susan finished the job only a few minutes before Lisa came tearing into the living room the next morning."

Andrew chuckled, then stopped as if deep in thought. "I've never had to do that. The pre-Christmas assembly, I mean. I had to work every Christmas when Chris was growing up."

Susan noticed the wistfulness in his voice before he diverted her attention by picking up the cardboard box and stuffing it with the plastic bags and packing paper.

"I've always just trusted my instincts about putting things together," he said, changing the subject.

"Sometimes, though, things are easier when you have help. At least, that's what I find."

"Yeah, I guess so." Andrew turned and flashed her a warm smile. "We did a pretty good job tonight. Thanks for the help."

"Any time." Susan was nearly disarmed by the crooked grin. "Would you like something to drink before you leave?"

"A tall glass of tea chock-full of ice would hit the spot about now. Where do you want me to put this?" Andrew asked, dragging the trash-filled box down the stairs behind him.

"On the back porch will be fine."

"Isn't there somewhere I can put it so you won't have to take care of it later?"

"Well, yes. I guess you can go ahead and carry it out to the dumpster behind the back fence."

Andrew nodded in satisfaction as he maneuvered through the back door.

Susan brewed the tea while he was gone. The man was such an enigma. He was so dogmatic, so sure of himself. But at the same time, he had a vulnerable, considerate side. For an instant tonight, he'd seemed almost sad that he had never put together a bicycle. And he'd carried out the trash, just so she wouldn't have to do it later.

She was surprised that after their initial quibbling, she had actually enjoyed working with him. They made a pretty good "baby bed" assembly team, she thought.

After Andrew came in the back door he said, "When you asked earlier about the ad for a baby-sitter, I forgot to tell you that I gave out your number for them to call. I hope that's all right?"

"Of course. It makes the most sense."

"As a last resort, I called around for references about day-care centers, but I don't really think that was necessary. Surely there'll be several applicants. I need to find someone tomorrow because I've got to head back to Houston on Wednesday." As though he needed reassurance, he continued, with concern in his voice, "It shouldn't be too hard to find a nice, organized woman to care for the baby here in your home."

"Not with the job market the way it is. But, Andrew, I think it's important to find someone who will not only care for him, but care *about* him."

"That may be true, but the book also says that a baby needs to be kept on a regular schedule. He needs to eat and sleep at set times."

"You can't raise a baby by a book," she countered.

Ignoring her comment, Andrew finished the last of his tea, then glanced at the red-and-yellow teapot clock. "It's getting late. I'd better run. See you in the morning."

"Goodbye," she said before closing the door and leaning against it. Just what made this man tick?

She stacked their glasses in the sink, locked the back door, turned out the light and headed upstairs to put Colton in his new bed. *After tomorrow,* she thought, *I won't have to wonder. He'll be gone. And not a moment too soon!*

"BETSY, I don't have the time," Susan protested to the assistant principal the next afternoon.

"But you promised. It's too late to get someone else. I've already given your name to Mr. Garcia. And the meeting will only take a minute." Betsy cleared her desk and reclipped her long black hair with a red bow. "How do I look?"

"You always look stunning," Susan assured her.

"I wish." Betsy reapplied her scarlet red lipstick and rubbed her lips together a few times before asking, "You do want to save those poor creatures..."

"I don't know anything about 'those poor creatures,' but of course I want to do my part. It's just that things have—"

"Great. I knew you'd be willing to help. We need to get started now so that we'll have everything in full swing by Earth Week in April. All we're going to do today is form committees."

Betsy maneuvered Susan down the hall to the library where the Corpus Christi Elementary School Earth Watch group was getting organized.

Mr. Garcia, standing behind a counter shuffling papers, nodded his head in acknowledgment when Susan and Betsy entered the room. Pushing his glasses up on the bridge of his nose, he glanced at the other five people gathered around one of the tables. "Uh, we'll wait a few more minutes to see if anyone else is coming."

Betsy scanned the room, then settled in a chair at the table near the rear of the group. "I've been dying to talk to you all day. Grandma called last night and told me a man has been at your house with a baby. What's going on?"

Susan smiled as she took a seat beside her. "Whoever said that news travels faster in a small town than a large one isn't familiar with you and Agnes."

She laughed and leaned forward. "Come on, tell me the whole story."

"I don't think even *you* are ready for my news. I sure wasn't. It seems that my darling Lisa had a little boy in July. His paternal grandfather was kind enough to deliver him to me."

Betsy was speechless for several seconds, then her words ran over each other. "A baby? You're kidding. That makes you a grandmother. Where's your daughter? What are you going to do?"

"I honestly don't know." Susan whispered. When she caught a glance of a bleached-blond hairdo filling the doorway, she turned her attention toward the front. Milly Adams and her cleavage had just breezed in and taken a seat. As usual, by the time Milly arrived, the meeting was five minutes behind schedule.

Mr. Garcia stood a little straighter, cleared his throat and launched into his speech. "Earth Watch is an organization where the senior citizens, teachers, students and parents work together as equals." He smiled at the parents.

"Its purpose is to protect our dwindling resources, and, of course, to educate our children to do the same. Because of our proximity to the ocean, the preservation and cleanup of beaches is our primary target— that and the protection of the few remaining Kemp's ridley turtles."

Susan's mind wandered to what awaited her at home. Her primary target was a good night's sleep, not turtles. Colton had kept her up much of the night again. She was tired and didn't feel like arguing with Andrew over a baby-sitter.

An elbow nudged her side. Betsy pushed a notepad closer to her. Susan glanced at the scrawled words.

You didn't know about the baby when you let me talk you into taking this job last week. I'll get you out of it.

Susan kept her gaze focused on Mr. Garcia's wide girth as she wrote a response on the same notepad. *That's okay. I'll figure out a way to do it.*

You're sure?

. *Yes.*

Good. You'll be perfect. I'll help. Then, as an afterthought, Betsy scribbled one last statement. *Wow!!! A grandmother!*

Mr. Garcia's voice stopped the note writing as he announced, "Susan Montgomery, a teacher new to our system, has kindly volunteered to be the chairman, uh, chairwoman, uh, whatever the politically correct term is this year...has volunteered to chair the Kemp's ridley turtle committee. Their preservation is a major concern of fourth-grade children across Texas. Would you please stand, Mrs. Montgomery?"

Susan hated such moments, but she smiled and nodded to other committee members.

"Thank you, Mrs. Montgomery. Betsy Johnson, the assistant principal, will organize the beach cleanup. Betsy, would you stand, please? And Milly Adams—" Mr. Garcia smiled in her direction "—whom we've been lucky to have on our staff for, uh, many years, will chair the clean oceans committee. Would you stand?''

After Milly had stood up as though making a grand entrance, Betsy leaned over and whispered to Susan, "Do you think he's sleeping with her?''

Susan bit her bottom lip to keep from laughing. "Stop it,'' she whispered back as she gathered up the environmental-information materials being passed to her. "You'll get us kicked out.''

"Impossible. We're the chairmen, uh, chair-women, uh, chairs,'' Betsy repeated under her breath. "You have to admit, it's an interesting possibility. Can you just imagine his belly and her hair? There wouldn't be much room in the bed for anything else.''

Susan closed her eyes at the thought, which was a mistake. Amusement welled up inside until her shoulders began to shake in response. She conjured up the least funny thing she could think of... Lisa having a baby... Still, she couldn't keep the silly grin off her face as Mr. Garcia droned on.

"We are all aware of how the petroleum industry and tourism have destroyed our natural resources. We feel the best way to fight this terrible circumstance is a grass-roots approach to...''

Her mirth under control, Susan wondered how the man thought his students' parents made their living. If it weren't for tourism and petroleum, most of the people on the coast of Texas would be unemployed. The oil industry made her think of Andrew. She looked at her watch and whispered to Betsy. "You said this would only take a minute.''

After ten more minutes of laying out the format of the committees and stating the basic direction each was to take, Mr. Garcia dismissed the group. "We'll meet next Wednesday at the same time, review what's been done, then break into our respective committees."

Betsy stood up just as he got the last word out of his mouth. "Let's get out of here. You have to tell me everything. I still can't understand why you didn't say anything earlier."

"I've been in shock." Susan shifted her book bag. She didn't understand how some teachers managed to leave school without taking a mountain of paperwork home to grade.

"Do you have time to stop by the house for a glass of tea? I'm dying to hear all the details."

"I really don't. I'll call you later tonight if I have time. Now, I've got to go because Mr. Bradley, *the* grandfather, is baby-sitting until I get home...and he isn't too thrilled with the job."

CHAPTER FOUR

PUSHING THE FRONT DOOR open with her shoulder, Susan balanced papers and books, then hurried to the sofa to dump them before they ended up scattered all over the floor. Noises that sounded like nails scratching a chalkboard came from the kitchen, causing Susan to shiver. Peeping inside the doorway, she saw Andrew bent over the sink wielding a large crescent wrench on her leaky kitchen faucet.

"Dripping faucets drive me crazy," he said without looking at her.

The drip had bothered Susan, too, but she just hadn't gotten around to calling a plumber. And while she appreciated Andrew's help, it made her feel negligent. If she could just keep her composure for one more day, then she probably wouldn't have to see him for a long time. "Where's Colton?"

"Trying out his new bed." Andrew gave the fitting one final twist and turned to face her. "How did the day go?"

"It wasn't one of the better ones."

"What was the problem?" He leaned back against the counter and wiped his hands with a paper towel.

Susan plopped down in a kitchen chair and studied him. Maybe he was genuinely concerned, she thought, but then quickly dismissed the notion. But she found it impossible to ignore his unaffected masculine appeal. It had been a long time since she had been so intensely aware of a man.

"Are you going to tell me?" He shot the paper towel at the wastebasket and missed.

She grinned as he strolled over, picked it up and deposited it in the trash. "Among a host of other things, there's a little boy named Billy Lupton in my class who won't do his work unless I prod him every two minutes. He stares at the wall, stares at his paper, stares at everyone in the room."

"When he does the work, is it right?" Andrew asked.

"Sometimes. But his learning is getting to have real gaps. And it's not just his work that I worry about. The other students don't like him at all—he's always taunting them or hitting them."

Andrew listened with seeming interest, nodding as if he understood.

"Even when I see it with my own eyes, he'll point-blank deny touching the other kids. Then he'll finally end up saying they started it."

"Aren't most kids like that?"

"Not this bad," Susan explained. "He's living with his grandparents right now. Betsy, the assistant principal, told me his mother died last year and his father hasn't been able to handle it, so Billy has been left to deal with his grief on his own. Oh, and yesterday he brought a snake to school. It turned out to be the nicest thing he's done for the other kids all year, because I turned it into a science lesson."

Andrew smiled.

"He was disappointed that I wasn't scared, though. I feel sorry for him, and at the same time he gets my goat. Today I caught him pushing a classmate's head in the toilet."

"I went to school with a kid like that. Ended up in the pen."

"That's what I want to prevent."

"You can't save everyone."

"I don't believe that." Susan kicked her shoes under the table and scrunched her toes, then propped her feet in a chair. "At least I have to try."

Andrew looked at her shoes for a second, then at her red-tipped toes before he swallowed and said, "You said a host of things went wrong. What else happened?"

"Well, I was gently nudged by a friend into chairing an Earth Day committee." She resisted the urge to cover her feet, though they felt naked and exposed to his gaze. "It seems that it's very important to Texas fourth-grade students to save the Kemp's ridley turtles."

"Kemp's ridley turtles?" Andrew's eyes darkened momentarily.

"Yes. To tell you the truth, the last thing I need right now is another job. Not with Colton."

Andrew started to say something but seemed to think better of it. "Hey, would you like something to drink?" he asked.

Lowering her feet to the floor, Susan nodded. "Sounds wonderful." She licked her lips, surprised at how dry they were. The fact that she found the man attractive was unsettling. "Did you find a baby-sitter?"

"Three women called about the job. Two of them came over for an interview." Andrew shook his head and gave her a lopsided grin. "The first one came at about ten this morning. I guess she needed the job to buy soap...she sure smelled like she was a stranger to it." He handed Susan a soft drink and a glass filled with ice.

"Thank you." It was a nice change to have someone wait on her, but she wasn't sure she liked Andrew making himself at home in her kitchen. The familiarity made her uncomfortable.

Andrew continued with his story. "She had on a pair of rubber shower thongs and a big sloppy tent of a dress. It was so thin that I could see the safety pin holding up her brassiere."

Smiling at his description, yet feeling pity for the woman, Susan poured part of her diet drink into the glass, stopping just before the foam poured over the edge.

"The second one—" Andrew paused, turning a little red "—was this big-boobed redhead, and she seemed more interested in me than in taking care of a baby."

The situation struck Susan as amusing, but it caused the beginnings of a headache as the implication sunk in and panic swelled. "So you struck out."

"For a while I thought so. Then, while I was rocking the kid in the porch swing, Mrs. Johnson came over to welcome me to the neighborhood with a loaf of freshly baked bread. Still hot from the oven."

Susan smiled and visibly relaxed. "She couldn't stand it any longer."

"Right. I gathered that she'd decided I was your husband, but she couldn't figure out the baby."

"She's a dear, but because she's lived on this street for the past fifty years, she feels entitled to know everything that's going on."

"Not just entitled. She sees to it that she *does* know what's going on. After she grilled me for half an hour over bread and butter, she had the basic picture and offered to help out."

"She'd give up her work at the center? That work is her life."

"She only does volunteer work three days a week every other week, so she'll stay with it the days she's off. Perfect solution to our problem, I'd say."

"It's part of the solution, at least. What about the other days?"

"I have it all mapped out. I'll come back on my weeks off for a while. Mrs. Johnson said she could arrange her schedule to run opposite mine, and if she gets sick or anything, she'll find a friend to fill in. I have to be at the Freeport dock to fly to work at around seven on Thursday morning. I'll stay there a week, then go back to Houston and take care of business. You can take care of it on the weekend, then I'll roll in here late Sunday, ready to take over Monday morning." Andrew looked proud of his solution. "How does that sound?"

"You're coming back?" Susan asked in dismay.

He didn't answer her question but continued his explanation. "The good thing about this whole setup is that Mrs. Johnson will come over here to keep the baby. The book says that it's better for the baby to stay in familiar surroundings. It's been shuffled around enough lately as it is. This way he'll never have to leave here.''

"You're coming back?" Susan asked again as she stood up to face him.

"Yes, next Sunday night. If you need me for anything, I wrote down a number where you can reach me on the platform. Here's a check that should cover any expenses while I'm gone." He indicated the slip of paper lying on the table.

"You're coming back? I thought you were in a hurry to be out of here."

"I am. I have enough to do without this, believe me.''

LITTLE DID HE REALIZE how prophetic his words were. When he reported to the Muchiwich docks in Freeport at six-thirty Thursday morning, he was still not fully awake. Keith Pierce, who was in charge of supplies on the beach, called him over. "Hey, Bradley. Got a minute?"

Andrew nodded, matching his stride to the shorter man's. "What's up?"

"I don't really know. Maybe trouble, maybe not. I tried to get you yesterday at home several times."

"I've been gone." Andrew wasn't about to tell anyone that he'd been baby-sitting his grandson—not even an old buddy like Keith.

"Yeah. You weren't home all week. You need to let us know where we can reach you in case of emergency."

"I'll give you a number." He pulled out a pencil and scrawled Susan's phone number on the edge of the yellow legal pad he was carrying, tore it off and handed it to Keith. "You can reach me there on Monday through Wednesday when I'm off duty."

Keith studied the number for a second. "That's a Corpus number. I know 'cause I got a son going to school there. What're you doing down there?"

"You wouldn't believe me if I told you." They were nearing the chain-link fence that separated the helipad from the beach office.

"You got a new woman."

"No." Andrew was emphatic. He turned to enter the gate when he noticed someone sitting in the front passenger seat of the helicopter. "Who's that in the helicopter?"

Keith cleared his throat. "Uh, that's what I was meaning to tell you. A man from the office called to tell me they were sending out someone to visit on the platform for a few days."

Andrew let the news sink in. He knew what the visit meant. Potential layoffs. Their staff of five men was already cut to the bone. They couldn't spare anyone else. "Fine by me. He's not going to find anyone slouching, and he's not going to ride in my seat."

Keith's face erupted in a broad Cheshire smile. "She."

"She?" Andrew's eyes clouded. "Damn."

"Yeah, and she's waiting for you . . . in your seat."

"Damn."

"You've already used that one." Keith was obviously trying not to laugh outright. "Try something more original."

"You wouldn't like it if I did."

"Maybe she'll get all the info she needs in a day or two."

"Sure. See you next Thursday and see if you can't have some good news for a change."

Keith turned and headed back to the office as Andrew strode toward the helicopter. A woman! He'd had his fill of women lately. First Lisa, then her mother. He hadn't been prepared to like Susan, but he found her fascinating. No, he thought, he definitely didn't want to meet another woman. Not that he had anything against them, but they tore up the sleeping arrangements on a platform. And the bathroom. Now, instead of sharing two bathrooms among five guys, they would have only one. She would have the one he usually shared with Dan, one of the operators, all to herself. Dan wasn't going to be happy to hear that he and Andrew were going to have to move in with the other men.

For the first time, Andrew was glad the roar of the helicopter prevented conversation. The flight out would give him time to size up the woman.

Fully prepared to dislike her, Andrew hopped into the helicopter and was immediately disarmed by the smile the short, heavyset woman flashed his way. She looked friendly and harmless. He nodded in her direction and decided not to gesture for her to vacate his front seat. He could sit in the back this once. Might even be able to catch a nap. He hated flying, but it beat a boat ride all to hell.

As the glass-like surface of the unusually calm gulf waters passed below him, he began to relax, glad that it was late October and the hurricane season was almost over. So far this year they had escaped a storm, but any low-pressure system like the one responsible for the smooth seas below could pull in a storm from the Yucatán. And a tropical storm was all he needed right now.

He studied the woman in his seat. She was on the homely side, unlike another woman he knew. He grinned as he remembered Keith asking him if he had a new woman. He could just picture Susan's reaction to that news. With Susan in his thoughts, he leaned back in his seat, his headphones drowning out some of the hum of the chopper.

Fifteen minutes later a change in the pitch of the helicopter-engine noise woke him from a light sleep. The production platform lay below like a gray dot on an enormous blue-green canvas. Other orange and gray specks dotted the painting as far as the eye could see in any direction. Peering down from the window, Andrew was reminded anew of the mind-boggling quantities of oil and gas being pumped out of the gulf and the enormous amounts of money involved.

"We're here!" The helicopter pilot's voice boomed out of the headsets, causing the woman to jump in surprise.

Andrew unbuckled his seat belt and hung the headset above the console before removing his life vest and stepping onto the helipad. Ingrained good manners made him offer his hand to help the woman out of the helicopter.

"Thanks," she yelled over the noise.

Andrew pointed out the metal grating stairs that led to the lower levels, then turned to wave the helicopter on. He followed her down the stairs, eager to get his mind on his work. He had a lot to do...a wire line crew on well number twelve...a jack-up boat acidizing crew on number eighteen...and now a woman watching their every move, just waiting for someone to prove he was superfluous.

He caught up with her at the bottom of the stairs and edged past her. "This way," he said. "I'll show you to your quarters."

Stopping him, the woman held out her hand and double-checked the name on his coveralls. "Mr. Bradley, I'm Diane Weathersly. Before we get started, let me say I'm just here to note the day-to-day workings of the platform. I'll be following you around and asking a few questions...well, maybe a lot of questions." She fell into step beside him as he led the way to his and Dan's room. "Other than that, try to ignore me."

Andrew stopped before a door and turned to face her. "We both know it will be impossible to ignore you, but we'll make the best of it." He pushed the pocket door open. "You can put your things in here."

She chuckled as she dumped her bags on the lower bunk and turned to survey the tiny six-by-eight room. Other than the built-in bunks, a metal chair was the only furniture. "You don't mince words, do you, Mr. Bradley? Let me assure you, this is just my job."

"And it's *my* job that's on the line," he countered, "and the jobs of my men." No one could be at ease while being evaluated. Just as Susan had said. Susan would know how he felt. She'd said that she knew she did a good job, but being observed so closely always made her feel a little inadequate. He understood that feeling all too well.

"I'll just get my things out of here." He unlocked his locker and removed the personal items he needed for the next few days.

"I'm sorry about putting you out of your bunk and bath. I know it's a problem when women come off-shore. I'll try to stay out of your way. I wish there was... I'm talking too much, aren't I?"

"I know enough not to answer that," he said, thinking that the woman was not unfriendly. Maybe she wasn't going to push her weight around and make them all miserable for a week.

She laughed again. "When do we eat?"

Andrew looked at his watch. "Breakfast is still on and lunch begins ten-thirty or eleven, depending on Three Can's mood."

FIVE DAYS LATER, from his perch eighty feet above the dark water, Andrew studied the reflection of the setting sun in the gulf. After Diane had left with the contents of her report unknown to him, the rest of the week had been inordinately boring. He'd kept up with his work, which was mostly completing production and environmental reports. He'd still had time to read the *Houston Post* bow to stern.

He'd gone to the recreation room the evening before and rummaged through the boxes of crackers, nuts and candy stashed on the top of the refrigerator. He flipped through the television channels in less than a minute before clicking off the set. Next, he'd read the notes that were haphazardly tacked to a bulletin board hanging next to the wall phone. He'd tried running on the treadmill and riding the stationary bike, but hadn't been able to shake his quiet ache. He felt different. Sort of nervous. Like a cat.

He turned and leaned against the handrail. Though he lived half of his life in close quarters with up to fifteen other men, he often felt isolated, lonely. Today had been worse than most. And it wasn't Diane and her report that bothered him. She'd turned out to be just one of the guys. At least, that was the impression she'd left.

Instead of worrying about job security, visions of the baby and its grandmother intruded upon his concentration. Susan. The image warmed his heart and cooled his feet. He couldn't allow himself to become involved with her, no matter how desirable she looked. It was going to be hard, he thought with a sigh, to be around her day in and day out and not touch her.

He had a feeling she wasn't the type to get involved in a purely physical relationship. He, on the other hand, wasn't the type to get involved in anything else. He knew he was lousy husband material. He was gone from home too much. And what Susan needed was a good husband to take care of her. He didn't like the way that made him feel—the thought of her with another man.

His past had taught him that feelings were painful. Little other than hurt had come from his marriage to Marilyn. Except Chris. Being a father had been no picnic, and that in itself made him feel guilty. He didn't want to experience that betrayal and hurt again.

He could remember his father telling him as a child to dry up the tears, that real men didn't cry or show emotion. Anger was the only strong emotion allowed. He and most other men of his generation had been raised that way. Self-sufficient. Tough. It was hard to relearn something so deeply ingrained.

He certainly hadn't passed his toughness on to his son. He couldn't help loving the kid, but—damn, where was he?

Finally, Andrew strolled back to his tiny office sandwiched between the steel decks of the platform and called his ex-wife. Maybe she'd know the whereabouts of their son. Even if she didn't, she needed to know what was going on.

Moments later, he hung up the phone and pushed his chair away from the desk in frustration. Marilyn wasn't happy about being a grandmother. That was the first common feeling they'd shared in years. After her initial shock had worn off, she gave Andrew the name of one of Chris's friends in Houston. Jack Green. Jack, she'd said, would know more about Chris's plans than anyone else. That was a start, at least.

He envisioned Chris and that girl out in California mooching off someone. No worries. Just having a good time. In frustration, he slammed his fist against the desk.

ON A BLUFF windswept by a different ocean, Christopher Bradley held Lisa Montgomery in his arms and tried to comfort the crying girl. "Lisa, baby, don't cry. You know it was for the best."

"But I—I didn't know it would hurt so bad," Lisa sobbed. "We've been gone two weeks and each day gets worse."

"Shhh, baby. Colton is better off with my dad. He can take care of him. We weren't ready...it's just too much to handle right now."

"Ready or not, he's our baby. Your dad can't be too happy about taking care of him."

"Aw, he's probably called my mother to come get him by now. Put everything on her back."

"Maybe we should have taken Colton to my mom."

"We didn't have the money for you to go back home, and you said you'd never take the baby there as long as..."

"I know, but my mom doesn't even know she's a grandmother. It all happened so fast...our leaving Houston, I mean... I should have written to her or something...." Lisa bit back her words and pulled away from him. "Chris, this doesn't feel right...like we thought it would."

"We've been through this before, Lisa. I didn't twist your arm. You *wanted* to come out here. Now, come on. We need to get back to the rest of the group."

"I like it out here where it's cool." Lisa held the neck of her blouse open to allow the breeze to caress her warm skin. Her fingers brushed the crystal pendant hanging around her neck. "Do we have to go back in there?"

"You know the rules as well as I do."

"I don't like the rules. I thought the whole idea of coming to California was to be free, to learn about ourselves, to become centered. All we've done so far is follow stupid rules and make faith offerings with what little money we had."

Chris looked around furtively. "Don't let them hear you say that."

"It's the truth. What have we got left? Ten dollars?"

"It doesn't matter. Let's get back." Chris took Lisa by the arm and led her across the clearing toward a long log building that housed the commune's meeting hall and kitchen.

"I don't care if they do hear me," Lisa mumbled as she reluctantly followed him. "That's what the rules are—stupid!" Her lowered voice assumed a mimicking tone. "'Get up. Eat this. Don't eat that. Chant. Listen to the prophecies of Venus. Sell flowers to help Venus spread the message. Don't ask questions because Venus knows best. Go to bed.'"

"Venus has been like a mother to us. She took us in and gave us food and a place to live when we had nothing. Stop and take a breath, Lisa. Can't you feel the peace and love here?"

Lisa drew in an exaggerated breath. "No. I feel even more trapped than I did at home. Even Dad allowed me some freedom. Here, we don't even get to think for ourselves." She fell silent as Chris, shaking his head, held open the door and allowed her to precede him.

Candlelight flickered, casting ghostly shadows around the circle of faces that looked up when the two entered the room. A plump woman with purple-tinted hair hanging down to her waist stood and greeted them as though they had been gone much longer than their brief thirty-minute respite. "Come, my children. The stars have a special blessing for you tonight." She gave them each a hug. "While you were gone we spoke of needs and took up a special collection. To show your concern for all of our needs—" she picked up an etched crystal bowl "—I know you'll also want to make a love offering."

Lisa looked at Chris. Tears glistened in the corners of her eyes before she bowed her head when he withdrew a five-dollar bill from his pocket and deposited it in the incandescent bowl Venus held before him.

CHAPTER FIVE

A SMALL SHAFT of light reflected off the bowl of relish Susan slid to the back as she dug through the refrigerator looking for something to munch on while Colton slept upstairs. She'd put him to bed early after he had fussed all afternoon. Sunday afternoons were no longer lazy, unencumbered days to read or take a nap. She couldn't remember the last book she'd read or real nap she'd taken. Those were luxuries she might as well forget about until Colton got a little older. But the sweet little boy more than made up for any inconvenience he caused.

The peal of the doorbell brought her upright. She bolted from the kitchen through the living room to the door before the bell rang again and woke Colton. After his rough afternoon, she sure didn't want to risk having him wake up cross and having to rock him back to sleep.

She figured it was Andrew at the door. After all, he'd said he would be back in ten days. She would deny it to her grave, but after putting Colton to bed she had been unable to settle down and concentrate all evening. She listened for the sound of tires crunching the shell on the driveway, the sound of his firm steps coming up the stoop or the peal of the old doorbell.

Because her head had been buried in the refrigerator, she had missed the first two.

Wanting to see him, yet not wanting to see him, she unlocked the door with apprehension. Thoughts of his silent appraisals appeared unbidden several times a day, only to be replaced by thoughts of his helpfulness.

Andrew stood outlined against the black velvet night. He nodded a greeting. Why did the mere presence of this tall, slender man affect her so strongly? When his crooked grin spread over his face, she knew it was his rugged good looks that attracted her to him, certainly not his easy manner. "Hi. Come on in." Her voice sounded much more composed than she felt.

"Sorry I'm late," he said. "Had you given up on me?"

Her voice was husky from sleep. "No, you said you'd come." He was obviously a man of his word. Maybe that wouldn't be so bad, she thought suddenly, considering all she had been through the past twenty years. Lisa's father, George, had been more of a hindrance than a help. She needed some steadiness in her life, even if it was from a stuffed-shirt Adonis with blue eyes.

Determined to stem his anticipated criticisms, she had pulled out the old bulky Electrolux she'd inherited from her mother and vacuumed the area rugs and the upholstered furniture. Even now, the pungent aroma of lemon polish wafted through the air from gleaming wood surfaces. On a corner of the table next to her overstuffed armchair lay an orderly stack of her work. She wasn't about to admit, even to herself, that she had done it to impress him.

With raised eyebrows, Andrew looked around the room, nodded and chuckled. "I see you've been busy. There *was* furniture under all of that paper."

"I told you that two weeks ago." Running her fingers through her tangled curls, she renewed her determination to avoid a confrontation. She needed this man's help. "I dozed off on the sofa after putting Colton to bed."

He looked her up and down, but this time, instead of a critical appraisal his gaze was a warm caress that made her cheeks turn pink. She knew she looked as if she had just gotten out of bed and even though it had been a long time, she could still read a man well enough to know when he was thinking about getting her back there.

She asked, "I was making a pot of coffee. Would you like a cup?"

"Sure." He followed her through the living room to the kitchen and leaned against the counter. "How was your week?"

"It went pretty well. Colton and Mrs. Johnson get along fine. What about yours?" Susan set two coffee mugs on the cabinet top.

"It wasn't what you'd call typical. We had extra personnel most of the week, but it beat what the hitch out there this week is doing."

"What's that?" She poured the mugs full of hot steaming coffee. "Do you take sugar or cream?"

"Black," he said before explaining. "They are going through an oil-spill drill."

"You practice for that sort of thing?" She handed him a mug. As he took it from her hand, his fingers brushed hers. Deliberately? She wasn't sure, but she could still feel his warm touch as she led the way back to the living room.

Sitting down in the big stuffed chair, he answered her question. "We have to be prepared for any emergency, and I guess because there have already been so many spills in the gulf this year the bosses decided we needed more practice."

Susan sat down on the couch and carefully tucked her bare feet under her. The man sitting across the room made her aware of every part of her body in a new way. To avoid thinking about his eyes on her, she asked, "What caused the spills?"

"Lots of things. Archaic equipment. Carelessness. Cutting corners." He leaned back and set his mug on the end table. "In one instance, a tanker was lightening."

At her puzzled look he explained, "That means pumping oil into a smaller craft to reduce the draft so the tanker can make it into the shallow Houston ship channel. An electrical spark on the tanker caused an explosion. Usually that kind of thing takes place in international waters where our government has no control."

Susan enjoyed the mellowness of his voice, and wanted him to continue. "That doesn't make sense. We're all victimized when the oil drifts onto our beaches."

"Yep, that's true. Ocean currents wash just about everything that is thrown into the gulf back onto our shores."

"Can't something be done to stop it?"

"Are you asking if there's anything I can do personally about the ocean currents or the dumping?" He picked up his mug and cradled it in his hands as he leaned forward.

Susan's brown eyes widened when she raised an eyebrow. "No, I didn't mean that at all. It's just that...it doesn't seem right for a company's profit margin to take precedence over the welfare of the environment and animals..."

"That company's profit margin employs a lot of people."

"But can't they compromise? Can't they make a profit and still protect the environment? Take the turtles for instance...there should be laws—"

He set his mug down on the table with more force than necessary. "Every one of those damn laws means more people out of work. Even now, most of the large oil companies are moving their business overseas where they can make a profit. A few men are being given the option to work overseas—Nigeria, Brazil, Russia—without their families in tow. It's one helluva way to live. And they're the lucky ones. For others, it's goodbye Joe. I know at least twenty men who've been laid off in the past six months—older men, with fifteen, twenty years with their company. In fact, this week a woman visited our platform. Her job is to find someone who isn't necessary. I may be next."

"I didn't mean...I didn't know..." Susan was uncomfortable. "I don't want anyone to lose their job...it's just that I think there should be a happy medium where a profit can be made, but not at the expense of an entire species or our children's future."

"I agree," Andrew said, leaning forward again in his chair, "but government regulations and environmentalists are a sore spot with me. It seems like I deal with 'em thirty hours a day. Put 'em together and you've got a peck of problems, Susan. We need some regulations to protect the environment, but, Lord, it would help if there was just a *hint* of forethought about the implications."

"I know what you mean. It's the same way with schools." Susan set her coffee down.

Andrew grinned, his guarded expression softening. "There's no escape, I guess, unless we want to become hermits." He thought for a moment, leaned back in his chair and studied her before adding, "Sometimes I feel like I'm held personally responsible for anything that goes wrong in the oil industry. Already, we carry back to shore all of our waste and trash from the platform. We aren't even supposed to take a leak over the side. It might pollute the ocean. I wonder where the environmentalists think the fish urinate?"

Susan couldn't help but smile at the way Andrew tried to lace his bluntness with humor. "I didn't know such care was being taken. I wish all of the industries were so careful. From what I've been reading, a lot of the marine animals, including turtles, ingest plastic thinking it's food. Some die of abdominal infections."

"I've heard that, too. All of us could do more, but since I'm not one of the powers that be, I don't suppose my opinions count for much in the overall scheme of things."

"I sometimes wonder if anyone's opinion or plans count for much...about anything," Susan mused.

"What do you mean?"

"Think about us. Our plans for our 'golden years' sure got changed now that we've got a child to rear. I'll bet a month ago you didn't plan on that."

"I still don't think much of the idea. Not the way it happened, anyway."

"Right. Even though I love Colton, having him to rear wasn't a free choice. It's just something that happened. Something out of our control that changed our lives."

"I believe that people are responsible for what happens in their lives, barring things like being struck down by lightning, of course. Perhaps the way we handled our kids many years ago has led to this."

Susan sat up straighter. "Are you saying I'm responsible for Lisa getting pregnant?"

"Not at all. Just that we never know where any of those seemingly insignificant choices we make every day will lead, no matter how well-intentioned we are. Ultimately we have no one to blame for our condition but ourselves."

"I don't know that I agree with you. Sometimes things just happen. I didn't get pregnant and have

Colton. And I sure as heck didn't encourage Lisa to become an unmarried mother. To the contrary.''

"But you had Lisa, and that resulted in Colton.'' Holding up his hand to stifle her response, he added, "You don't have to agree with me about that. It's only my opinion. But you do have to agree that right now we are faced with a choice that will affect our lives for a long time to come.''

She was well aware of that but wanted to know what Andrew had in mind. So far, all of their plans had been short-term. "What do you mean?''

"We have some options concerning the kid. We can turn him over to child welfare, which might eventually put him up for adoption, or...''

Susan caught her breath. "You don't mean it,'' she gasped, standing up to face him across the narrow rug.

"No, I don't, but let me finish. Our careless kids are responsible for having had him. If Chris had controlled his raging hormones and kept his pants zipped we wouldn't be in this mess. But like it or not, we're responsible now. We can turn the baby over to someone else or we can raise him ourselves.'' Andrew aimed his index finger at her to make his point. "And I'm telling you that what we're doing now is not a long-term solution.''

He was right, she knew. They had to make some kind of a decision. About Colton. For Colton. "Well, I'm not giving him up.'' Susan picked up their mugs and headed toward the kitchen. "He's my grandson!''

Andrew nodded his head as he followed her. "Yeah. Flesh and blood and all that. But that isn't going to make it easy."

"I realize that." She put the dishes in the sink and turned to face him.

"Okay, so can you keep him like we're doing now for the rest of the school year?"

"Probably." If her health held up, she added to herself. After hearing Andrew suggest adoption—even if he hadn't meant it—she was afraid to let him know how tired she was after only two weeks. Two weeks of interrupted sleep—just catnaps, it seemed. She had no time to call her own since a simple task like going to the grocery store was now a major accomplishment. "No, I mean, yes, I know this arrangement will work for me, but what about you? Can you continue to come here every other week?"

"I don't have much choice, do I?" He crossed his arms and leaned on the counter.

"Yes, you do. You can wash your hands of this whole affair."

"You're wrong. I can't do that," he insisted, "any more than you can."

"Flesh and blood and all that?" she echoed.

"Sort of." He grinned, dropping his protective stance and taking a step closer to Susan. "Okay, we'll keep this up till the Christmas holidays, or maybe the end of school. Come summer, you'll have plenty of time to find a lady who'll come here to keep the baby. Be sure you get someone who'll keep your house clean, too. I'll pay."

"That would be nice." She chose to ignore the subtle dig about her housekeeping. "I don't really want to take Colton out to a day-care center if I can help it. Those kids catch all kinds of childhood diseases, apparently."

"Been reading the book, haven't you?" He reached out and brushed a stray curl away from Susan's face.

She caught her breath, then slowly exhaled and muttered, "Damn book."

Andrew laughed at her expletive. "And speaking of the damn book—" he continued outlining his plans as though he had not touched her "—while I'm here, I'll get him on a regular schedule."

As if on cue, Colton began crying. "You can start right now," she offered in a honeyed voice. Sometimes the confidence of the man really grated on her nerves. Wiping her hands on a dish towel, she asked, "You do want to see him, don't you?"

"Sure, I guess so."

Susan bounded up the stairs, needing to get away from the disturbing man and determined to let him begin his scheduling miracle without delay.

Entering the kitchen a few minutes later with the hungry baby nestled on her shoulder, she paused and watched Andrew wash the countertop. The dishes were done. Shaking her head in consternation, she didn't know whether to curse him or thank him. She'd never known a man so neat and orderly. Andrew turned, caught her staring and shrugged in concert with that disarming smile of his.

Irritation melted. She returned his smile as she thrust the whimpering, wriggling baby in his arms.

"Here, why don't you hold him while I warm his bottle."

Holding Colton gingerly, Andrew tickled the baby's developing double chin with the finesse of a sumo wrestler. "Coochie-coo, coochie-coo," he said awkwardly.

Susan watched the two males out of the corner of her eye with amusement. The big one was jumping around trying to stop the little one from crying. The little one was winning. Her attention riveted on them, she inadvertently spilled some formula onto the cabinet.

"The book suggested using a funnel to pour formula into a bottle," Andrew observed. "It'll save cleanup time."

"If I hadn't been paying attention to how funny you looked bouncing Colton around, I wouldn't have spilled it. Besides, I'm sure the book said something about how too much bouncing makes babies spit up." *On you, I hope.*

MONDAY AND TUESDAY were uneventful days, with Susan and Andrew earnestly trying to keep their swords and their growing awareness of each other sheathed. On Wednesday, after the Earth Watch committee meeting, Susan walked to her car with Betsy Johnson. "It's only midweek and I'm pooped already. How you talk me into these things, I'll never understand." Susan unlocked her car and tossed her purse and books on the front seat before turning to her friend. "Mr. Garcia was more verbose than usual."

"He was trying to impress Milly. I tell you, there's something going on there."

"Only in your imagination."

"Maybe so, but it spices up an otherwise dull meeting." Betsy leaned back against Susan's car, allowing the late-October sun to glint off her black hair.

"You're hopeless."

"I know, but it's fun. What do you think of this shade of nail polish?" Betsy held out her fire-engine red fingertips for inspection.

"Lovely." Susan surveyed her own colorless fingernails. She hadn't had the time, since Colton had arrived, to manicure her nails. From the corner of her eye, she saw a little boy dart around the building, climb on a bike and pedal off. "I still can't get over Billy burying his head in all that information about the Kemp's ridley turtle, rather than his fist in someone else's stomach."

Betsy offered a satisfied smile. "I told you something good would come out of saving the turtles."

"There was no way you could have known that Billy would show more interest in them than he has anything all year."

"I could be psychic, you know."

"Not psychic, just nosy. Like your grandmother Agnes."

Betsy laughed. "Actually, I know from the school records his dad is director of animal husbandry at the state aquarium."

"That would explain Billy's interest. I wonder why he didn't tell me."

"Couldn't say." Betsy changed the subject again. "How'd your postevaluation conference with Mr. Garcia go?"

Before Susan could answer, Betsy continued. "I saw you go into his office, then Milly Adams brought two fifth-grade boys to my office for writing something about her on the bathroom wall."

Susan grinned. "What did they write?"

"The usual four-letter word with her name attached. They misspelled her name, and that's what had her the most upset. She made such a big deal out of it that they'll probably write something else tomorrow."

"I'll bet they get the spelling down this time."

"Anyway, I heard you did great on your evaluation. You have excellent rapport with the students. You encourage problem solving . . . and . . ." Betsy began to tick off the compliments on her fingers.

"Is there anything that gets by you?"

"Not much. I told you, you would do fine."

"Thanks for the vote of confidence. I'd better get home before Grandpa Bradley comes looking for me."

Betsy laughed. "From what Grandmother says, he looks more like a movie star than a grandpa. She says he's 'a real hunk.' I'd swear she has a crush on him, the way she carried on over the phone."

Visions of the man with sand-colored hair leaning against the counter entered her head. No, Susan didn't consider him a hunk. That expression reminded her of an overdeveloped body builder, not of Andrew. But there was something about him . . . something she hadn't quite been able to define . . . something that made her breathing irregular and her heartbeat dance when he touched her. "No doubt she does have a crush on him. You ought to see the shameless way he caters to her."

"How does he get along with the baby?"

"Surprisingly, pretty well, considering how he enjoys playing the martyr. Still, I'd better rescue Colton before he learns to be a stick-in-the-mud like his grandfather."

Betsy peered at Susan over her sunglasses. "Stick-in-the-mud?"

Susan nodded affirmation. She didn't want to admit to anyone that she was beginning to find the man as attractive as Mrs. Johnson did. "I don't have time to go into details, but the man was probably the bossiest, most self-righteous kid in his class." She paused for a moment. "Though he *can* be interesting to talk to. It's been fun bouncing ideas about the environment off him. He has rather definite ideas on the subject."

Betsy grinned and winked before asking, in a conspiratorial voice, "So where does he stay while he's in town?"

"At a place called The Palms." Susan shot her a withering look. "Certainly not with *me,* so wipe that grin off your face. He goes home this evening," she added.

SUSAN STOPPED in her tracks. Her lawn was freshly mowed, and nail heads shining like polished medals adorned the new railing of her porch. Damn! Couldn't he leave her stuff alone for one day? She wished she'd

never told him that her rent had been reduced on condition that she do some of the repair work. She *was*
going to get around to it. Soon. If only he'd left well
enough alone!

Andrew opened the screen door. "Hi."

"What's this?" She indicated the porch.

He leaned against a turned post. "I was bored."

She knew she should be thankful for his help, but
somehow she felt insulted—the same way she'd feel if
her mother-in-law had started dusting her furniture.
"You didn't have to go to the trouble. I was planning
to hire someone to do all this stuff."

"That would've cost money. There's no need for
you to spend your money when I can do the job free."

Susan felt terrible for being so ungrateful. The urge
to tell him off pulled hard, but she forced herself to say
the proper thing. "Thank you for fixing my porch,
and mowing my grass...and repairing the kitchen
faucet."

"You're welcome." He checked his watch. "You're
home later than usual. Any problems?"

"No. I should've called to let you know that I had
a turtle committee meeting this afternoon."

"How was it?"

"Long. But at least one good thing seems to be
coming out of the project. Billy has developed an avid
interest in the turtles."

"Is that the little troublemaker you were telling me
about?"

"Yes, but today he scoured the library for information and took a stack of books home. It seems his

dad works at the Texas State Aquarium. He told me how industry had nearly eliminated the turtles."

"Hmmph," Andrew grunted. "Before you get buried in all the propaganda, let's get the facts straight. The oil industry isn't responsible for the demise of the turtles. If anything, it's the loss of habitat caused by egg harvests in Mexico—"

Susan interrupted, "But that was stopped years ago."

"Let me finish." Andrew crossed his arms over his chest and faced her. "Yes, most of that has been halted, at the expense of some poor Third World village's way of life. But that's just the start. Every beach that becomes a tourists' paradise and every shrimp dinner you eat means fewer turtles."

"What does eating shrimp have to do with anything?"

"Turtles get caught in the shrimp nets and they drown."

"But I thought shrimpers have to have turtle excluders in their nets. I read that in my committee materials."

"Don't believe everything you read. Excluders cost money and cut down on the catch."

"But... it's the law."

"Yeah, and everybody obeys the traffic laws, too. Don't be so naive, Susan. All shrimpers don't have excluders." Andrew held the door open for her to precede him into the house. "By the way, I'll be painting the new railing next time I come."

Tensing up at what she thought to be another criticism, she looked up into his sea blue eyes, eyes filled

with warmth and teasing. He meant well, she knew—
so why did she overreact to everything he did or said?
The answer to that question was buried somewhere
deep inside her, so she veered to a more neutral subject. "How was Colton today?"

A little twitch pulled at Andrew's mouth. "He was
fine. Upstairs napping now. He was a little late getting to sleep."

"So the 'it' is now a 'he'," she said with a chuckle.

Andrew let the comment pass. "Maybe you'll have
time to unwind a little before he wakes up."

"That would be nice for a change." Turning to hide
her amusement, Susan sensed that Andrew had been
unsuccessful getting Colton on a schedule but was too
proud to admit it. "Did you have any luck with the
schedule?" she asked over her shoulder before turning around to gauge his reaction.

"Sort of," he mumbled, then checked his watch
again and announced, "Say, I've gotta go."

"So soon?" The words came out unexpectedly.
During the past three days, she had rather enjoyed
their verbal sparring.

"It's a four-hour drive to Houston."

An attack of conscience hit Susan. Knowing how
tired Andrew must have been after mowing her lawn,
repairing her porch and taking care of Colton, she was
worried about his long drive. It would be easy for him
to fall asleep at the wheel. "You be careful, okay?"

"Sure. If you need anything, call. Otherwise, I'll see
you next Sunday." Andrew started out the door, then
turned and gave her a long, searching look. "You're
not turning into one of those environmentalists, are

you?'' He said it as if it was a dirty word. "It's us or them, you know."

Susan pondered what he'd said for several minutes after the back door closed. Maybe she *was* turning into an environmentalist. The more she learned about Kemp's ridley turtles, the more sympathetic she became to their cause. There had to be answers that everyone could live with.

CHAPTER SIX

FRIDAY AFTERNOON, because of the traffic leaving the low-lying barrier islands above and below Corpus Christi, Susan had to slow down even though she was in a hurry to get home, anxious about the weekend and the storm that lay ahead. When she turned the corner at the end of her block she saw Mrs. Johnson, fists propped on her hips, standing on the front porch and staring at the blue sky.

"What's the update on the tropical storm, Mrs. Johnson?" Susan asked, joining her neighbor in studying the clear sky and glaring sun. It certainly didn't look stormy.

"It's still headed straight for us. They say this is one of the latest storms on record—this is the first week of November, mind you." She shook her head.

"I still can't believe a storm is coming. The weather has been beautiful all day."

"That's usually the way it is. Gorgeous one minute and then the blackest clouds you ever saw will roll in from the ocean. I've been through a few bad ones myself, but James was alive then." She wrung her hands. "Oh, dear, I do wish Andrew was here."

"Let's go in," Susan suggested, wanting to get off her tired feet. Following Mrs. Johnson into the house, Susan asked, "Why do you wish Andrew was here?"

"Why, I'd just feel safer. Even though the storm may not be a threat where he is, it worries me just the same." Mrs. Johnson seemed to forget about the storm when she thought of Andrew. Smiling from ear to ear she added, "Isn't he the most wonderful man?"

"What makes you say that?"

"Everything. For example, Wednesday, I didn't have to go down to the center until noon, so he helped me in my yard for part of the morning with the heavy stuff that I just can't do anymore. Colton rested in his little seat and took it all in." The older woman giggled like a schoolgirl as she pulled a chair up the table. "After that, Andrew repaired the railing on your porch and mowed your lawn. Putting it to rest for the winter, that's what he was doing."

"I know I should be grateful for his help because the railing had loosened and was probably dangerous, but still, it irritates me for him to just up and do it without a word to me."

"Would you have allowed him to do it if he'd asked?"

"Of course not."

"There you have it, dear." Mrs. Johnson shook her head. "I'm sure he knew that and was just trying to be helpful."

"I don't know how to explain it." Susan motioned toward the coffeepot, fully convinced that nothing would sway her neighbor from taking Andrew's side.

Mrs. Johnson nodded her acceptance. "Decaffeinated, dear. I can't sleep at night if I drink the real stuff this late in the day."

Susan took two cups from the white cabinet. "Everything he does is measured and precise. I could never be that perfect."

"But you are, dear, in matters that count. Bets tells me you're a wonderful teacher. You're sweet and caring, so don't sell yourself short." Agnes patted Susan's hand. "It takes all kinds to make this world go round. Andrew's type and your type."

"I suppose you're right." The corners of Susan's mouth relaxed as she set the coffee on the table. "Thanks. You always have something good to say about me, and it makes me feel better, whether it's true or not."

Agnes must have remembered the storm again as she sipped her coffee. "If the wind picks up and you need any help closing the hurricane shutters, I'll show you how, though I can't climb up on a ladder anymore to reach the high windows. Andrew made sure your shutters work."

"He did that, too?"

"Yes, the same day he repaired one of mine."

Susan shook her head and refilled her coffee cup. She didn't know what to say.

Agnes continued. "My mother survived the Galveston hurricane in 1900. Wiped out the whole town. The best I remember from the stories, about six thousand people were killed, though I don't think they ever knew for sure how many were dead."

Realizing that Mrs. Johnson was truly frightened of storms, Susan tried to reassure her. "That hurricane took them by surprise. These days we're warned and can evacuate in plenty of time. Besides, the seawall built after that will probably keep that kind of destruction from happening again." Susan patted Agnes's hand. "This is only a tropical storm."

"If you say so," Mrs. Johnson glanced uncertainly toward the window. "But I have a feeling about this one."

Uneasy after Agnes left, Susan turned on the television and flipped through the channels as she played with Colton and graded math papers. She couldn't dismiss the older woman's foreboding. And by nine o'clock it looked as if Mrs. Johnson was right. On all the local television stations, weather watches and warnings ran like banners across the bottom of the screen. Wind speeds were up to sixty-five miles per hour. The late-season storm in the Gulf of Mexico was predicted to make landfall in twenty-four hours, a little farther down the coast. Other than delivering cold, drenching rains and high winds, it looked as if the brunt of the storm would miss Corpus Christi, but the town and barrier islands remained in the watch area.

She worried about Andrew out on the platform. She knew, from the rough map Andrew had drawn her on a napkin one night, that it was located off the coast somewhere between Freeport and Corpus Christi. Surely he was far enough away to be out of any danger, she reasoned.

Flexing her fingers unconsciously, she didn't understand why she was so worried about him. She'd only known him for three weeks. But she had to admit she was beginning to like him—most of the time, that is. She didn't want him in any danger. She had to agree with Mrs. Johnson. She'd feel better if Andrew were anywhere but in the gulf right now.

As she rocked the semidozing baby, a ring pierced the warm, humid air, startling her. Hurrying to intercept the second ring, she grabbed the receiver and readjusted Colton to an upright position with his head nestled on her shoulder. She held her breath for a second. Who would be calling at this hour?

"Susan? Is that you? This is Andrew. Anything wrong? You sound breathless."

She released her breath, thankful that it was Andrew on the line. "Oh, hi. No. I'm fine. What about you?"

"Fine."

"Let me put Colton down." A quilt spread out on the living room floor served as his playpen. She gently laid him in the middle of the pallet where she could keep an eye on him. She laid her hand against her chest as though to slow her heartbeat. Satisfied, she settled herself on the sofa, tucking her bare feet under her to get comfortable. "I'm back."

They spoke simultaneously. "I've been worried."

"Wait," he said, "you go first. I've been watching the weather. How are things there?"

"It looks fine here."

"Be serious, Susan. Have you latched the shutters? And what about drinking water? It sells out fast."

Susan smiled to herself. "I promise, Andrew, everything's fine. Mrs. J. is taking care of me. Now, how are things going out there? Will the storm affect you?"

"Probably not much. It looks like it will track west and south of here. We'll only get high winds and tides tomorrow. In any case, we spent the morning preparing."

"It sounds scary to be out there where the only thing you can see is water. What do you have to do to prepare?"

"Surely you don't want me to bore you with all the details?"

"It wouldn't bore me."

"Oh, we put away a lot of the tools and other junk—little things that take a while to do. Why?"

"It's just that I was concerned about you, Andrew."

There was a pause on the other end of the phone. Finally Andrew spoke in a halting voice. "That's a switch. It's the first time anyone has worried about me since I was a kid. Usually it was the opposite—me worrying about everybody else."

Susan didn't know how to respond. That he was touched about her concern was evident. What kind of life had the man been leading, for no one to care about him?

Andrew continued in a stronger, more matter-of-fact tone. "Things are calm for now. I had a little time, so I thought I'd better check on you and the kid."

"We appreciate it."

"Since your house is on elevated land, the tidal surge shouldn't flood it—unless it's a lot higher than expected."

"Andrew, I've been getting advice all day. Don't worry." Susan looked at the sleeping baby and changed the subject. "Colton's trying to fidget himself awake right now."

"Oh."

"He rolled over yesterday. He hoisted one fat little thigh over the other one and surprised himself. Mrs. Johnson said he practiced all day long. She's wonderful with him. She sings him nonsense songs all the time, and he stares at her and purses his lips like he's trying to sing, too."

With a hint of wistfulness in his voice, Andrew said, "Sounds good. You've probably got him on a schedule by now."

"Uhhh, not really. But he's sleeping better. He only woke up once last night."

"The book says a baby will do better if you feed him and put him to bed at the same time every night. Just one or two changes will foul everything up."

"I know what the book says, but things just haven't worked out yet," she told him, thinking that she had no intention of forcing a schedule on such a little baby. She would feed Colton when he was hungry and let him sleep when he was tired. "I can't decide what to do about his formula, though. He's been spitting up the stuff Lisa had him on. I've wondered if I should try something else, or if I should take him to a pediatrician before I do anything."

"Will it hurt him to try a different kind?"

"No, probably not." Susan twirled the phone cord around her finger, unwrapped it, then twirled it in the opposite direction.

"Then I don't see that you have anything to lose. Try another one. If it doesn't stay down, then take him to the doctor."

"Yes. I could do that." She didn't know why she had told Andrew about the formula, as though it was a problem he could help her solve. Perhaps she just wanted to prolong their conversation, to keep hearing the mellow tones of his voice.

"I've got another call, Susan, so I'll let you go. Call me if you have any problems with the storm, or... or with anything. It'll probably be Sunday before I get back to Corpus. There are a few things in Houston I need to take care of if I'm going to be spending my off time baby-sitting."

"Take care," Susan whispered before hanging up the phone and studying Colton, now fully awake and lying on his back trying to grasp a plastic Miss Piggy hanging from a play gym. "How could anyone abandon you? So precious, so sweet. But don't you worry. Your grandfather and I will take care of you."

Your grandfather!

Though he was nothing like a grandfather, the man she'd just talked with was quite different than she'd first thought. He was more reliable, more caring. Occasionally a crack appeared in his rough exterior, and she got a glimpse of a kinder man underneath. Like the way he treated Mrs. Johnson, or his obvious affection for Colton even if he refused to call him by name. He would have called the Children's Protective Services if he had not wanted to assume any responsibility.

Susan was relieved that the impending tropical storm in the gulf would miss the man. Colton needed him right now. *Not only Colton* was her next, unbidden thought.

THE TROPICAL STORM didn't miss Andrew Bradley. In fact, it dealt him a lot of grief. While Susan was eating breakfast, Andrew had his hands full.

"Hey, Bradley. You might want to see this." The heavy Cajun accent spilled from the PA overhead just as Andrew sat down at the table in the galley.

"Damn, this better be important," Andrew mumbled as he rose and pushed a steaming cup of coffee toward the center of the table. Worrying about Susan, the baby and the coming storm had kept him awake most of the night, so he was already dog-tired. He glanced at his watch. It was almost seven o'clock.

Sprinting down the steps to his office, he wondered what was so important that he had to miss breakfast. He looked up at the sky. The weather had been beautiful for the past couple of days. The seas were calm and the skies clear, but that was common before a big storm.

Dan Hebert was waiting for him when he opened the door. Andrew could tell by his stance that the news wasn't positive. "What you got?"

"Weather report. It don't look so good."

Andrew studied the fax from Air Routing/Wilkens Weather Division. In the past hour the storm had turned northward and been upgraded to a category-one hurricane. She still lay 180 miles to the southeast.

"Looks like we'll have an unwelcome visitor before long, maybe as early as sundown."

Noise emitted from the fax machine as a second message came in. Andrew tore it off and scanned the brief words. Glancing at Dan, he abbreviated the message. "We've got to prepare for evacuation."

"Sounds smart," replied the portly Cajun. "What else do you want us to do first?"

Andrew raked his fingers through his hair, grateful for the earlier precautions they'd taken. They'd already filled all the tanks with oil or water to make them too heavy to move around when the winds hit. Now, there were only a few last-minute things to be done before they evacuated the platform. "Get everyone in the galley for a meeting."

After Dan hurried out, Andrew radioed to find out how long it would take for their helicopter to arrive. He wished he had more than four men to help him secure the platform, but he was also glad few men had to be evacuated.

Andrew returned to the galley, picked up his cold cup of coffee, poured it out and turned to greet the men entering the room. "We want everything secured and shut down ASAP. Dan, you and Joe take Maurice and shut in all the satellite platforms. I'll do this one for you."

Dan scratched his head. "Tell me something."

"What do you want to know?"

"Think you can remember how to shut in a well? What's it been, five, six years since you done any operating?"

Andrew smiled. It had been several years since he had done any of the actual manual labor involved with shutting in a well, but it was something a person didn't forget. "Maybe I won't blow it."

Shaking his head, Dan picked up his hard hat and started for the door.

"Leroy—" Andrew nodded toward the oldest roustabout "—put up the storm shutters and make sure the life ring buoys are collected and stored. Then load out the boat with those crates that need to be sent back to the docks. We don't want them weathering the storm here."

As Leroy was double-timing it to his duty station, Andrew called out a reminder. "And don't forget to secure the crane boom when you're finished." Andrew remembered the time some fool forgot to secure the boom and a chunk was knocked out of the railing. It could jut as easily have knocked a hole in a separator or broken some piping.

Dan opened the door. "Maurice, you and Joe ready?"

"Yep."

Watching the backs of the men as they descended the stairs, Andrew was grateful for the capable old Cajun and for having Maurice and Joe with him. Dan was careful and efficient, just the type of person Andrew liked to work with.

With everyone split up, Andrew went about his work. The gas and oil to the platform had to be turned off in case worse came to worst and a fire broke out. After checking the computer, he switched the surface valve of the one well remaining in what a few years ago had been a block of ten good wells. If something should happen to this last well they would lose the lease on the block, and Andrew would have to either move to a different location—no telling where—or he would be out of a job.

Ten seconds after he blocked the master valve, an alarm went off that could be heard over the entire platform. "Damn." He had forgotten to kill the alarm before he blocked the valve. He was going to catch it from the other crew members for not knowing how to operate a platform, and he was the boss. *Boy, Susan would love this,* he thought. To catch him in a mistake would make her day. He hurried to kill the alarm before Leroy came to check.

Too late. Leroy stuck his head around a tank, took in the situation, then walked off with a shake of his head. He would tell Dan and the others, so Andrew might as well get ready for the ribbing that would be coming his way.

As he worked, Andrew went through a checklist in his head. Pneumatic valves closed. Manual valves closed. Hydraulics bled off. He glanced up at the sky, noting the bands of high-level ice-crystal clouds stretching overhead to the southwest. The seas were beginning to pick up, but it was nothing like they'd be seeing by early afternoon.

He was glad he and the crew would be spending the night in a hotel in Freeport instead of on the platform. Even though it was built to withstand 200 mph winds, it had never been tested and he didn't want his team to be the guinea pigs.

About an hour later, the helicopter returned with Dan, Joe and Maurice. Motioning at the guys who were already heading toward him, Andrew wanted one last review of what they'd done.

Dan reported, "Everything's down."

"Shutters are up. Anything loose is in the tool house. It's locked tighter than Scrooge's vault. Everything that's not welded down is tied down." Leroy pulled at his mustache, something he always did when he was nervous. "Anything else?"

"No, that's about it." He nodded toward the waiting helicopter. "Dan?"

"Nah. I'll wait and go in with you. We can handle things from here."

Andrew turned to face Leroy and the others and yelled over the helicopter noise. "You guys go on. The hotel's expecting you…and go easy on the booze. We may be back out here tomorrow. Dan and I will wait for the last ride."

Andrew had never felt so alone as he did when the gray dot of a helicopter blended with the larger gray of the sky. He looked around and all he saw was gray. Even the platform was a tiny gray dot isolated in a sea of sloshing waves.

He and Dan headed back to the office. Dan picked up a fishing rod. "I'm a gonna go down to the fishing deck and catch me a fish or two."

"Are you crazy?" The walk-around, located around the legs of the platform, was normally twenty feet above the waterline, but not now. The winds were driving the sloshing waves up and over the deck.

Dan grinned and shook his head. "Couldn't be better fishing weather. Fish bite like crazy when a storm has 'm caught up."

Andrew shook his head in disbelief as he watched Dan ease down the wet steps. "Crazy Cajun," he muttered.

After he shut down the generators and bolted the office door, he decided to check each level one last time while he waited for the helicopter to return. The winds were reaching close to thirty-five miles per hour. Any higher and the helicopter couldn't shut down when it landed or it would be blown off the platform.

The winds buffeted him, making it difficult for him to negotiate the narrow walkways. He shielded his stinging eyes with his hand and studied the bar of low clouds building on the horizon. That's when he spotted it. A five-gallon can of lubricating oil. "Damn it to hell," he swore as he climbed the ladder, put the can inside the cab of the crane and retied the door. Leroy would hear about this. This was just the type of thing that could become a dangerous projectile, cause a lot of damage. Little things mattered.

His brow furrowed when the image of a little baby boy flashed through his head. Andrew needed to survive. Little things mattered.

THURSDAY MORNING, Andrew pulled out of the Muchiwich docks in Freeport and turned on to the blacktop that led to Houston. Even though it was only nine o'clock in the morning, he was tired. He always felt this way after a week offshore.

This week, the added pressure from the hurricane had taken more out of him than usual. Because the storm was a small one by gulf standards, the crew had spent only one night in a hotel before they went back out. Despite his warning to take it easy, the guys were all hung over the next day. The platform had weathered the storm better than its crew.

The previous night, he had given in and called Susan again. To check on the kid, he told himself. He hated talking on the phone. As far as he was concerned, it was for business matters only.

But the past couple of days had been different. He had enjoyed the calls and found he was reluctant to hang up. For one thing, he wasn't sure Susan felt comfortable taking care of a baby by herself. Why, she couldn't even decide on a formula change. Thank goodness Mrs. Johnson was there.

When Susan had asked him about the hurricane, he'd made light of their emergency evacuation of the platform. Any storm out in the middle of the Gulf of Mexico was a potentially explosive situation, but one that turned so quickly could have led to fatalities. He knew they had been lucky this time.

If something should happen to him now, Susan would be left as sole supporter of the kid. One of the first things he intended to do was rewrite his will and change the beneficiary of his life insurance policy.

He had refrained from telling her about the surprise he had in store for her. Dan had hauled up a turtle during his fishing expedition. He had recognized it as a yearling ridley and decided not to throw it back into the water because its mouth had been torn when he tried to remove the hook. It was a tenacious little devil. A fighter. It wouldn't even let go of the hook for its own good. Andrew looked down at the creature. It kind of reminded him of himself sometimes.

He had put the tan plate-size sea turtle in a box lined with shredded computer paper and fed it bits of shrimp. At the time he hadn't considered the legality of keeping an endangered species, but he couldn't just throw it back in the water with a ripped mouth and let it die. So now it lay on the seat beside him, seemingly oblivious to its change of habitat. Andrew didn't understand what had come over him, but he'd decided to give it to Susan for her classroom. *She* could worry about the legal stuff. Maybe the little boy who was always in trouble would like it.

TOSSING DOWN his offshore bag in the entry hall, Andrew began going through the mail he had picked up at the post office. He stacked the mail into junk, bills, personal and guess stacks. Methodically, he tended to the bills, writing a check for each one before progressing to the next.

He then turned to the personal mail. One envelope had a North Carolina postmark. Maybe his ex-wife, Marilyn, had discovered Chris's whereabouts, he thought hopefully. Wrong. She wanted some of the furniture or wanted him to pay her for it. His mouth twitched. He'd already paid her for it twice. Money— that was all she'd ever wanted from him. He deposited the letter with the other junk mail before heading for the backyard.

He knew the one thing he had to do after filling the bathtub for the turtle was mow the lawn—if it wasn't too wet. His neighbors, with their perfectly manicured yards, would have his place condemned. Already his grass stood inches above theirs, something he would never have allowed to happen were it not for the interruption of his orderly life by Chris and Lisa and the kid.

Two and a half hours later, he stood before the bathroom mirror and looked at his torso, beaded with water droplets after his shower. He had worked up a sweat by the time he'd finished mowing, but that was what he'd needed. Something to quell his frustration and anger toward Chris. Or maybe it was more anger toward himself, for having been such a lousy father. The idea hit him like a fist. He'd always known it but had never openly admitted it. Was Chris just doing what he'd been taught? Absentee fatherhood?

Andrew stood sideways in front of the full-length mirror. He didn't like the man he saw. But the body wasn't bad, he conceded as he pushed out his stomach, then pulled it back in. Pretty firm for a forty-two-year-old.

Using a hand mirror, he looked at the back of his scalp. He noted with relief that his hair was still quite thick. Turning his head sideways, he leaned up close to the mirror and looked at his temples. A little gray, it was true—but surely not enough for anyone to know he was a grandfather. He didn't want anyone to know. Just the idea made him feel old.

Susan didn't seem old, he thought suddenly, and she too was a grandparent. He grinned when he remembered Susan admitting that she didn't have the kid on a schedule. She might appear docile in some ways, but she didn't concede defeat easily. He kind of liked that. He was looking forward to the next few days in Corpus Christi.

LOG

AFTER A LUNCH BREAK, I continued telling my story to the Corpus Christi Senior Citizens' Quilting Club. "If Andrew had known what was in store, he wouldn't have been looking forward to the week, I'll tell you."

"Why not?" asked Era Sullivan, holding one corner of the quilt.

"Just a minute and I'll explain the whole thing." I walked around the quilting frame to loosen the metal clamps and turn the quilt two rolls. I enjoyed taking my time because I knew it annoyed Bertha.

"Has he been back to help you in your yard again?" Bertha asked.

"Oh my, yes. He's the dearest thing. All this rain from the hurricane just left my yard in an awful mess. Right after he said hello to Susan and Colton, he came over to check on me, to see if I needed any help. Why, he does things just like my James used to—"

"Has Colton started teething yet?" Bertha inquired.

"He's really not old enough, but he's slobbering a lot. Probably precocious." I changed the subject. "Andrew brought Susan a Kemp's ridley turtle."

Virginia asked, "Isn't it illegal to keep one?"

"I'm sure it is," Bertha said confidently, as though she actually knew.

"Susan called someone important who said it would be okay to keep it till a man from the state aquarium could pick it up," I informed her. "Now, where was I?"

"You had told Susan about the measles, and Andrew had come back to Corpus with a turtle instead of a baby this time," Bertha answered.

"Oh, yes. Anyway, after I told Susan about the measles going around, she called the doctor. The earliest appointment she could get for Colton's vaccination was early the next Monday afternoon."

"Then she had to miss school, didn't she?" Virginia inquired, pushing up the sleeves of her sweater.

"No, not at all."

"Well, how did she manage to be two places at once?" Bertha prompted.

"Andrew took him."

"Oh!" Three voices chorused in sympathy.

CHAPTER SEVEN

ANDREW FIDGETED in the straight-backed vinyl chair, trying to look at ease. Being the only man in a sea of women and kids, he felt totally out of place, like a crawfish on dry land. Stretching his legs in front of him, he looked around at the fresh faces of the women who sat in the pediatrician's waiting room with him. They made him feel old.

Directly across from him sat a young mother whom he would have sworn was no more than nineteen. He didn't think much of her frizzy hair. It looked as if it was the result of her sticking her finger in an electrical outlet. She must have had it styled that way so no one could tell if it was combed or not. A shapeless dress made from a fabric that reminded him of mattress ticking hung stiffly from her shoulders. Not attractive. Tacky, in fact. She needed to spend more time on herself.

Andrew watched her struggle to placate her curly-haired twin sons who were two, maybe three, years old. Since they had arrived, the boys had been constantly whining for something. Finally the woman yielded to their high-pitched pleas and bought them a soft drink to share. To Andrew's dismay, the boys didn't seem to have mastered the concept of sharing yet. They immediately began squabbling over who got to hold the can.

"Boys, shh." The woman furtively glanced around the room. "I don't have the money for another one. Please be nice and share."

While thumbing through a parents' magazine, Andrew listened to the squabbling kids for several minutes before he slammed the magazine shut and fished some money out of his pocket. "Here, is this enough to get another pop?" He would have given her ten dollars to stop the boys' fussing.

The woman looked at the outstretched palm holding two quarters. "Yes, but I really shouldn't."

"Nonsense, take it."

Taking the money, the young lady said, "That's very kind of you. You seem to understand that twins need to assert their individuality. Thank you, sir."

The "sir" made him feel even older. That, and the fact that he wanted to tell her that she needed to let the twins know that their mother could assert herself, too.

While she was gone to the vending machine with one boy, the other boy spilled his grape drink, splashing Andrew's canvas shoes with the sticky purple liquid.

"Sowwy," the little towheaded boy muttered as he squatted on the floor and wiped the mess around the tiles with his hands.

When the woman returned, she emitted a loud sigh. "I'm sorry, Sir. Would you watch them while I run and get paper towels from the rest room?" Without waiting for an answer, she hurried away from the waiting area.

Andrew had just about had it, but he wasn't too sure what to do. He could use his now purple-spotted shoes to move himself to another seat and abandon his unsolicited charges. Instead, he took the toddlers by the hand and led them to the plastic play table in the corner of the waiting room. He set each child in a small plastic chair, plopped a truck in front of one boy and a toy telephone in front of the other before saying, "Call someone."

While he was staring down at the startled youngsters, the woman returned with a stack of towels. After she'd cleaned up the mess and sat back down, the boys decided they wanted to play tent under the full skirt of her dress. Maybe she hadn't had time to comb her hair, he decided. With those monster kids of hers, she had enough work to keep three people employed full-time. No wonder she looked harried and tired.

"Colton Bradley." A young, dark-haired uniformed nurse holding a folder stood in the doorway next to the registration desk.

What those boys needed was a little discipline. A good swat on the bottom would do them a world of good. He wasn't going to allow *his* grandkid to behave that way.

"Colton Bradley." This time, the nurse was more emphatic.

Andrew jerked his head up. He had been so bored and irritated waiting that he had quit listening for the kid's name.

"Bradley?" the nurse repeated a third time as she scanned the waiting room.

Andrew got up and carried the infant seat to where the nurse stood impatiently waiting. He gave her his most disarming smile and watched her demeanor change almost instantly.

With a bright smile of her own, she pushed open a door. "Can you wait in this room, Mr. Bradley? The doctor will be right with you."

"Sure thing. Thanks." Andrew set the infant seat on the paper-covered examination table and surveyed the cramped little room. Other than walls covered with painted figures of giraffes and of monkeys swinging from trees, it looked pretty much like any other examination room. A narrow counter holding a sink, antiseptic soap, tongue depressors, thermometers, hypodermic syringes...

Andrew swallowed. For the first time since he had agreed to take the kid for his shots, he felt a twinge of remorse. All parents had to do this. He could handle it. Shots had never bothered him. And he'd had plenty when he'd entered the military.

Andrew was awkwardly digging the kid out of the surrounding blankets when the pretty nurse stuck her head back in the room. "The doctor will be with you in just a few more minutes," she assured him.

He certainly hoped so. Andrew was only here because Susan couldn't bring the kid during office hours.

He wondered what Susan was doing at this moment. Was she in her classroom? He could just imagine how she looked, bent over a student's desk while explaining a problem. How come he'd never had pretty teachers like Susan when he was in school?

Teachers with long silky hair, smooth, soft skin and chocolate eyes?

A friendly voice interrupted Andrew's reverie. "Hello, there. I'm Dr. Felano. Let me see this little fella. Your grandson?" The doctor washed his hands in the small sink. Without waiting for a reply he continued, "How old is he?"

"A little over four months."

"Needs his shots?"

"Uh, yes," Andrew replied. "Isn't that what I wrote on the questionnaire?"

Dr. Felano laughed. "This must be your first time in with a little one. I scan the questionnaire and you answer my questions. It's a safeguard so there'll be no misunderstandings." He picked up the questionnaire and added, "You'll need to undress the little man."

Andrew pushed aside the strap on the infant seat and laid the baby on the paper-covered table. Big blue eyes stared at him with absolute trust. Eyes that reminded him of his own. This was going to be more difficult than he had first thought.

While Andrew was struggling to get the kid out of its clothes, the young nurse returned with several vials of liquid.

"Would you like some help?" she asked.

"No. I can handle it," Andrew assured her though he didn't really understand why Mrs. Johnson had put so many clothes on the kid. He slipped off the tiny socks and the bottoms of the sweat suit with no problem, but Colton balked and let out a cry when Andrew tried to slip the top over his head. Then he untied the undershirt and left the whimpering baby lying on the table dressed only in a blue-and-white striped diaper.

Gathering his equipment, the doctor instructed, "Considering the information here, I'd say the young man needs a complete checkup as well as immunizations. We can't really be sure if he's had a total workover."

Dr. Felano fell to the task of examining the baby with Andrew following his every move. The doctor checked Colton's reflexes and visual tracking. He weighed and measured him. When he removed the diaper, Colton began kicking and cooing with evident delight at being relieved of the restricting clothing.

Looking from the baby to the doctor, Andrew felt a moment's anxiety as the doctor examined the boy's testicles. "Is something wrong?"

"No...no. Everything seems to be right on track. He's an alert little tyke. Follows you around with his eyes, Grandpa. It's a good thing he trusts you, because I'm going to make him a little mad in a moment." He turned and took the syringe his nurse was holding out for him. "This will hurt a bit, and he may run a slightly elevated temperature tonight. I'll give you something for it. Nothing to be concerned about. Now, Mr. Bradley, if you'll just step over here while we get this over with."

Andrew looked at the sharp, shiny needle aimed at the tiny thigh. His knees turned to jelly and his vision blurred as he gripped the edge of the examining table. At the last moment he turned his head away unable to watch but all too able to hear Colton's piercing cry.

Then his surroundings began to fade as he felt his body sliding downward. He clutched at the table but his fingers didn't work. He didn't remember anything except a sinking sensation for several seconds after that.

"Mr. Bradley. Mr. Bradley." The nurse's voice penetrated the fog in his brain.

"Uhm . . . what . . . where?" he muttered.

"You fainted," explained the doctor.

"Nah . . . I couldn't . . ." Andrew stopped when he felt the chill of the floor and heard Colton's cries from the examining table above him.

Dr. Felano was kneeling beside Andrew, checking the pulse in his neck. "Don't be embarrassed. It happens all the time. Usually the fathers. You'll be fine in a few minutes. Just put your head between your legs," he ordered as Andrew struggled to get up.

The nurse swabbed his forehead with a damp cloth. "Take a few deep breaths now."

Feeling like a first-class fool, Andrew followed their instructions. Here he'd weathered a hurricane with hardly a moment of anxiety, and then a simple task like taking a kid to get shots had proved too much for him. He shook his head in embarrassed confusion.

Trying to calm his own nerves, Andrew drove around town until the baby quit crying and went to sleep. For a moment there in the doctor's office, he'd thought he was going to have to call Susan to come get him, wobbly knees and all. That would have been embarrassing.

If he'd known taking the baby to get his shots was going to be as bad as it was, he'd have made up some excuse and let Susan take the kid. It had taken him a full fifteen minutes to get the baby's cries reduced to sniffles before he could put him in the car seat. He hated crying. It made him feel helpless. He never knew what to do when someone cried.

ANDREW CARRIED the infant seat up the steps carefully so as not to wake the baby. He took a couple of deep breaths before he unlocked the door. Susan was already home, and he didn't want her to know how much the visit to the pediatrician had affected him.

Susan rushed from the kitchen into the living room to greet them. "I left school just as soon as the students were gone so I'd be home before you got here. I was beginning to worry—I thought you'd be home earlier." Ignoring the fact that the baby was asleep, she took Colton from his seat and cuddled him against her shoulder. "Was it bad?"

"Nothing to it."

"I'm so glad you took… Andrew, are you all right? You look a little pale."

"Oh, I'm fine." Exhausted, Andrew plopped down on the sofa and ran his finger around his shirt collar. It was damp with perspiration. He explained, "It's just a little warm out."

"It's the coolest day we've had so far this fall."

He watched Susan try unsuccessfully to suppress a smile as she sat down in the big Victorian rocker. What did she think was funny?

She swallowed and said, "Tell me what happened. What did the doctor say?"

Andrew didn't see the need in boring her with all the trivial details, so he gave her an abbreviated and slightly altered version of what had happened in the doctor's office. "Oh," he said, reaching into his pocket and pulling out a small bottle of red liquid, "Dr. Felano gave me this sample of Tylenol drops."

Susan reached for the drops to read the directions and uttered soothing sounds to Colton as she rocked him. "I'm so glad you took Colton," she repeated. "I don't think I could stand to watch him get a shot."

"Of course you could. It's just part of life."

Susan fidgeted in the rocker a few seconds, grinning all the while. Then, in a silky voice filled with gentle amusement, she let him in on her secret. "Dr. Felano's nurse called about ten minutes before you got here. She didn't want to know how Colton was. She wanted to know how *you* were doing."

Andrew leaned back against the sofa and closed his eyes to Susan's amused expression. "A man can't even be humiliated in private around here."

"Now, what *really* happened?"

"I didn't have lunch, so I fainted. Okay? That's all there was to it." He was still too embarrassed to talk about it. He'd been around blood and gore many times and handled it with stoicism. Never, absolutely never, had he fainted. Before today.

"You fainted?"

"Let's drop it, okay?" Andrew sat up and pointed to the sleeping baby. "I guess I'd better be going now. He seems to have calmed down, and you probably need to rest for a while."

"Don't go." She stood up and laid Colton down on the sofa beside Andrew before turning to face him. "That is, if you don't have anything you need to do."

Andrew was pleased that she wanted him to stay, and no, he didn't have anything to do. Nothing except going back to his motel room and watching television until he fell asleep from boredom.

Susan sat on the edge of the sofa next to the baby. "Thank you for taking Colton to the doctor. I'm sorry it was so difficult." She reached out and touched his hand where it rested on his knee.

Her fingers felt like velvet as they caressed the back of his hand and her voice was lower when she continued, "And thank you for bringing the turtle. Billy was so excited about it that I had a hard time getting him to go home today. We couldn't get a permit to keep it, though. In fact, we're lucky we weren't fined."

"You're welcome. I'm glad that I could help, though I can't imagine why there's all this fuss to save a few turtles." First, the turtle, now taking Colton to the doctor. He had to admit it—pleasing Susan made him feel good.

To his surprise Susan asked, "Are you going to be doing anything special for Thanksgiving?"

"I—I'll be offshore."

LATE INTO THE NIGHT, Susan sat up with Colton who was running a temperature from his shots. Pacing the floor to calm the fretting baby, she smiled as she remembered Andrew's frazzled appearance when he walked in with the baby. She never would have guessed that Andrew was the fainting type. He seemed too controlled.

She had seen the concern in his eyes and a new gentleness in his hands when he returned from the doctor's office with Colton. And he'd gone to the effort to save a turtle for a troubled little boy he'd never even met.

Locked away in Mr. Bradley were a lot of good qualities that he tried very hard to hide. Somewhere, maybe in one of her educational psychology classes, she had learned that people who needed others the most tried the hardest to pretend they didn't need anyone. They pushed love away. Maybe Andrew Bradley needed love in his life. A baby was a wonderful, unthreatening way to learn to love. Andrew needed his grandson, she decided, as much as the other way around.

As she rocked and sang to the whimpering Colton, she began planning for an early Thanksgiving. She would ask Andrew to stay. It wasn't that she really enjoyed his company, but... Suddenly remembering the feel of his hand beneath hers, she knew she was deceiving herself. She *did* enjoy his company. Besides, Andrew needed to start a tradition of spending some holidays with his grandson. She'd have Mrs. Johnson and Andrew to Thanksgiving dinner on Wednesday afternoon before Andrew had to leave. It would be fun.

Colton might be too young to know what was going on, but Susan was determined to give him a sense of security, of belonging. Apparently she had not instilled that feeling in Lisa. Maybe she'd taken on too

much, rearing a daughter alone, making ends meet
year after year, going back to school to earn her
teaching certificate. The hardest part had been leaving her friends and her hometown in West Texas town
so she could move to Corpus Christi to be near her
daughter, only to find that Lisa had disappeared.

Susan clutched Colton more tightly, thankful that
he was unaware he'd been abandoned. His tiny fingers stroked against her neck. With a tear-dampened
cheek, she nuzzled the softness of his head.

"Where are you, Lisa? Is what you're doing so
much more important than your baby?"

FIVE LANES of vehicles flashed past an oblivious Lisa
who stood on a nearby curb rehashing the previous
night's conversation with Venus. Venus had sensed
Lisa's resistance to her control. Lisa bit her top lip,
recalling the deep melodic voice reassuring her that she
was responsible to a new family, that Colton, no
longer her family, was unimportant in the cosmic
sense. The litany had continued for hours. Finally, she
nodded in understanding in order to stop the weight of
the hypnotic persuasion.

Glancing at the changing traffic light, Lisa knew it
would soon bring the cars to a screeching halt. That
was her signal to get to work. Taking a deep breath,
Lisa stepped toward the red Mazda that was coming
to a stop at the curb. "Would you like your windshield washed, sir? Just two dollars."

Getting his go-ahead, she leaned across the car and
sprayed window cleaner over the dirty windshield.

"Hey, get the side mirror, will you?" he asked as she gave the windshield a last swipe.

Spraying the mirror, she bent forward to wipe it and check her reflection. All of a sudden, the man reached his hand out the window and slid it up her thigh. "Wanna earn some extra money?" he asked.

Shrieking in surprise, Lisa jumped backward. "You—you bastard," she sputtered.

The man laughed at her response. "Thanks for the free wash job." His car bolted forward at the light change, splashing her with water as it sped away.

Shaking from the encounter, Lisa doubled her fists. "I hate this place, I hate this place, I hate this place," she sobbed. Craning her neck to spot Chris, she finally got his attention from the other side of the freeway and waved frantically to him. She needed to talk to him now, not at their designated break time. Now.

Reacting to her exaggerated gestures, Chris hopscotched his slender frame through the lanes of cars rather than waiting for traffic to come to a stop. "What's the matter? Don't tell me you've already reached your quota?"

She rubbed her eyes, reddened by tears and smog. "Funny, ha ha. I hate it here, Chris."

"What happened, honey, that you needed to talk to me now? One of Venus's people could come up at any time to check on us and we'd be in deep trouble. We've got four more hours on duty."

Lisa related her experience in graphic detail. Chris threw his rag on the pavement in disgust. "We didn't bargain for this, Lisa. We didn't bargain for this." Retrieving his cloth, he looked at her with determination. "You told me before and I didn't want to listen, but you're right. We've got to do something. I won't have you subjected to this kind of thing again."

"How much money have you made today?"

"I don't know. Let's go count." Plopping down on the damp grass by an evergreen, away from traffic, he kept his money low to his lap and counted it. "Eighteen dollars."

"I've only got sixteen. Thirty-four dollars won't take us very far."

Chris buried his hands in his shoulder-length hair and propped his elbows on his knees.

Lisa patted him on the leg. "We could wire our parents for the money."

His head shot up. "No way! This time we do it on our own. I'm not crawling back to my dad for anything."

"My mom probably won't even speak to me when she finds out what I've done. And I don't blame her."

"Maybe if we get back to work and make over our quota, we can keep a little money every day and stash it away somewhere. If we work extra hard we can make enough for a bus ticket home."

"Chris, can you imagine keeping money back from Venus? She'd know."

"Yeah. You're right."

Lisa dropped her head on her knees. "I can't believe the mess I've made of my life. I have a son I ran away from. My mom will probably never want to see me again after the things I said to her before I left, and she'll never forgive me for not telling her about the baby. We're trapped with no money. Chris, what's going to happen when Venus is through with us?''

Chris put his arm around her slender shoulders and pulled her close to him. "Lisa, we both thought we were so smart when we came out here. Now look at us. Standing on a freeway washing windshields—" a wry chuckle escaped his lips "—which is supposedly a step up from selling flowers."

"Degrading is what it is."

Chris hitched himself up from the grass-covered ground and offered his hand to help pull her up. "Yeah," he agreed. "I guess a lot of what we've done is degrading and now is as good a time as any to try to get our act together."

Something about Chris's tone gave Lisa confidence. "How?" she asked, dusting herself off.

"For starters, let's go talk to a justice of the peace, then buy some stamps and envelopes. We have some letters to write. After that..." Chris draped his arm over her shoulder, gave it a squeeze, and outlined the plan for getting their lives back on track.

CHAPTER EIGHT

"I CAN'T BELIEVE another Thanksgiving has rolled around." Mrs. Johnson was bustling about the kitchen, helping Susan prepare dinner when Andrew banged on the kitchen door. Drying her hands on her pumpkin-design apron, Mrs. J. smiled at him through the windowpane as she hurried across the spotless linoleum. "Why, Mr. Bradley," she said, beaming as she opened the screen door. "Your errand didn't take very long, did it? My, my, what a load you have in your arms." Taking one of the top boxes, she exclaimed, "What on earth could this be?"

Andrew tried to downplay his purchase. "Oh, nothing really. I stopped by and picked up a camcorder and a VCR. Susan is always going on about what the kid is doing while I'm gone."

"I'm what, and you did what?" Susan asked from the sink where she was peeling potatoes.

"I was afraid you'd already whipped out a plastic card to buy one of these." Andrew stacked the boxes on a corner of the kitchen table.

"I'll let that pass." Susan exchanged knowing smiles with Mrs. Johnson realizing that this purchase meant more than pictures. It meant that Andrew didn't want to miss any more of Colton's development than he had to.

While the women finished putting the meal together, Susan watched as Andrew slowly read the directions for assembling the equipment. She was amazed at how much he had changed in the month she had known him. He had previously refused to follow written instructions. Now he would rather incur the embarrassment of reading instructions than of needing her help again.

That he had agreed to stay for the Wednesday-afternoon meal, even though he said he didn't like to make a big deal out of holidays, was a change. And money. A month ago he wouldn't have spent that much money on a video camera. Realizing that Colton meant more to Andrew than money, Susan felt a warm glow.

Two hours later Andrew groaned, half in pleasure and half in pain. "I ate like a pig on the way to slaughter, ladies. You may just have to haul me to the cemetery." He slowly leaned back from the table. "But—" he nodded toward the desserts "—bury the rest of that pumpkin pie with me. Everything was so good, I must've died and gone to heaven. Thank you both."

"Don't thank me," Mrs. Johnson explained, blushing with pleasure as she dabbed at the corner of her mouth with a linen napkin. "Susan did all the cooking. I just helped dish it up."

It had been ages since he had eaten a meal like that. He was a little surprised that Susan was such a good cook. He had her figured as someone who couldn't do much except open a few cans, microwave a frozen dinner or place an order from a fast-food place. He looked at her across the table. Her cheeks were rosy from the steamy kitchen and her brown eyes twinkled with happiness. The woman was full of hidden talents.

Andrew stood and gingerly patted his full stomach. "I think I'll just take myself into the living room and kick back on the sofa for a while. I need to let that dinner settle down."

"Oh, no, you don't, young man," Mrs. Johnson clucked, looking over the top of her bifocals as she stacked the dishes together. "You don't get out of doing dishes that easily. Good meals aren't free."

Andrew feigned shock. "You can't be serious, Mrs. J. You mean that you want me to help with the dishes?" He enjoyed kidding the older woman. His instincts had been right. She was a perfect baby-sitter. That she loved the kid was obvious.

"Well, I'll tell you what. I'll put the food away while you finish getting that video contraption set up. Little Colton seems to be in a fine mood to have his picture taken," she replied, taking a load of dishes to the sink. "Yes indeed, he's in a fine mood."

Andrew looked at the little boy who was lying on the old quilt pallet, studying his foot in between sticking it in his mouth. The baby was so content, so happy. Thank goodness he didn't know what irresponsible clods he had for parents. "I'll go for that. Anything to keep from getting dishpan hands."

In the center of the kitchen floor, he wrestled with the camera and tripod while Susan and Mrs. Johnson cleared the dining table. Finding the whole operation more difficult than he imagined, he muttered to himself, "Blasted instructions must have been written by someone who doesn't speak English." Finally, satisfied that the camera was operable, he refolded the instructions and trained the camera on his grandson. After an hour of having his "piggies" videoed by his grandpa, Colton began to fret.

"I think you've had all the attention you want for one day, haven't you, Baby?" Susan lifted Colton's sweat top and blew on his stomach, enjoying his squeal of delight. "Let's get you ready for beddybye." She scooped him up in her arms and started for the bedroom.

"Oooh, it's already dark out, isn't it?" Mrs. Johnson peered out the living room window to confirm her fear. "I should have left earlier. Well, I guess that's that. Good night, all." Pulling on her heavy cardigan, she paused at the front door and looked up and down the dimly lit street.

Andrew rolled his head from side to side as though he were working out a kink, then walked over beside her. "Would you mind if I tagged along with you, Mrs. J.? I could sure use a little fresh ocean air to help put some life back in my stiff bones."

"Suit yourself." Mrs. Johnson dangled her door key in front of him.

When he returned from escorting Mrs. Johnson home, Andrew sauntered up the stairs to the nursery. Susan was bent over Colton's crib. His gaze traveled down the sheath-style dress encasing her rounded curves, stopping to admire how the fabric clung to the right places, places he wouldn't mind clinging to. She sure had nice buns for a grandmother, he thought, walking over to stand beside her. He had been right when he'd thought it would be hard to keep his hands off her. In fact, it had become much more difficult than he'd imagined.

He stuck his hands in his jeans pockets to curb the temptation to give her bottom a little pat. She would think he was a lusty old man if he did something like that. And she would be right.

He gave the rounding contours of her rear one last longing look before he cleared his throat and said the first thing that came to mind. "The little fellow's all tuckered out, isn't he?"

"He should be." She gently nudged his feet into the bottom of his sleepers, then snapped the grippers. "He really put on a show for you."

"I'm not so sure about that. I think that show was for you and Grandma J."

"Not true. But it was nice of you to walk Mrs. Johnson home. There've been some muggings a few blocks away, so she's afraid to be out at night."

"No problem. She's a pretty special lady." Muggings? Andrew hadn't heard about any muggings. "What muggings?" he asked.

"I thought I told you. One night last week, two houses were broken into two streets over. One was across the alley behind Milly's house. In both cases, the women were beaten and robbed. It's made all of us a little leery about being alone at night."

"Any clue as to who did it?" Andrew, feeling apprehensive about leaving Susan, was glad he'd replaced her old door locks.

"Yes, in fact the police arrested the young hoodlums the next day. One of them was the great-nephew of one of the women. They were after some money she kept hidden, and when she refused to give it to them, they beat her. I don't think there's anything for the rest of us to be worried about."

"Oh." Andrew felt a little relief that the culprits had been caught, but it made him realize how much he wanted to protect the people in this house. They seemed like a family tonight. He reached down and clasped the baby's tiny fingers and felt an unfamiliar warmth inside himself. "Good night, little fellow."

Reluctantly releasing the tiny fingers, Andrew shrugged off the feelings and turned to Susan. "Now, let's get those dishes done," he said, taking her elbow and guiding her to the kitchen.

"You've got a long drive before you. I'll get them tomorrow."

"No. Mrs. J. was right. Nothing worthwhile's free. Besides, they'll be harder to wash tomorrow and you need the day off so you can rest a little. It won't take long if we get after it."

Susan nodded. "All right. I'm not one to pass up such an offer twice. You finish the stacking, and I'll start the washing."

"Dinner really was delicious," Andrew said, scraping food from the dirty dishes into the garbage can. "I think it might have been the best Thanksgiving spread I've ever had."

"Thank you very much, sir. But I couldn't help noticing that you picked the onions out of the cornbread dressing."

Andrew had the grace to look sheepish. "I thought you wouldn't notice."

"Only a dolt wouldn't have noticed. Why didn't you tell me you didn't like onions when you saw me chopping them up? I could have left onions out of part of the dressing."

"It wasn't that important. I can usually eat around them. As hard as I've tried, I just can't learn to like onions. Even the smell of a raw one gets me."

"Now I know how to get rid of you when you've overstayed your welcome. Put onions in everything."

"That would do it." Andrew grinned. "I can't believe you like them."

"I love 'em. And garlic, too. Haven't you heard that onions and garlic are great for your health?"

"I'd rather meet an early death. If you can eat those, you can eat anything."

"Wrong. There's lots of stuff I won't eat. Some of it looks good, like bananas. They smell wonderful, but I can't swallow a bite of one to save my life. It's the texture. And liver!" Susan shivered at the thought. "It looks awful, it smells awful and it tastes awful." When the deep, old-fashioned sink was full of hot water, she switched off the tap and set the plates at the bottom before dumping all the flatware on top of them.

"Aren't you going to wash the glasses first?" Andrew asked.

"This is how I always wash dishes."

"There's no way you can see the blades on those knives you just dropped in the water. Aren't you afraid you'll grab an edge and cut yourself?"

"No."

"I always wash the glasses first. That way they don't look spotted."

Susan looked at Andrew for a long moment. "Do you want to wash the dishes by yourself?"

"Uh . . . no, not really."

"Then I'll do it my way."

"I didn't mean to imply that . . ."

"Yes, you did. I haven't done anything to suit you since I met you, except for the meal we just finished."

"That's not true."

"Yes it is, Andrew, and you might as well admit it. You couldn't keep your hands off the clutter in my living room the first time you set foot in my house. But you did restrain yourself for a day or so before you attacked the railing on the porch."

"When I fixed the railing, I was bored. I knew you didn't have the time now that you have the baby to care for. I meant to help."

"Okay, I withdraw the comment about the railing, even though I thought you were being critical. But you can't deny that you disapprove of the clutter."

"All right. Yes, the way you keep house does drive me crazy. Out on the platform, anything left lying around creates a hazard. Same thing applies here. If you would just change a—"

Susan interrupted his criticism. "Besides the way I take care of Colton and my housekeeping, is there anything else you'd like to change?"

"Yeah. Now that we're on the subject, there is." Andrew grinned and pointed to the teapot clock over the range. "That's absolutely the ugliest clock I've ever seen. I'd rather not know the time than look at it."

"It was hanging on the wall when I moved in, and I haven't bothered to change it. If you'd been looking at collectibles lately, you'd know that clock is the height of style. Early-fifties memorabilia. That clock is quite expensive, I'll have you know."

"Ummph," Andrew grunted, staring at the clock. "I've always had my doubts about collectors. That clock was ugly in the fifties, and unlike fine wine, it hasn't improved with age."

"You don't have to hurt my feelings, Andrew. I'm particularly fond of the dingy white electrical cord trailing out the bottom."

Andrew gave her a strange look for a split second before he realized that she was baiting him, then he laughed. "Now that you've revealed your tastes, I know what to get you for Christmas."

"Don't you dare."

He gave her a wicked grin.

She added, "I guess it's a good thing you and I aren't a couple. We'd be at each other's throat."

"We would if you insisted on keeping that clock and never picked up your junk."

Susan wiped the last plate and reached for the pots and pans, hesitated, then washed the glasses. "When it doesn't matter to anyone, it's easy to get in the habit of not picking things up. I always think I'll get to it later." She gave a short chuckle.

"I can't do that. I have to attend to things as they come up so I don't lose track of what has to be done."

"That's probably because you're away from home half the time. You can't let things slide."

"Maybe." He paused and thought for a minute. "Sometimes I think I pay attention to the details because I don't want to examine the whole or find out what's missing in my life. The details keep me so busy that I don't have to think." Andrew stopped when he realized that he had revealed too much. "Never mind. Where do you keep these?" he asked, indicating the crystal glass in his hand.

Susan nodded toward a far cupboard door. Having finally washed all the dishes, she studied the disappearing soapsuds in the sink for a moment before pulling the plug and watching the water swirl down the drain. "I think we all sometimes wonder if we've missed something." She turned around and leaned against the counter as she dried her hands on a cotton towel.

There was something different about Andrew tonight, something bordering on melancholia. Before, she had thought him a man whom women would notice when he entered a room, but be a little afraid to approach. Initially she, too, had thought him handsome, but cold and brusque. Now she knew he wasn't cold. Efficient would be a better description. It was in the way he walked and carried himself—a sort of presence, a self-assurance that most other men lacked.

Tonight she found him very appealing, emotionally and physically. The muscles in his face lacked the tenseness she often noted in his jaw. His eyes radiated warmth and depth. And the way he smiled—his crooked grin made her chest tight and her stomach tingle, both of which she hadn't felt in years.

Her physical responses to his nearness felt good but dangerous, under the circumstances. She realized that she needed to change her avenue of thoughts.

Andrew stared out into the darkness that hid everything lying outside the security of the kitchen. True, he wasn't old, but he was no longer young, either. The path he had chosen was narrow and rather straight, unadorned with frills. Work. No wife. A girlfriend, maybe. That was all he had time for. He was at a crossroads in his life.

Before this evening, he had hardly given any thought to the future except for stocks, annuities and an IRA account. And to what end? A lonely retirement? Hospitals? To leave to that ingrate of a son? No!

Colton.

He had another chance with Colton.

And maybe with Susan.

The thought startled him. He felt the warmth radiating from Susan's body as she stood next to him. Did she feel the same way he did? Were they both getting another chance? He felt a sudden spiritual closeness to the woman so near to him and yet so far. Sure, he had problems with some of her habits, but then, she had been letting him know that she had problems with him, too. Not too many, he hoped, thinking he'd like to engulf her in his arms, feel her flesh pressed against his. He'd like to...

When Susan gingerly laid her hand on his arm he was startled at the diffusion of warmth that was transmitted from her bare flesh to his. "Penny for your thoughts." The soft, soothing, honeyed words enticed him to tell her what he was thinking, but he was afraid to let her know how much she appealed to him. How much he wanted her.

He closed the blinds and turned away from the empty blackness back to the brightly lit kitchen to give Susan a halfhearted smile, determined not to reveal the lust-filled thoughts that had come unbidden. More pressing concerns needed to be addressed first. "That's about what they're worth."

"Nonsense."

"Among other things, I was thinking of the little fellow. He's sound asleep, completely oblivious to his predicament, and I'm wondering what kind of life he'll have. It seems a little early to start worrying about that, doesn't it?"

"It's never too early. What happens now will probably determine what kind of life he has. What kind of life do you want him to have?"

"Oh, I could say whatever makes him happy, but that's not true. Or, at least, it's not enough. I always thought Chris was pretty happy, but I don't like the mess he's made of his life up until now."

"Then what?"

"I don't really know. I want him to be organized, a person people can count on. Not necessarily a go-getter, but a doer. I want him to have a sense of fulfillment, like he's contributed something to society."

"I'd like that, too."

Looking at the teapot clock hanging on the kitchen wall, Andrew hung up the wet dish towel he'd been using. Somehow, the clock didn't look as ugly as it had before. "I'd better get a move on. Tomorrow's a workday, and I won't get home until way after midnight as it is."

"What time do you have to get up in the morning to be at the docks?"

"Around four-thirty."

"You won't get much sleep tonight. You'll hardly have time to climb into bed before you have to get back up." Susan walked him to the door.

"It doesn't matter. I don't usually sleep well the night before I leave to go offshore. Lying in bed, I start thinking about all I've got to do when I get to work. Then I worry about what I might be leaving undone at home."

They were silent for a few seconds.

She liked him tonight. Colton was lucky to have him for a grandfather. Some men would have backed away from caring for a baby. That Andrew didn't, showed a man of warmth, of concern. Tonight, it felt as though the four of them—Mrs. Johnson, Andrew, Colton, herself—were a happy family.

"Susan?"

"Mmmh?"

Jacket slung across his shoulders, Andrew grinned broadly while holding the doorknob with one hand. "Thanks for nagging me to stay."

"I did not nag." She emphasized the word *nag*.

"Even though I'm glad you did, you didn't have to work so hard on the dinner. Anything, even wieners and cheese, would have been infinitely more enjoyable than eating a hamburger and fries in the car on the drive home.''

Susan laughed aloud. "You...you..." Finding no words, she whacked at him with the wet dishcloth she still held in her hand. "Get out of here." She really didn't want him to go, wanting instead to bask in this newfound friendliness. She wanted to watch a movie with him, or sit on the sofa and watch the videotape he'd made of Colton. More than anything, she wanted a reason to touch him again.

Andrew grabbed the end of the cloth and with a devilish smile pulled her toward him. "The gods of hospitality will punish you if you're not nice to guests.''

She pulled back on the cloth but allowed him to close the distance between them inch by inch until their hands touched. Her tongue flickered over her dry lips as she whispered, "I'll bet the gods of hospitality would have to change their rules if they'd ever entertained the likes of you.''

He was so close that she could feel his breath as he said, "Are you saying I'm a bad guest?"

She looked into his eyes. "No, tonight you were..."

"I do mean it, you know. The food, the conversation, you..." His gaze held her transfixed as he hooked a finger beneath her chin and raised her face still closer. He lowered his lips to hers.

She trembled as he first teased her top lip softly, then covered her mouth with his. The dishcloth fell to the floor between them as the kiss deepened.

Before she was ready, he ended the kiss and leaned back. "I don't want to go but if I don't leave now..." The rest of the sentence he left unsaid as he gave her a quick peck on the tip of her nose.

With a look of contentment on his face, Andrew opened the door. Taking one last look, he stepped off the porch into the darkness. "Good night, Susan."

Sighing, Susan leaned against the counter after he had gone, remembering the lingering look he had given her. Gingerly she touched her lips where the taste of Andrew remained. She had wanted to ask him to stay. The desire she felt and how close she had come to acting on it filled her with uneasiness. She wasn't free to do as she wanted.

Tonight had been one of the most enjoyable times she'd had since, since... Her mind flashed through the past and came up barren. She couldn't remember ever experiencing the kind of pleasure that was now co-cooning her. And Andrew Bradley was responsible.

She parted the blinds to get a view of his car pulling away from her driveway. "Good night," she whispered.

CHAPTER NINE

THE BEGINNING of December was sunny and warm. It wasn't like any winter Susan had experienced on the High Plains. Leaves were still clinging to the trees and a profusion of fall flowers adorned the neighboring yards with varying shades of yellow and orange.

Susan nudged her car door closed with her right hip as she precariously balanced student sketches of the ridley turtle on top of a wooden art box. Holding the papers in place with her chin, she hurried up the steps of her house, opened the front door and stumbled into the living room before her load toppled to the floor. "Oh, crumb!" She wanted to say worse, but had stopped using her favorite expletives so she'd be a better influence on Colton.

Mrs. Johnson poked her head into the room. Colton was nestled in her arms while he nursed a bottle. "My goodness, what happened, Susan? Did you hurt yourself?"

Emitting a loud sigh, Susan surveyed the chaos. "No. It just looks like I made a mess sooner than usual. It's been a typical Monday. Right down to this."

Agnes Johnson put Colton on the sofa and kneeled down on the floor. "Here, let me help you while you tell me what happened."

"Oh, really nothing big. The students acted like they were on a sugar high all day. They fought and called each other names and wouldn't do their work. I hope tomorrow'll be better."

"They're probably excited and counting the days until Christmas."

"So am I. Billy reminded me three times—as if I didn't know—that there are only twenty-one shopping days left."

"Poor dear. That sounds like a hint for you to buy him a present."

Susan nodded. "And not a very subtle one at that."

Handing the last stack of papers to Susan, Agnes pulled herself up. "I hate to rush, but I promised Bertha I'd drive her to the clinic to check her blood pressure this afternoon. She's been in a dither all day, so she's probably got it worked up high enough that she'll be happy. She gets grumpy if I'm five minutes late. One time she even called Betsy to see if something had happened to me, so I'd better be on my way." She patted Colton on his head, then bustled out the door.

Leaving Colton happily playing with his fingers, Susan carried her mess to the kitchen. She'd just be a minute, then she'd go play with him. First, she wanted to get her work out of the way so she could really relax and enjoy him. She needed to prepare for the turtle committee meeting tomorrow.

She tossed her work on the big table and began rolling the Save the Turtle posters that needed to be

hung in rest rooms and snack bars along the beach.
The posters would inform readers that they could be
fined up to $20,000 if they had a Kemp's ridley in their
possession or if they messed with one that was laying
eggs. She bet Andrew didn't have a clue what he'd
risked by bringing one to her.

The posters also asked people to be on the lookout
for nesting females returning to Padre and Mustang
Island. She had to admit that she was becoming more
interested in the ugly little creatures every day. If for
no other reason, she was doing it for Billy.

She was almost through with the rolling when she
heard a sickening thud from the next room. Hearing
a piercing scream, she bolted for the living room.

THE HEADLIGHTS caught the gleam of Milly Adams's
blond hair as an exhausted Susan turned into her
driveway. Milly yanked open her car door. Susan gave
her fellow teacher a look that spelled exhaustion,
barely noticing that Agnes and Betsy were also there.

"Susan, what happened?" Milly asked, glancing
over at Colton in his car seat. "All that blood...we
were so frightened...after what happened to the lady
who lives behind me."

Susan slumped her head on the steering wheel,
weariness claiming her control. "Everything's okay,
Milly. Give me a minute."

Betsy peered in at Susan, then ran around to the
other side of the car and took the whimpering baby in
her arms while Milly helped Susan out of the car.

Agnes immediately ran and engulfed her in a big
hug. "Oh, dear. Oh, dear," she kept repeating. "Oh,

dear . . . I was so worried. . . . What happened? I came over to bring you some cobbler after I got back from taking Bertha to the clinic. . . . Your door wasn't locked. . . . When you didn't answer I went on in. . . . I thought you might be upstairs changing Colton's diaper. That's when I saw the blood in the kitchen. . . ."

Susan tried to calm the hysterical woman. "It's okay."

"So I called the police. I didn't know what else to do," she sobbed. "All I could think about was those muggers. I had a feeling something terrible had happened to you and Colton."

The young, slender policeman who had been patiently waiting on the porch while the women talked, finally spoke up. "Ma'am, is there a problem?"

"No, my little boy fell on the corner of my art box and cut his head. I've just returned from the emergency room," Susan explained. "He'll be all right now." Susan began giggling. "You know what I thought when I saw those lights flashing when I rounded the corner? I thought I'd been robbed. Wouldn't that have been funny?" Tears began to flow as Susan giggled.

Taking a step backward, the policeman asked, "Are you sure you're all right, ma'am?"

Wiping away tears with the back of her hand, Susan nodded her assent.

"She'll be fine, Officer. Thank you for coming," Milly assured him.

Flipping his notebook closed, he mumbled, "If that's all, I'd better be going," then hurried down the driveway to his patrol car.

Milly patted Susan's shoulder. "Here, honey, let's go in the house and have a cup of coffee. I brewed a pot while we were waiting."

"Thanks, Milly." Susan felt guilty for all the wild thoughts she'd had about Milly. There was a kind, caring woman beneath the makeup and blond hair.

Susan sipped on the hot liquid as she tried to explain what had happened. "I would have sworn I was watching Colton. I just turned my back for a minute. Then he screamed. By the time I got to him, blood was gushing from his head and trickling into his eyes."

"There, there, dear. I just hate it that you had to handle it by yourself." To calm her shaking hands, Mrs. Johnson twisted her skirt into knots.

Susan closed her eyes. "I thought I was going to faint, but I knew I couldn't." Sighing at the memory, Susan looked at Betsy who was whispering to the still-whimpering Colton. "Do you want me to take him? He's got to stay awake for a while."

"No, let me hold him. Babies feel so good. This may make me want to have one." Betsy flashed a smile at her grandmother.

"I do hope you choose to get married first." Agnes gave her granddaughter a pointed but affectionate look, then turned to Susan. "Oh, Susan, I feel like such a fool calling Betsy and Milly," she explained, "but if anything had happened to you or the baby, Andrew would skin me alive. We all decided that we'd better call the police."

"I'm glad you cared, Mrs. Johnson, and I'm sorry for having given you a scare. It's nice to have neighbors like you. I appreciate it."

Agnes patted her dress back into place and confessed, "Susan, there's one more little thing."

"What's that?" Susan asked, falling back into the overstuffed chair. She was exhausted mentally and physically.

"I . . . called Andrew."

"You what?" Susan stiffened, thinking of the implications. How would she ever explain to him what had happened?

"I thought maybe he'd heard from you or something. I hope you're not too upset."

"You did what you thought was best," Susan assured her. "What did you tell him?"

"Just that the door to the house was open and there was some blood in the sink," Agnes said, pausing as the impact of her words hit her. "I think you'd better call him and explain what really happened before he catches a boat back to Freeport."

"He wouldn't?"

"I think he would. He sounded really worried and told me that he was coming in as soon as he could get a boat to pick him up. That was about ten minutes before you came back."

Susan tapped her fingers against the tabletop while she waited for what seemed like an eternity until the phone call went through. Her friends had left only after they were sure that she was calm. Mrs. J. had urged Susan to call Andrew "the minute" she was alone. This was the first time Susan had called him offshore. "Andrew?"

"Susan? Is that you? Are you all right? What happened? Where were you?" His voice took on an urgency she hadn't heard before.

"It's Colton." She tried to remain calm. She really did. But the past few hours at the emergency room, then finding the police and her neighbors at her house, had left her overwrought, and she began to cry.

"Calm down. I can't understand you. What about Colton?" Andrew's voice caught.

"He fell...and cut his head open.... He had to have...three stitches." She sobbed between words.

"Is he okay?"

"Yes. He's not sniffling anymore."

"What happened?"

"He rolled...off the sofa and...hit his head on the edge of my wooden art box."

"That's what I've been trying to tell you!" his raised voice accused over the phone line. "All that clutter is an accident waiting to happen."

"I just..."

"You were supposed to watch him! You knew he was rolling around like crazy. And the book says dangerous objects should be kept away from infants."

She had been through enough during the past few hours that his censure was more than she could take. "Andrew Bradley, you can take your bloody book and shove it!"

"Wha..."

Susan interrupted. "I wasn't neglecting him. I only turned my back for a—"

"A second is all it takes. He could have hit his eye on the corner of that box! What am I going to have to do? Quit my job and take care of him myself?"

Susan had reached her breaking point. Sighing, she laid the receiver back in its cradle even as she heard Andrew's voice on the line. She felt guilty enough already without Andrew making her feel worse. Shifting Colton to her shoulder, she rocked him and silently let tears run down her cheeks unchecked as she chanted over and over, "Oh, baby, I'm sorry. I'm so sorry."

Hardly had she started rocking when the phone began ringing. Suspecting it was Andrew calling her back, Susan ignored it. She didn't want to talk to him. Not now. Not ever, if she could avoid it. Compassion was foreign to the man. He only knew how to cast guilt. How she could have ever deluded herself into thinking that they shared something special was beyond her comprehension. Well, she wouldn't make that error in judgment again.

Reaching over, she flipped on the mute switch to keep the ringing from disturbing Colton. It was the same as it had been when Lisa was little. No understanding, no support, no comfort. Lisa's father, George, had been there in body, but he had refused to have anything to do with rearing his daughter. The fact was, he had to be babied himself.

Her father had warned her about marrying George. He'd seen past the captain of the football team that had so enchanted his cheerleader daughter. "Pick the right man, Susan," he'd warned, "because you only marry once."

Well, she'd married George, anyway, and realized her mistake almost immediately. Right from the start, he proved unable to hold down a job. What success he'd had ended with his last high school football game. When Lisa had come along a year later, they both felt a responsibility to keep the marriage together. So Susan had found herself with not only a daughter but a full-grown man to raise as well.

She relived the pain of that loneliness during the four hours she kept Colton awake as the doctor had suggested. Four long, miserable hours before she could finally put him in his crib.

Standing in front of the mirror and studying her tear-swollen eyes, Susan realized the residual pain from her marriage was nothing compared to the new ache caused by Andrew's attack. Just when she thought they'd become compatible, if not soul mates, he'd turned on her when she'd needed him most.

Ignoring the stacks of ungraded papers still lying on the kitchen table, she changed into her nightgown, flipped off the mute switch and climbed into the lonely bed. Immediately, the phone rang again. Susan looked toward the ceiling in a silent prayer, then rolled across the bed and pushed the intercom button. "Yes."

Muffled by static, Andrew's low voice filled the room. "Susan, why didn't you answer the phone? I've been calling constantly since we were cut off."

Though she didn't want to admit it to herself, his voice was a welcome sound. Her temper had cooled, though the hurt inflicted by his words remained. "We weren't cut off, Andrew. I hung up."

"Oh. I thought maybe you did, but... Hey, look, I'm sorry."

"Sure you are." She thought she'd learned not to be vulnerable, but Andrew sounded sincere.

"No, really, I am. I know that things just happen sometimes. I don't know what got into me. I imagined the worst when Mrs. J. called and said your door was standing wide open and there was blood in the kitchen. And I couldn't do a thing. It was already getting dark, so I couldn't even catch a helicopter to the docks. I should've been there to help, to drive you to the hospital. That must've been agony for you, being there alone."

Susan appreciated but was still unwarmed by Andrew's confession. She just couldn't trust him yet—not after the years of empty promises and apologies from her husband.

"I'm used to handling things by myself, Andrew."

"I should've been there," Andrew repeated.

Andrew's not George, she reminded herself. There was no similarity. "You couldn't be. I understand that's just part of your job." Susan snuggled down in the bed for physical warmth, although she was starting to feel a warm glow from Andrew's apology. So much for remaining invulnerable. "Don't be so hard on yourself, Andrew. Everything turned out okay." Maybe sharing her pain with him would lessen it. "I haven't been so frightened in years."

"And I berated you. There's no way for me to take back my words, Susan. I let you down."

"It's okay," she sighed.

When at last they hung up, Susan sat up in her lace-covered bed. "He loves Colton. He cares," she whispered to the moonlit room. And deep amid her stirring emotions was the knowledge that she cared for Andrew.

EVER SINCE his last phone conversation with Susan, Andrew had rehearsed his speech. Talk about low. He'd never felt as low in his life as he did after he lashed out at Susan for Colton's accident. *He* was the guilty party. She was having to cope with the baby by herself. Who did he think he'd been fooling? Her? No. He'd only been deluding himself into thinking that he was a full partner in sharing the responsibility for the kid's well-being. Sure, he was there three days every other week, but she had Colton the rest of the time. She was never off duty. Maybe she understood, as she'd said on the phone, but he didn't. Not anymore.

After pacing the floor of his Houston house for half an hour that morning, he'd decided to drive to Corpus right away. He'd been too anxious to wait until evening. The shell driveway brought back memories of the first time he had pulled in, eager to find relief. Now he wanted to provide relief. Cool wind whipped around his body as he stepped out of the car, erasing the stiffness from his legs.

Looking at the doorbell, Andrew grinned, then depressed it with a firmness of purpose. He was still grinning when Susan opened the door.

"Andrew Bradley, when that bell kept ringing, I knew it was you. You'd better be glad that Colton was already awake."

"Mrs. Montgomery, I presume?" He forgot his speech.

"And may I ask why you need to see Mrs. Montgomery?"

"To apologize for boorish behavior. May I come in?"

Susan laughed. "Oh, Andrew. Come on in. I didn't expect you until tonight." Pointing to a chair, she asked, "Can I get you something to drink?"

"No." He ran his tongue over his parted lips, remembering the kiss that had developed into more than he'd intended. "I thought maybe you had a hemmed-in feeling today and would like to get out for a while. Why don't we go get something to drink?"

The pleasure in her chocolate brown eyes confirmed Andrew's belief even before she spoke. "That sounds wonderful."

"Then we could drive around a little. You could point out the sights of the Texas Riviera."

"Sights? I've missed the Riviera part. The only sights I could point out are the school, the bank, the grocery story, the church and home. We can see the sights together. Let me grab a coat. Would you wrap a blanket around Colton?"

Andrew watched Susan dash up the stairs. He turned away, trying to get his mind off her curves. He couldn't get involved with her. He couldn't.

He picked up a blue quilt that Mrs. Johnson's club had made, spread it on the sofa and placed the squirming baby in the center. He carefully folded the corners around the little boy until only a cherub face peeped at him from the covers. There wasn't a man alive who could remain immune to that angelic look, he thought, hoisting the baby against his shoulder before calling up the stairs to Susan. "Your car, okay? The infant seat is already in it."

Her soft voice floated down. "If you'll drive."

Moments later a pink mirage appeared at the top of the stairs. He was reminded of pink taffy, pink dreams. He stared as she slowly descended. He'd never seen a coat as feminine as the one that encased Susan. He wanted to slide his hands inside. Yes, they needed to get out of the confines of the house.

She stopped in front of the mirror and lifted her dark hair out of the collar of the coat. She caught his eye in the reflection. Her eyes were filled with concern. "Are you too tired? You've already had a long drive." She turned to face him.

"No." He took the keys she handed him. "This kind of driving I enjoy."

She held the screen door open for him and his precious bundle, locked the door behind her, then hurried down the steps to help him get the baby in the car.

He buckled the baby in the back seat, started the car and pulled into the street. "Where to first?"

"There's a drive-in a couple of blocks from here. We can get something to drink without having to get Colton out in the wind."

He liked that. They could sit in the car and talk. That would be better than being separated by a table.

When both of them ordered a Dr. Pepper, Susan laughed. "Finally we agree on something."

Her laugh made him feel good. By the time their drinks arrived, the interior of the car was warm.

Susan unbuttoned her coat and started to shrug it off. When she couldn't get her arm out of a sleeve, he reached across to help her. That was a mistake. His knuckles accidentally brushed the side of her breast. Both of them froze for a second, then after carefully extracting her from the coat, he took a gulp of his Dr. Pepper.

"Susan, about that phone call . . . I lost it, I guess. I'm really sorry."

"Andrew, have you worried all this time about what you said to me?"

"Yes, I have. I was a total ass—just as you'd suspected all along." He started to lay his hand on her knee but stopped himself. "Is there anything I can do to erase that impression?"

"I forgave you that night. Honest. I know it took a lot for you to apologize." She turned to face him. "And, Andrew, thank you for worrying about me and Colton."

"It's not enough." That's how he felt, anyway. He finished his drink and started the car.

"You don't know how much it means to me."

He pulled onto Shoreline Boulevard and headed to the downtown Bay Front while Susan sat just inches away, sipping on her drink. It was hard to keep his eyes on the street and away from those pink lips puckered around the red-and-white straw. Damn! This arrangement with the baby was never going to work unless he could think of something besides Susan.

He was grateful when she pointed toward the bay. "Hey, look, there's a barge."

He pulled the car against the curb above the sea-wall and stopped. An oil barge was slowly making its way from the refineries on Nueces Bay into the Gulf of Mexico. He looked over his shoulder at the sleeping baby. "Do you want to get out?"

"Yes." Susan tugged on her coat and took the hand he offered.

After assuring themselves that the baby would be fine, they walked the six or seven feet across the boardwalk to a lovely white observation gazebo that sat on the seawall overlooking the bay.

Susan stopped and looked out over the gray-blue water toward the lumbering barge. She tilted her head into the wind. "It's so peaceful. Where I came from, there isn't anything to compare to this."

Andrew stopped behind her. He could smell the fragrance of her hair inches from his face. The wind caught a stray curl and blew it against his cheek. He reached up and caught it. He liked the way her hair felt between his fingertips.

Susan looked over her shoulder and smiled at him when he settled the curl and his hand on her shoulder. "What's that noise?" she asked.

He listened to the low-pitched roar. "Shrimpers in the bay. December is the end of the season. See all the boats docked on the T head?" He put both hands on her shoulders and turned her toward the pier. "You can buy shrimp right off the dock."

"Do you want to buy some and we'll fix them for supper?"

"Sure." He didn't want to release her, so he shifted his hand to her elbow and guided her back to the car.

''Colton hasn't even stirred,'' Susan observed, getting into the front seat.

They drove down the People's T head. The piers were lined with shrimp boats and luxury sailboats. After making their purchase they headed back to Susan's house. Andrew settled back against the car seat, content, certain this would be a good week.

CHAPTER TEN

DECEMBER FLEW BY until, as usual, Susan had her last-minute panic the night before school closed for the Christmas holidays. She always said she meant to get things done early, but even she had to admit that she liked the bustle of last-minute activity.

Warm fragrances of brown sugar and chocolate wafted through the air as Susan nibbled a lump of dough on the tip of her finger. She wiped off the residue, stepped over Colton and shoved a pan of cookies into the oven. When she had first begun teaching, she'd gotten into the habit of baking extra holiday cookies to take to her students, a habit she still retained. Year after year, the youngsters seemed amazed that their teacher could cook.

She smiled, remembering how Andrew was also amazed at her culinary skills. His method of thanking her had amazed her. How could one kiss deliver such a wallop? And the wonderful Sunday-afternoon drive along the bay? The memory still tantalized her.

"Hey, Colton, cookies come from Grammy's kitchen, don't they?" As if on command, he got up on all fours and began rocking as he blew spit bubbles from his mouth. "You're absolutely right," Susan said. "They're going to be mouth-watering good. And what are we going to do with all of them? Eat them and get fat?''

Lying down on the pallet beside him, she continued talking. "We've been so busy, haven't we?" Even though her students weren't going to present the official Christmas program, she had them working on a play in her room. Then there was the classroom Christmas party and the faculty Christmas party. But most tiring of all was the task of keeping her twenty-two students' excitement down to a manageable level.

All that activity, coupled with shopping, had made the two and a half weeks since the accident pass in a blur. Well, almost. There had been moments she would never forget, like having the stitches removed from Colton's head, or taking him shopping one night and stopping at a huge musical Christmas tree covered with twinkling lights.

The best of all may have been the night Betsy, Mrs. Johnson, Milly, Colton and she had gone to see Santa turn on the harbor lights. Yachts and shrimp boats were decked with colored lights for the annual festivities. Colton's wide eyes filled her with an excitement she had not felt in years. It was so much fun to imagine what he must be thinking when the brilliant colors flashed. It would have been perfect if Andrew had been there to share it with them.

Colton rolled over next to Susan and pulled himself up to his knees. "Hey, little one, that's Grammy's hair." With some difficulty, she dislodged Colton's fingers from her curls. Sitting up, she took the plump baby in her arms. "Guess what. Tomorrow is the last day of school. Then you and I will have nearly two weeks to romp and stomp and have a good time. Of course, that's what you and Grampa have been doing all week.'' Susan was eager for him to come back from Mrs. Johnson's.

Rolling onto her back, she held Colton overhead. ''We'll sleep in if we want to. We'll sing and talk. And, who knows, if it's warm enough, we may go down to the beach and look for driftwood or some pretty pink shells. Would you like that?'' The jarring sound of a buzzer interrupted Susan's discourse. ''Oops, time to put in the next batch.''

Even though it was the twentieth of December, the weather was warm enough in Corpus Christi to keep the kitchen window open a few inches. A cool evening breeze that smelled faintly of the ocean mixed with the warm cooking scents in the kitchen. This kitchen . . . this house . . . felt more like home than any place Susan had lived in her adult life.

The main reason was the contented little boy on the floor. It was impossible not to love him. He'd become much more cheerful now that his formula agreed with him. And he slept all night long, so she wasn't as tired as she had been. Starting a new job and then getting her grandson had been a huge strain on her. Now that she and Colton had established some workable routine, she could come home and relax. And they had done it without the help of Andrew's blasted book!

She grinned as she recalled Andrew's expression the previous day, when she'd told him again in no-nonsense terms what to do with that book. It had made her feel good. She bet that the author of that book had never had a child, or if he had, that a nanny had taken care of it. To Susan's great surprise, Andrew had good-naturedly laughed at her tirade.

"Is *everything* in the book wrong?" he'd asked. When she'd replied in the negative, he'd added, "Then don't throw out the baby with the bathwater." And that expression had reminded her of her mother.

It was amazing how much better she and Andrew were getting along since Colton's accident. She'd found it easy to forgive Andrew. Besides, this was Christmas, a season of peace, of understanding.

Of love.

Of forgiveness.

Lisa.

It seemed as if everything eventually came back to Lisa. Christmas with Lisa had steadily deteriorated over the past years. She, like her other teenage friends, seemed to be more concerned with the cost, or the brand, or the style of their gifts than with the spirit of the holiday. Then, the last Christmas Lisa was at home, it had meant nothing to her. Superficial, she had called it.

Lisa had grown more reclusive—never openly rebellious, but cynical. Susan had shrugged it off as "senioritis" at the time. In fact, she had been grateful that Lisa had attended summer school and graduated a year early. At sixteen, she'd planned to go to college back East, but her father wouldn't hear of it. He wasn't going to waste his money, he had repeated often. Not that he had any to waste.

And Susan hadn't stood up for her daughter, but had given into George's demands that Lisa get a part-time job and attend the local community college. Lisa had been disgusted by her parents' relationship and openly hostile to Susan's indecisiveness. After a final showdown between the three of them, Lisa had disappeared.

Using her finger to push the last bit of dough from the spoon onto the cookie sheet, Susan glanced down at Colton. "She left, Colton. The week after she graduated. But, honey, she's coming back. I just know it. You'll see." She wondered at the conviction of her words.

How could Lisa and Chris go off and leave him? She knew that Lisa had a stubborn streak, but that didn't account for her leaving her baby.

And Chris? What kind of person was he? Like Lisa? Self-centered? Rebellious?

What had gotten into them? Andrew had mentioned some guru or religious cult. She had tucked that bit of information away as though it didn't exist. That was on television. It happened to other people. Not to Lisa. She was too bright.

Only an indirect communication from Chris's friend Jack in Houston had let Andrew know Chris and Lisa were okay. Susan stopped in midthought, greatly irritated with herself. Her daughter had run off to California, and all Susan had done was hope. Maybe she should actively try to find Lisa. Maybe she could enlist Andrew's aid.

Andrew.

He liked the idea of their children abandoning the baby even less than she did. She smiled, remembering how he continued to avoid admitting he felt any paternal affection for Colton. But she had stood outside the door and listened to him play "this little piggy went to market" with Colton more than once.

He still maintained that the only reason he kept coming back to Corpus Christi was because she needed his help to care for Colton properly. And he had said he would help until they located a suitable, responsible person to take over the baby-sitting. So far, he had not found anyone who suited him.

Susan was glad, though she felt somewhat selfish that he was enduring such a long drive every other week. It was a shock for her to realize how badly she wanted to see Andrew. Every day since he'd kissed her, she relived it in her dreams. Always, an eternity passed as his face neared hers until his breath fanned across her skin.

She didn't know what she'd expected when he'd returned, but Andrew gave no indication that he'd ever kissed her. Occasionally she would catch him looking at her with longing, but then he would look away. The drive to the T head that Sunday afternoon had been truly magical. Didn't Andrew feel the same way? Didn't he know she wanted him to take her in his arms?

His schedule had been changed, so Andrew would be in the middle of the gulf on Christmas Day. That bothered her. He should be with family or at least with Colton since he had worked the Thanksgiving holiday. Christmas was a topic they had not discussed. It was almost as though they were avoiding it.

Susan's pulse increased just slightly when she heard Andrew's footsteps as they hurried up the steps and across the back porch. He knocked and opened the door at the same time. "Hi. Ummm…smells good in here." Andrew swung Colton up in his arms and held him over his head. "Have you been a good boy while I was gone?"

Colton, arms reaching toward Andrew's face, gurgled and cooed as if he understood.

"He's been perfect. He's a self-entertainer, unless he gets tangled up in chair legs and has to be pulled out, of course. Did you get Mrs. J.'s work done?" Susan peeked in the oven to quell her jitters. The heat from the oven in no way masked the heat emanating from Andrew.

"Sure did. She wanted me to secure a couple of window screens she thought were loosened by the wind last month. She was afraid someone could break in too easily. After checking the screens, she said I could change a light bulb in the guest closet if I wanted."

Susan grinned. "And of course you wanted to."

"Of course I did. That's one of my favorite pastimes. Mostly I think she just wanted company."

"Mostly I think she wants *your* company." Susan tilted her head to the side and surveyed the man standing in her kitchen before she shook her head as if in disbelief. "I'm sure she has a crush on you."

Andrew flashed her a flirtatious look. "You act like that's impossible to imagine."

"Maybe not impossible to imagine, only hard." *Liar,* she thought to herself, knowing that she too had a crush on Andrew. Maybe more than a crush. Susan took the final pan of cookies from the oven and set it on a rack to cool. "Oh, good, these aren't burned. Mark that as a first."

Andrew perched Colton on his knee and reached for a cookie. "What's a first?"

"Not burning at least one batch of cookies." Swatting at him with a spatula, Susan stopped his hand in midair. "Those are for my kids at school."

"You'll never miss one or two. Let me eat the ones you planned on burning. Besides, you've got enough there for an army. Even you couldn't be so cruel as to expose me to that smell and not let me have a bite."

"Do you promise to never ever, as long as you shall live, bring up that stupid child-rearing book again?"

Reluctantly, he agreed. "Okay, I promise."

"That sounded like a halfhearted promise to me. One that could be broken." She got a plate out of the cabinet and heaped it with cookies. "Would you like a glass of milk?"

"What do I have to promise to get that?"

"Let's see . . . Never criticize my housekeeping."

"Now you're stretching it." Andrew stuffed a cookie into his mouth and chewed slowly. "Lord, this is good. How about if I don't say a word as long as there's a clean place to sit down?"

"That's good for half a glass." Grinning, she opened the refrigerator and took out a half gallon of low-fat milk.

"You win. I'll keep my mouth shut about your disorganized clutter." He nodded toward the cabinet top strewn with canisters, bowls and spoons.

"You couldn't resist that one last dig, could you?"

"You set yourself up for it, and it was too tempting to let pass. But I promise—" he held a hand up in the air as an act of contrition "—that is absolutely the very last time. You are now the best housekeeper in Texas, and you cook a mean chocolate-chip cookie to boot.''

"Flattery will get you very little.''

"Will it get me a full glass of milk?''

"I guess.'' Susan filled the glass to nearly over-flowing and handed it to him.

Andrew finished his last cookie and washed it down with the cold milk before he set Colton on the floor. Unfolding his long legs, he said, "I forgot to tell you earlier. A man called for you today while you were in school.''

"Who?''

"I don't know.''

"Didn't he leave a name or message?''

"No, he just wanted to know what the hell I was doing here and where you were.''

Susan's stomach knotted before she shrugged as if she didn't care and turned away to hide her expression. Darn! She was afraid it was George. How had he gotten her number? She hadn't deliberately tried to hide from him, but she hadn't volunteered any information, either. Maybe he'd just go away. "Well, if it's important, he'll call back. What did you tell him?''

"I told him it wasn't any of his damn business why I was here, and, yes, he said he'd call back.'' When Susan didn't offer an explanation, Andrew asked, "Is there anything you need before I leave?''

"No, Colton has everything he needs.''

"That isn't what I meant. What about you? What do you need?''

"Oh, I'm fine," Susan emphasized. "I don't need anything." *Except comfort, reassurance, love. You.*

Andrew pulled out his wallet and took out a couple of bills. "Uh, would you buy something for him from me for Christmas?" He nodded at the little boy sitting on the floor gnawing on his vinyl-coated animal book.

"I thought you bought him a savings bond for Christmas."

"I did, but, hell, he needs something else. I don't know what to buy. It'll be a while before he can ride a tricycle or play ball, and I can't think of anything else. You'll have time to get him a little something from me, won't you?"

"Sure." Susan had not broached the obvious, afraid of the confirmation. "You have to work Christmas Day, don't you?"

"Yeah, I always volunteer. Most of us who don't have small children work so the men with kids can be at home for the holidays."

The consideration he had for his co-workers revealed how thoughtful a man he was. She appreciated his kindness, but still...

Andrew stuffed his wallet into the pocket of his cotton canvas trousers. Standing with his back to her for a moment, he propped his hands on the kitchen counter and looked out the kitchen window as she'd seen him do a number of times. The miniblinds rattled in the slight breeze, almost covering the softness of his voice. "I've never regretted missing Christmas until now." As if afraid he would reveal too much, he stopped and turned to face her. "It isn't that important right now, though. He's young. Colton won't know that I'm not here.''

"It is important now. I wish you . . ." Susan took a step toward him. What did she wish? That Andrew was going to be here with Colton? With her? With the two of them? Yes, that is what she wanted, but she couldn't make herself tell him that.

"What do you wish?"

"Oh, nothing."

Andrew raised one eyebrow and leaned against the kitchen counter. "That isn't fair, you know. To start a sentence and drop it." During the silence that followed his words, he slowly crossed the vinyl floor until he stood only inches from Susan.

She stared up into his blue eyes. Deep. Magnetic. Warm. Warmer than she could ever remember. How could she have ever thought them cold and hard? He didn't touch her physically, but her skin prickled with his nearness. He just stood inches away, hypnotizing her with his eyes.

"Now. What is it you wish?"

Swallowing and rubbing her lower arm to erase the goose bumps, Susan searched his face for some clue to what he was feeling. Faint lines radiated from the corners of his eyes and there was just the hint of a five-o'clock shadow across his jaw. His lips were slightly open. But nothing gave away his thoughts.

"I wish you were going to be here for Christmas," she whispered, remembering the pleasure she'd had sharing Thanksgiving with him. The pleasure of his kiss.

"So do I." Andrew expelled the breath he was holding. "So do I," he repeated. "But I can't."

"I know." She watched the sinews in his neck tense, then relax. To hide the confusion she was feeling, she looked at the floor. "It was just a thought."

"And a good one."

Raising her eyes to meet his, she became bolder. "It bothers me that you'll be alone on Christmas."

"You can't call being with four other men alone," Andrew reminded her.

"You know what I meant." He was so close that she could feel him breathe, almost feel his pulse.

"Yes, I do." Andrew's gaze burned into her. "And much of the time I do feel alone out there. After a while, you get used to the isolation. And as far as the guys are concerned . . . I spend more time with those men than I do with anyone. In a way, they're my only family."

His voice sounded wistful. Susan reached out and brushed his sleeve before dropping her hand as though it had encountered searing heat. "You must have smudged your shirt when you were over at Mrs. J.'s."

Andrew studied the spot where her fingers had touched his sleeve, ignoring her sidetrack. "On the platform, we usually try to make things as pleasant for the men as possible. We get together and prepare for what passes as a big feast, then do as little work as we can get by with. The crew spends a lot of the day watching the football games on television or napping."

"It sounds rather empty. You have to want more than that."

With a work-roughened fingertip, Andrew reached out and tenderly stroked her soft cheek and let his hand glide to rest around the nape of her neck. "All I want for Christmas is for you to call me. Let me know how things are going here."

"I will. I promise. As soon as I get back from Mrs. J.'s Christmas dinner," Susan whispered from between dry lips. She would promise him anything at that moment. He was going to kiss her again. She knew it. She had waited for it. Moistening her lips with the tip of her tongue, she waited. Her heart felt as if it was going to erupt from her chest with each beat.

Andrew clasped her shoulders in gentle hands and pulled her against him. He lowered parted lips to meet her waiting ones. His lips were warm as they covered hers. She wound her arms around him, running her fingers through his hair. Andrew's hands slipped down her back, his open palms stroking her willing flesh as he deepened the kiss. Susan, lost in an eddy of desire, matched his fervor in each succeeding kiss.

Moments later, when he trailed kisses down her neck, she realized she had to get control of herself. She couldn't give in to their passion until she got some of her personal life worked out. She was aided by a loud bang coming from the living room. "Andrew?"

"Umph?" he muttered against her warm flesh.

Pulling away, she asked, "Where's Colton?"

Andrew looked disoriented for a second, then released her to find the source of the noise. She followed him into the living room, where he rescued a frightened Colton from under the coffee table. He handed her the sniffling baby and picked up the books

Colton had knocked off. Satisfied that all was well, he ran his fingers through his hair. ''Nothing like a kid to keep us on the straight and narrow.''

Nodding agreement, she gazed at him with eyes still warm with desire.

''Well, I'd better be going. Merry Christmas, Susan.''

''Merry Christmas.'' Susan choked the words out as she watched him stride out the front door.

CHAPTER ELEVEN

ON CHRISTMAS DAY, Andrew looked at the stark white face of the wall clock hanging above his metal desk, then at the sheet of paper in his hand and back up at the clock. He thought of the clock in Susan's kitchen. It was three o'clock there, too. Susan had said she would call when she returned from dinner at Mrs. J.'s house. After their passionate goodbye, he realized that he cared more deeply for Susan than he'd been willing to admit.

The day had stretched on forever. Because it was a holiday, the duties were limited to essential tasks. Once these were completed, the other men on the platform had gone to the recreation room to watch a football game. Not being able to concentrate on the game for his anticipation of Susan's call, Andrew had come back down to his cramped office that he shared with an operator.

Dan Hebert's Cajun accent and way of looking at life were sometimes amusing. Since Andrew could remember the days when Texans and Cajuns didn't choose to work together offshore, he'd wondered a time or two why Dan worked off the Texas coast where he took a lot of ribbing from the other men, rather than the Louisiana coast. He decided, though, that it wasn't his business to find out.

Working should have helped pass the time, but it didn't. He tossed the production report he'd been filling out onto his desk as he stretched his long legs and got up to pour himself one more cup of coffee. He didn't really want another cup. Dan had brewed it and when Dan brewed his Cajun coffee with chicory, it was true to its name—mud. The last cup had turned cloudy and cold before Andrew had finished drinking it. But it gave him something to do. He checked the black hands of the wall clock one last time before he left the office to go to the galley. Five after three. Five minutes had passed.

Holding his free hand over his steaming mug of coffee, Andrew paused on the metal decking. The misty gray sky blended at the horizon with the dark green waters surrounding the platform. Whitecapped swells, ten to twelve feet high, heaved repeatedly at the intrusive pilings anchored deep into the gulf's floor. The wind seemed to have its own color—a steely gray—as it played hide-and-seek around the metal behemoth laboring to provide energy for a tireless world. Even on Christmas Day.

Andrew nudged open the door to his office with his shoulder and heard the sharp ring from the phone sitting at the edge of his desk. Its ring pierced the lonely silence twice more before he could cover the distance to grab the receiver. Though he was certain it was Susan, he answered it as he did all calls. "Brazos 576. Bradley."

"Hi, Bradley." Susan's soft Southwestern accent floated over the line. "Merry Christmas."

Hearing her voice lifted the gloom from Andrew's shoulders. "And Merry Christmas to you. How's your day going?"

"This morning was so much fun. Even though Colton's too young to really understand, he picked up on the atmosphere and got into it. Particularly the packages. Mrs. J. came over for a few minutes to watch him with his presents. They made quite a pair. She'd rip a piece of the wrapping paper loose and show Colton how to pull it. He loved it—so much so that he wanted to eat the paper. We had to fight him tooth and nail to tear the pieces of paper away from those death-grip fingers of his."

"How about the presents?" Andrew inquired, wondering what Susan had bought for Colton with the money he had given her.

"Well, I tried to follow your lead and be practical, so I bought a few clothes, which he ignored, and one quacking rubber duck."

Andrew was somehow disappointed. He thought that Susan would have gotten some big toy for Colton. "Did he like the duck?"

"He grabbed at it a little, but he's not interested in presents yet. Just pretty paper."

Susan thought she heard Andrew sigh. "I've got it all on videotape so you can see it, except for our lunch." She paused. "We missed you."

"I missed being there." It was true. He did feel as if he had missed something. Something he had never experienced but sensed was there. "Maybe next year."

"No, not next year. When you get back, we'll have our own Christmas."

"Whatever for?"

"Because I want to." The line was quiet for a moment before Susan asked, "You told me once that you weren't often home at Christmas, but you didn't tell me why."

Andrew thought for a moment. He could brush off the unasked question, but he didn't want to. He wanted Susan to know how he felt about the past and about the future. "I was in the army for several years, two of which I spent in a rice paddy in Southeast Asia. When I came back to the States, I went to work for an oil company. Things were really booming then. I wasn't used to being at home with a wife and kid, and they weren't used to having me there. Actually, I felt like I was in their way."

When Susan didn't say anything, he continued. "As long as the money kept coming in, Marilyn preferred it if I wasn't at home. During the holidays she'd go to her folks or have friends over. She'd taken care of things for so long in my absence that she didn't want or need me interfering when I returned. I could understand that, so I poured all of my energy into my job and stayed away as much as I could. I guess that caused the marriage to last several years longer than it would have otherwise. Anyway, holidays seemed contrived to me at that time."

"That's sad."

"It doesn't matter now." He took a sip of his coffee and frowned. Cold. "Until these past weeks, I didn't really figure I'd missed much."

"Well, you did. I'll show you how much fun Christmas can be when you get here. Now, since I'm paying for this call, even with the holiday discount I've exceeded my chatting budget, so I guess I'd better say bye. Aren't you proud of me?''

Andrew leaned back in his squeaky metal chair and absentmindedly ran his palms along its Naugahyde arms. Hang the damn phone bill! The call had left him feeling at peace yet high at the same time. Almost like a drug.

He was needing something he hadn't wanted. He hadn't wanted a scatterbrained, indecisive, disorganized woman in his life. Not until he'd gotten to know her. Not until he'd held her. Not until he'd kissed her. He'd thought the emotions that had swept over him from the first kiss were just a fluke, but the second time…well, it confirmed that his desire for Susan was more than lust. That scared him. He wasn't ready for a commitment. Was he?

ANDREW WAS STILL wrestling with that question the following Sunday as he drove the long road from Houston to Corpus Christi. His thoughts spun around in circles, never quite keeping up with his confusing emotions.

That he desired Susan he couldn't deny. But what if it was more than passion? That would be emotional suicide. Susan was warm but not sophisticated, sensual but not overtly sexy the way most of his girlfriends had been. True, she laughed a lot but didn't take life seriously enough. Planning was foreign to her. She just wasn't his type for anything permanent. And yet, he'd talked to her more than anyone he could remember. That was nice. To have someone with whom he could share his thoughts without censoring them. He could get used to that.

A grin appeared on his face as he thought about how silly she'd looked on the floor playing with the baby. Even now, as he drove into the town of Victoria, a familiar tightness spread through his groin when he remembered her soft lips responding to his kiss with her body promising more. No red-blooded man could ignore that. It had driven him crazy all week.

"No," he said the word aloud as he pulled into a convenience store to get something to eat. What he really needed was a cold shower and something else to think about—anything but Susan Montgomery.

He had to keep his distance, yet he wondered for the hundredth time about the man who had called for her. Andrew had little tolerance for people who called and then wouldn't identify themselves. Who did the guy think he was? Agent 007? He knew it couldn't have been a telephone huckster. A salesman would have given him a long sales pitch.

No, it was someone who knew Susan. A boyfriend? Susan didn't even speculate about who the caller might have been, and he really shouldn't have cared one way or the other. But he did. Damn! He felt like a thirteen-year-old whose hormones had just kicked in.

In the small store, he got a cup of coffee and a package of peanuts. Then, more to kill time than to shop, he wandered down the cramped aisles. There was everything a person could possibly need from sunglasses to laundry detergent. On his way to the checkout counter he passed a rack of condoms.

After looking up and down the aisle to satisfy himself that no one was watching, he stopped and studied the display. There were lubricated condoms, non-lubricated, natural skin, extra large and colored. The myriad choices left him dizzy. He turned to leave, then stopped. He thought of Susan, of her warmth and her softness, and he knew he wanted to make love to her. He selected one of the packages and strolled to the front of the store, whistling softly.

He was sure the young woman at the counter could see his embarrassment as he paid for his purchases. He remembered that the first condom he'd ever bought, on a double dare when he was twelve, decayed in his wallet before he'd gotten a chance to use it. That would probably be the case this time, he thought ruefully.

An hour and a half later, certain he'd gotten control of his hormones, Andrew knocked on Susan's back door. He took a deep breath of the cool evening air and willed his tense body to relax. She was only a woman. He wasn't going to get more involved than he already was, he reminded himself as he beat on the door more insistently.

After what seemed like several minutes, Susan, chocolate curls all askew, opened the door. "Come on in, Andrew."

She stood before him looking like spun taffy in—silk? Probably. It would be just like Susan to splurge on something so sensual. Without touching the shimmering pink fabric, he knew it was soft and smooth. His resolve to remain detached faded the minute he saw her. It was going to be difficult to keep his hands off her.

"I was upstairs and couldn't get here any faster," she explained.

Andrew followed Susan into the warm kitchen and stopped short, unable to believe what he saw. The round oak tabletop was clutter free and reflected light from its polished surface. Wanting to say something, he decided against it. He knew she had done it to please him. The thought made him feel as warm and comfortable inside as the kitchen was.

"Since the first time you set foot on my porch, you've been making noise at my door like you're in a big hurry." With her lips curved into a warm smile beneath her twinkling eyes, Susan hinted of the first time she'd seen him. "I hope you don't have another surprise like the first one."

"No, thank goodness."

"I was just about to sit down to a gourmet bowl of cornflakes. Do you want some, too? That's as good as it's going to get tonight." Susan opened the cupboard and took out a white-and-yellow box to make her point.

"Even that sounds good." Andrew opened the refrigerator to get out the milk. "Other than outdoor grilling and frying eggs, I don't cook, so I've been known to eat a bowl or two on more than a few nights. It's quiet in here. Where's Colton?"

Susan stopped dead in her tracks as she was getting out a couple of bowls and turned to face Andrew. "You called him Colton." She emphasized the last word.

"So?" Andrew set the milk jug on the table. "That's his name. Where is he?"

"Upstairs, playing his way into night-night. He should be asleep by now. And, yes, it does mean something."

"Okay, Miss Analyze Everything, what does it mean?" Andrew poured himself a heaping bowl of cornflakes and covered them with sugar and milk.

"It means you're beginning to see him as a person." Susan prepared her own bowl of cereal but left out the sugar.

"Maybe it does," Andrew muttered between bites. "How's teaching going?"

Susan saw that he was beginning to feel uncomfortable, so she allowed him to change the subject. "I have mixed feelings about tomorrow. The day after a holiday is always a little wild, but I'm looking forward to hearing their stories. They always try to outdo one another."

"How about that little kid you were having trouble with?"

"He was doing really great before the holidays. I think I told you that the turtle really started something. We didn't get to keep it at school because it's protected, but Billy's dad came from the aquarium to pick it up and tell the class about the steps being taken to save the species. It was wonderful, and Billy was so proud. He hasn't quit beaming. Maybe we can keep him out of jail yet."

Andrew nodded. "I sure hope so. The prisons are too full now. Teachers can make a difference, and I'm sure you're one of those who does."

The compliment warmed Susan. "I hope you're right." She picked up their dishes and carried them to the sink before turning to study him. He looked more comfortable in jeans and sneakers than he did in his usual slacks and loafers—more touchable. She brushed the dangerous choice of words from her mind.

"Leave them. I'll get them in the morning after you've gone to school," Andrew offered. "Let's go sit down."

Susan followed him to the living room, surprised that Andrew would leave a mess in the sink. She wondered if something was wrong.

"Colton sure has been quiet. I guess he went to sleep, huh?" Andrew asked, eyeing the stairs.

"You could go check while I pack up my things for class tomorrow," she suggested, amused that Andrew couldn't admit that he was longing to see his grandson.

She watched as Andrew crept up the stairs so as not to disturb Colton if he was asleep. Then she hurried to get everything together for school, trying to ignore the tantalizing desire she was feeling for the man upstairs. She didn't have much luck. All evening she had been aware of his every move, every look he'd sent her way. It had been so long since she had flirted with a man that she wasn't sure she knew how to let him know she was interested. She didn't know the rules anymore.

Soon a low voice and boisterous screeches could be heard coming from the nursery. Downstairs by herself, Susan felt left out. She could hear the giggles and laughs floating down the stairway as she stuck books and papers into her large bag. After only a few minutes, unable to take being excluded from the fun, she tiptoed upstairs and peered into the nursery.

She interrupted one of the most touching sights she had ever seen. Andrew was bent over the baby crib with Colton's big toe in his mouth. Colton howled in delight as his grandpa gave it a nibble. Both the plump little boy and the lean big boy looked wonderful to Susan. The emotion that squeezed her heart was almost painful in its intensity as she leaned against the doorjamb and watched the play.

When Andrew became aware of Susan, he dropped the foot, backed up and turned a bright red. "I... uh..."

"Cornflakes weren't enough, uh?" From the doorway Susan laughed at his discomfort.

"You weren't supposed to catch me."

"Do you still maintain that you only come to see Colton because you think I can't do a proper job of taking care of him without you?"

"I don't suppose it would do me any good to say...yes?"

"None at all."

After a few more moments of play, Andrew thumbed through the vinyl pages of an animal book, calling each animal by name while Colton watched intently. After those few moments of quiet time, they tucked the baby in for the night and stood at the door of the darkened room listening for his occasional angry whimper.

Andrew whispered close to Susan's ear, "Does he always do this?"

A whiff of his masculine scent weakened Susan in an instant. "Sometimes much worse. He can't make up his mind whether he's mad and wants me to know it, or if he's tired and sleepy. In just a minute he'll be sound asleep."

"I guess we'd better move before he spots us and decides to start another jam session."

"You're right." Susan ducked around Andrew, being careful not to touch him, and headed for the stairs. "Are you ready to see the video I made of him during the holidays?"

Before Andrew could answer, Susan led the way downstairs into the fire-lit living room. "I believe I promised you a Christmas when you got back here."

"I believe you did," Andrew said when he saw the holiday scene before him. He slumped down into the soft cushions of the sofa and looked around for a place to prop his legs. The fire crackling in the fireplace accented the Christmas music playing softly in the background. Colored lights adorning the tree twinkled in front of a long window.

After turning on the VCR, Susan joined him on the sofa and slung her bare feet upon the old coffee table. "You should have seen Colton go after those packages."

Andrew propped his feet up beside hers, then settled down to watch the antics of their grandson. It was impossible not to laugh at the little boy as he discovered each new experience. First the tree, then lights, then packages, and paper, and more paper.

"Well," noted Andrew, "he's going to be a cheap kid to buy for. Just go to the dumpsters and get a couple of boxes. Slap some colored paper on them, and he'll think he hit pay dirt."

"That's what you hope. In a few years when the first Saturday-morning commercial sinks in, boxes will be a thing of the past. He'll want Mutant Ninja Turtles and Lego to scatter on the floor for you to step on or wreck your vacuum cleaner with."

"Mutant Turtles? You've got to be kidding!"

Susan shook her head. "Teenage Ninja ones. That's what the kids like now."

"Better than the ridley turtles. I just won't let him watch TV," Andrew declared.

"Dream on." She twisted around so she could look him in the eye. "Maybe we can limit it, but stop it? Not likely. It's become part of our culture. Besides, it's an entertaining baby-sitter and allows working mothers some free time."

"Oh, that reminds me. I left something in the car. I'll be right back," Andrew promised before he disappeared out the door.

He returned a couple of minutes later carrying a rumpled brown paper grocery bag. "I didn't get a chance to wrap it."

"Andrew Bradley, you didn't do what I think you did, did you?" Standing, Susan took the package, then sat back down on the sofa. She knew what was in it even before she opened it.

She was right and wrong. Inside was a kitchen

clock, but... She looked up at Andrew standing in the center of the living room.

He was trying hard not to laugh. "Go ahead," he commanded. "Open it."

She removed the cellophane wrapping and stared at the most hideous clock she had ever seen: a red plastic rooster with purple and gold tail feathers and an orange beak.

"It crows on the hour."

"Somehow I'm not surprised." She turned the dials until the clock let out a screeching cock-a-doodle-do.

Andrew laughed at her startled expression. "Shh. You'll wake Colton. Don't you think it has more class than the teapot clock?"

Susan made the clock cock-a-doodle-do one more time. Then her laughter joined his until it was hard to tell who was laughing the hardest and what they were laughing about. Finally, wiping her eyes, she leaned against the back of the sofa. "Wherever did you get it?"

"Oh, I shopped for quite a while before I found just the right one." He sat down beside her, slightly closer than he was earlier.

"I'll bet you did. Not just every store would carry such a specimen." Susan rewrapped the clock and put it back into the paper bag. She was glad to know that Andrew had such a zany sense of humor. "Thank you from the bottom of my heart. I'll cherish it always. And now," she said, getting up from the sofa, "I have something for you."

She went to the carved fireplace mantel and took down a large stocking. *What if he doesn't like it,* she thought suddenly. What if he thought she was too sentimental? It's too late now, she told herself as she held out a red stocking that bore his name in gold sequins.

"Mrs. J. helped me make it," Susan explained. She was having second thoughts. Maybe she shouldn't have made him something that suggested tradition. Maybe she should have bought him handkerchiefs.

Momentarily Andrew was speechless. Then he muttered softly, "I've never had a stocking. Like this, I mean. When I was a kid, one of my father's work socks served as a Christmas stocking. I always chose the biggest one he had."

"Look inside."

Carefully he reached inside the red felt stocking and pulled out an oval-framed photo of Colton with his rubber duck. The grinning baby was proudly displaying his one and only tooth.

"The picture is for your desk."

Andrew's Adam's apple bobbed several times before he uttered a thanks. Setting the picture upright on the end table, he smiled at her. "Thanks a lot." Hurriedly he retrieved another item from the stocking. He pulled out a package of nuts. "What's this for?"

"As a rule, Andrew, nuts are for eating, unless you want to plant your own trees. A nut for a nut."

"I'm not even going to respond to that," he said, holding up a tin of peppermints. "And this?"

"Those are to sweeten you up."

Andrew returned his gifts to the stocking. "So you think I'm sour and nutty, huh?"

Nodding, she reached over him to retrieve the stocking. "Just a teeny bit."

When her breasts brushed against his uplifted arm, he felt a surge of electricity. He caught her hand in midair. "My stocking, remember."

"I was just going to get a peppermint ..."

"They're my peppermints. But if you ask sweetly ..."

"May I please have a peppermint?"

"Sir?" he coaxed, tightening his fingers around her wrist.

"Another dream."

"Well, you can't knock a guy for trying." Releasing her hand, he retrieved two pieces of candy from the tin and settled back amid the plump cushions to unwrap them. He popped one into his mouth and fixed his eyes on her. "Besides, I might like dreaming about you."

In a teasing gesture, he ran the other piece of candy close to her lips. She opened her mouth and closed it around the red-and-white striped treat. His fingers lingered against her lips for a second longer than necessary before he said, "Thanks for the stocking and for making the video. It's the best Christmas I've ever had."

"You're welcome." Susan could barely speak. Had Andrew really said that he might like dreaming about her? "How's it the best Christmas, Andrew?"

"I can't explain it, but somehow things seem different here with Colton ... and you. I can relax. Be myself." With a gentle hand, he nestled her head against the pillowy cocoon of his shoulder.

"I'm glad you feel that way."

He ran his fingers through her curls, feeling a sudden burst of tenderness toward her.

"Uhmmm." Susan closed her eyes and burrowed deeper into the warmth of his shoulder.

He tightened his arm around her and moved his fingers in an idle waltz down her silk-covered arm. "It's amazing how much things have changed in less than three months," he mused.

"Such as?"

"Such as . . . what I think about, what I want, what I'm interested in. Among other things, working all the time to make more money doesn't seem that important anymore."

Susan snuggled more closely. Her cheek pressed against his crisp starched shirt.

"Being around you and Colton—and Mrs. J., too—has taught me some things about life, about living, about myself." He stared at the fire. The red, yellow, and orange flames dueled, casting a warming glow over the room and its two occupants. His personal duel was coming to a close. He felt better than he could ever remember feeling in his life. He felt like he had found what he had spent the past forty-two years searching for. She was here in his arms.

"These few months have been a learning experience for me, too. I found a new strength in myself, a new reason for being. A joy and peace that has been missing until now." She opened her eyes and stared at the wispy curls of brown hair sprouting from the open neck of his shirt. Her fingers crept up to touch them.

A sense of security, of belonging and of mounting desire washed over her. She raised her face to look at him, her lips parted in dizzy anticipation as he lowered his head.

He lightly brushed the corners of her mouth and nibbled at her top lip, gently pulling it between his own. His fingers kneaded her neck, stroked her hair and turned her fully toward him. Slowly he deepened the kiss. While his mouth explored hers in gentleness and warmth, he pulled her around so she lay across his lap.

He smelled of after-shave and soap mingled with a masculine scent that was his alone, the scent that had pulled at her since the first time they'd kissed. Susan trailed her fingertips across his lips. They were moist from her kisses. "You taste good—like peppermint candy."

"So do you," he whispered. As if to prove it, he nibbled at her ear, flicked her tender skin repeatedly with hints of kisses and trailed his tongue to the hollow of her neck.

She felt herself drowning in the eddy of his sensual touch as he pulled at the small of her back, crushing her breasts against him. Teasing her flesh, he moved his hand upward until it reached the side of her breast. His fingers inched inside the lace cup of her bra. When he impatiently brushed the fragile fabric out of his way, Susan caught her breath and held it. As he found and caressed her softly curved contours, she rolled her head back and let a low moan escape from deep in her throat. Short breaths rushed from her parted lips.

"Andrew." She whispered his name just to reassure herself that he was really there . . . that it was him making love to her...not... She should tell him about George, now, before it was too late, but she didn't want him to stop.

"Uhmm...?" He planted a row of kisses on the exposed part of her neck, then blew into her hair. By the time his mouth took hers again, Susan was lost in passion and need. Only Andrew and his touch existed for her. She opened her mouth again to accept his probing tongue. He tasted of peppermint and desire. She could taste Andrew's hunger, a hunger matched by her own. Tongue danced with tongue until she thought she would explode. Of pleasure. Of pain. Of need.

He groaned against her cheek. "I want you. I want to make love to you so completely that you forget everything but us. I want to discover every inch of you. I've thought of how you look, how you smell, how you taste until I'm losing my mind."

Only the caressing timbre of his voice and the intent registered, not the actual words. He wanted to make love to her, that was all she knew. She should put a stop to the madness, but she couldn't. Never had anything so wrong felt so right.

"Yes." She knelt facing him and cupped his face in her hands so she could look into his eyes. They were full of warmth and desire. "Yes."

The words were barely out of her mouth before he tugged her top over her head and unfastened her bra.

The cool air of the room bathed her heated skin. She buried her fingers in his hair as he lowered his head to one of her breasts.

He worked his hands under the waistband of her slacks, letting his palms slide over the smoothness of her buttocks and digging his fingers into her flesh. "Oh, Susan," he groaned. Finally, frustrated that he could go no further, he stood and pulled her to her feet.

Standing silhouetted against the fire, he undressed impatiently, then sat back on the sofa. He pulled Susan to him and tugged her trousers down her legs until they were a puddle of pink silk on the oak floor. Then he lifted her to straddle him.

Brimming with anticipation, she felt the hair and the warmth of his legs against her inner thighs, then the searing heat of his desire as she settled above him. He clasped her waist as he guided her to him.

"Oh..." A deep moan forced itself from his throat as Susan sheathed his hot flesh. His head fell against the back of the sofa and he tightened his grip around her waist, holding her still when she began to rise. "Don't move...not yet...I just want to feel myself inside you."

"You feel wonderful," she whispered.

"So do you." The passion in his voice was almost palpable.

As the heat began to mount, Susan found it impossible to remain still. Nature pulled too strongly. Her hips started to move of their own accord.

"Slow, baby, we have all night," he muttered when she tried to quicken the pace.

It might have been hours or mere minutes later that Susan collapsed against Andrew's shoulder. Time had ceased to exist long ago. When she could finally talk, she whispered, "I think we just did what we were so unhappy with Chris and Lisa for doing."

"This is different."

"Is it?" She searched his self-satisfied expression for reassurance. "I believe the other day you said it was just 'hormones running away' when you were talking about Chris."

"I must have caught 'em." He tightened his arms around her and rolled her naked body beneath his on the sofa. "You Montgomery women must have something we Bradley men can't resist."

CHAPTER TWELVE

SHE'D TELL ANDREW about George tonight, Susan promised herself as she climbed her front porch the next afternoon after class. She had put it off too long already. She should have told him after George had called her to beg for a reconciliation, but she didn't know how Andrew would react. But she couldn't put it off any longer. She couldn't make love to him again without him knowing the whole story of her marriage.

And yet, their relationship was still so new that she didn't want to do anything to jeopardize it. If there was anything to jeopardize, that was. Andrew had made it clear that he never again wanted a permanent relationship. Her conscience warred with her heart. Maybe she would tell him on Wednesday night, right before he left. That way they'd at least have the next two days together.

"Afternoon," Andrew called out when the front door slammed behind Susan. "Was your day as difficult as you'd anticipated?" Andrew's lean frame stood silhouetted in the shadows at the top of the stairway.

Susan's heart lurched at the sound of his voice. "Not difficult. It was fine—just a typical first day back after a break. What about yours?"

"No problem." He slowly descended the steps toward her, his blue eyes focused on her brown ones. Her body prickled with a new awareness of his sensuality. He was tall, graceful, and she wanted to reach out and touch him. The memory of their lovemaking the night before had flooded her thoughts all day. It had been difficult dealing with children and their stories while she had such a momentous story of her own. One she couldn't share with anyone as she relived his touch and the feel of his lips on her skin again and again.

Before, his masculinity had made her nervous. Now it was overpowering. Every purposeful step he made toward her exuded sexuality. The room seemed too small for both of them when he reached the bottom of the stairs.

"Colton?" she squeaked. "Where is he?"

"Sleeping." Andrew walked toward the sofa, hesitated, then chose to sit in the overstuffed armchair.

She could nearly feel the heat of his eyes skimming her skin as she dumped her purse and books on an end table. Her hands shook when she pushed a stray curl out of her face and turned to face him. She wanted to kiss him but suddenly felt unsure of herself. What if the night hadn't meant as much to him as it had to her? What if he had been disappointed with her lovemaking, her body? What if he just wanted casual sex? Doubts assailed her.

"Sit down and rest for a minute." His voice was deep, warm and inviting, but he didn't make a move to touch her.

Susan settled back on the sofa, kicked off her shoes and propped her tired feet on a soft pillow. She said the first thing that came to her mind. "My tootsies are out of condition after a two-week rest. When I get rich I'm going to have a full-time masseuse just for my feet."

Andrew leaned forward in his chair and rested his elbows on his knees. "Uh...how about a masseur, instead? I'll rub them for you."

The desire for a foot rub and Andrew's touch overcame her anxiety and conscience. After what had happened the previous night, she should've had more sense. But logic, caution and sense had no part in her decision as she lay back against the armrest and murmured, "Mmm...that would be wonderful." Her heart won.

"Be right back."

Her chest constricted as he stood and smiled, then headed toward the kitchen. She couldn't be sure, but she thought she heard him humming the theme song from *Dr. Zhivago*. What was he doing?

She watched the doorway through half-closed eyelids. Waiting. As he entered the room, lotion bottle in hand, he seemed to be moving in slow motion. A calendar could have marked the time it took for him to close the distance between the door and the sofa. At his indication, she lifted her bare feet so he could sit at the far end of the sofa, then gingerly laid them across his lap.

Immediately the heat from his jeans-covered thighs burned the heels of her feet where they touched. She wanted to jerk them away and run, but even more, she ached to feel the strength of his fingers on her skin. She held her breath, waiting . . . waiting for that first contact between naked skin and naked skin.

When his fingertip gently brushed her little toe, she exhaled and closed her eyes. "Oh . . ."

His eyes glued to the task, he circled one of her feet with his warm hands and smoothed the milky liquid over her skin. Slowly he worked the lotion into her pores as he stretched each toe, pulling her flesh toward him. His thumb danced over the aching muscles in the ball of her foot.

"Oh . . . that feels so good," she moaned in pleasure. "Where did you learn how to do this?"

"In Southeast Asia. I'll tell you about it someday." He laid her relaxed foot on his groin and took her other foot in his hands. Again his fingers began to work their magic. "Now that you're relaxed, I want to hear about your day."

Relaxed? Hardly. She summoned up what seemed a distant memory buried by the pleasure Andrew was giving her. "Billy brought a regular turtle back to school." As she shifted to get more comfortable and allow him better access to her feet, her long cotton skirt rode up her calves. "You're probably tired of hearing it, but thanks for bringing me the other turtle."

He stopped and poured more lotion in his hand. Rubbing his palms together, he stared at the newly exposed skin. "Rubbing warms the lotion." With a firm touch, he kneaded the bridge of her foot before capturing her ankle in his palm. Stroking and pressing, he played havoc with her flesh and her heart. "You're welcome to any turtle I find."

"Billy has read everything he can get his hands on about them. Did you know that the eggs are considered aphrodisiacs in Mexico?"

"No." His voice cracked slightly before he cleared his throat and murmured under his breath, "That's one thing I don't need."

She had to strain to hear his last words. Surreptitiously she watched his face. His desire for her was clearly written in the tension along the sides of his mouth and eyes.

"That's one of the reasons the eggs were harvested at Rancho Nuevo in the '50s and '60s."

Andrew leaned back against the sofa and closed his eyes without stopping his caresses. His touch left a trail of tingling skin from the tip of Susan's toes to the swell of her calves. Each time his hand drifted up her leg it went slightly higher until he was circling her kneecap with a fingertip. She began to lose herself in the eddy of pleasure he was creating.

"Uh, a volunteer from the National Parks Service came to our classroom today and explained how a few years ago, when the female turtles landed on the beach to lay their eggs, volunteers would catch the eggs in sterile bags and pack them with Padre Island sand." Fertilization seemed to be the only thing on her mind.

Andrew opened one eye and looked at her as if she'd just said the sky was falling. "What'd they do that for?"

"They don't know enough about the locations imprinting on turtles, and there are some people who want to establish a nesting beach on Padre Island. So they brought the eggs back here and reburied them. The hatchlings were allowed to enter the water. Then they were netted and taken to a center in Galveston to raise. Since 1979 over 15,000 turtles have been released back into the gulf.'' Susan sat up in a burst of enthusiasm. ''Isn't that exciting?''

''If you say so.''

''After school today, Billy's dad invited me to go on a turtle watch this weekend.''

''Turtle watch?'' Andrew's fingers dug more firmly into her calf muscle.

''Yes, something to do with an oil company and explosives. We're supposed to patrol the area. I thought you might know what he was talking about.''

''Afraid I do.'' He gave her soles one last pat and gently moved her feet to the side. ''You're not going, are you?''

''I thought I would. I'm the chairman of the committee, and I've never even seen a turtle in the ocean.'' Susan reluctantly pulled her feet under her skirt. ''Why shouldn't I go?''

''Because the turtle watchers are just one more headache I and all the other offshore workers have to put up with.''

''I don't understand. How do they affect you?''

''For example…if we have an abandoned oil or gas well in the gulf, the caisson sticks up into the water. To keep ships and boats from hitting it, we have to either install a buoy and foghorn or set charges in the caisson. When the charge is blown, it severs the pipe so a crane can lift it off and set it on a boat.''

"Okay, but that doesn't tell me why you don't like turtle watchers."

"I'm getting there," he said. "Anytime we do any demolition, we have to notify the parks and wildlife people, and they send out turtle watchers. For three days before the charge is set, they patrol the area in a boat—the boat we normally use to ferry men back and forth between platforms to work or to get supplies."

"What do they need *your* boat for?"

"They're looking for *your* turtles."

"They're not *my* turtles, but in any case, what's wrong with watching out for them?"

"Nothing in theory, but those watchers can't see a damn thing except a lot surface water. You'd practically have to run over one of the blasted turtles before you could see it. But it ties up my boat for days. We can't get anything done."

"You're making this up."

"Don't I wish. Susan, it's too preposterous to make up. Not only do we provide them with a boat, we supply their meals and anything else their hearts desire. Last year one of them was walking around with his head up his ass and slipped on the boat deck and sprained his ankle. We had to fly him to Galveston for medical treatment." Andrew ran his fingers through his hair as he resumed his pacing.

Susan sat silently, her enthusiasm for the approaching trip waning.

"Then the morning of the demolition we have to let them use our helicopter so they can do an aerial surveillance before and after the charges are set. That way they can pull any stunned turtles out of the water, I suppose." Andrew shook his head. "Talk about priorities. People are starving in Somalia, and we're spending tons of money to save a turtle. Some of these dorks look like they wouldn't know the difference between a turtle and a mass of seaweed."

"I may be one of those dorks this weekend and I'm sure *I* know the difference. Besides, don't you think those people are trained?"

"In the classroom, maybe, but I haven't seen a lick of sense out of any one of those fellows. What I do know is that it costs the company at least ten thousand dollars extra—not counting the work we don't get done because they have our transportation tied up all day."

Wanting to understand the politics behind the procedure, Susan asked, "Is this a courtesy provided by the oil companies to pacify the environmentalists, or are the boats actually confiscated by them?"

"It's the law," he stated emphatically. "When I think of the waste, the expense, my blood boils. I'll bet the environmentalists hold bereavement wakes for the dinosaurs." Sitting down beside her, he drummed his fingers on the back of the sofa. "It sounds as if I don't care, but I do. I'm not advocating killing turtles, but, hell, these things should be put in perspective."

Although Susan agreed with some of his points, she refused to bow to what he wanted. "Good, because I'm working hard to save them."

He stopped and turned to study her. Their eyes met. "Don't you understand why I have a hard time with the turtle watchers?"

"I see your side, but . . ."

His blue eyes bored into hers. "You aren't going to go, are you?"

"I—I haven't decided."

"I see." He made a move toward the front door.

Susan reached out and caught his arm. "You don't have to leave just because we don't agree about turtles."

"You want me to stay?" He turned to look into her face.

"Yes. I want you to stay here tonight…with me…if you want to."

He pulled her into his arms. "How can you even ask if I want to?" He lowered his head until their lips were almost touching. "That's all I've wanted the entire day. Don't you know I'm crazy about you?"

SUSAN AWOKE with a start when she realized sunlight was beginning to filter into the bedroom. Stealing a delicious moment before she had to rush and dress for school, she kicked aside the blankets and hugged the extra pillow to her breast as she studied the sleeping man by her side. He had ignited the fire within her again and again during the night. By all accounts, she should be dead tired but adrenaline coursed through her veins until she felt she could do anything.

Andrew appeared dead to the world. His breathing was even and his face relaxed. She longed for him while at the same time she figured they had no future together. He had said he never wanted to remarry, and, also, they were as different as night and day. Their opinions about the turtles was just one small example. And then, of course, there was the big problem with George. A good opening had not availed itself for her to tell him she was married.

Why had she led Andrew on without telling him? It had felt so wonderful, so right, but she should have known better. It was too dangerous, dangerous in more ways than one. She knew better, but she wanted him so badly. The pain would only be worse in the end for having experienced his lovemaking. In the back of her mind she could hear her mother chastising, "Why, Susan Montgomery, I thought I taught you better than that!"

TEN DAYS LATER Andrew stood over the overhang sheltering his small front porch in Houston and thumbed through the stack of mail until a letter caught his attention. Eyes riveted to the postmark, he held the letter apart from the others as if it were a pariah. His throat constricted. Stepping into the house, he threw the letter onto his oak desk along with the bills, magazines and junk mail. He had a premonition he wasn't going to like its contents.

Curiosity nagged at him, keeping him from waiting too long. After setting his bag on the bedroom bench, he went to get a cold can of soda from the refrigerator and returned to his desk.

Downing half the drink, he picked up the letter again and tore it open. An ominous feeling settled in his gut as he pulled the single page from the envelope. He took a final swig from the soft-drink can, then tossed it into the trash can. Bull's-eye. Settling back in his swivel chair, he slowly unfolded the thin white sheet of onionskin paper and started reading. Once. Twice. His jaw set as his right fist wadded the paper into a ball that he rolled around in his hand like a worry stone. Finally he flung it toward the brass trash can. He missed. "Over my dead body," he swore to the empty room.

He sat immobile in his chair for a few seconds before anger spurred him to action. He strode to the backyard, unlocked the storage shed and grabbed a rake. He'd work. A little physical labor was good for a man. Make him forget his troubles. Besides, a light frost the week before had knocked some leaves off the trees. Today the weather was perfect—overcast but not too cool.

Pine needles lay thick around the edges of the cedar fence. Andrew raked and crammed the piles of dry needles into plastic bags, cursing more than once as he feverishly tackled the chore. He wished he could rake up his troubles and discard them as easily.

A half hour later, with sweat dripping off his forehead, he stripped off his sweater and tossed it on the damp ground before returning to his work. Work gave him a feeling of purpose... of something to do when he couldn't do what he wanted to do. Right now, what he wanted to do was to kick Chris's butt. What did he and Lisa think? That they could just sashay back home and pick up where they'd left off? That they could just take Colton back as though nothing had happened? He didn't give a ruddy rat's hair if they were married now. They had abandoned their baby. To him!

He stopped his frantic raking and leaned against the wooden handle of the rake. The gray sky had grown steadily heavier with moisture until a fine mist fell from the clouds and cooled his heated skin. He wished it would cool his heated emotions, too. But it was going to take more than rain to do that.

As ANDREW DROVE the now-familiar highway to Corpus Christi, he recalled his phone conversation with Susan the week before. He had thought of little else but their lovemaking for the entire week he'd been offshore. The oil company had not gotten their money's worth out of him this hitch.

He had placed his usual Sunday night call to check on the baby. After the preliminary niceties, he'd decided he should apologize for trying to influence her with his prejudices. But he hadn't really meant it, and she hadn't really bought it.

He wondered if she truly understood how perilously close to unemployment he was becoming because of the company cutbacks which were partly due to pressures from environmentalist groups. Every hitch he expected to be called in, laid off, then escorted to the platform to pick up his belongings.

She'd gone on the watch, too, he'd learned from the phone call last Sunday. So much for his influence. In a sense, he admired her for not allowing him to sway her.

"It was a lot of fun and Billy's dad was full of useful information," she had said. "But I have to agree with you that it does seem like a big waste of time and money."

"At least we agree on something." He was relieved that she had a little horse sense.

"I think we agree on more than turtle watches." Susan's voice had deepened seductively.

"Like what we're going to do the next time I'm in Corpus, perhaps?"

"Mr. Bradley! I'm shocked! Are you propositioning a grandmother?"

"You bet."

He made his regular stop at the convenience store in Victoria. The warm coffee helped ease his mind, though. He knew that Susan was going to be very upset when he told her that Chris and Lisa wanted Colton back. The little fellow had been a strain on both of them, of course, but the joy had far outweighed the trouble. They had witnessed his emerging personality, his curiosity and his ability to go to sleep alone. They had given him security. Now Chris and Lisa wanted to uproot the child again and destroy that security. God, how he hated to break the news to Susan.

He had to tell her even though he wanted to spare her the worry and the pain. He wanted to take care of her. That was a new feeling. This need to protect someone. Maybe his love would cushion her. It offered only sweet agony to know that he needed to protect her and Colton.

He would take care of this new problem just as he had all the other problems that had sprouted like careless weeds because of Chris's insensitivity. Andrew didn't need anyone's help. He never had. He would come up with a solution. Yet things were somehow different this time. More people were involved.

A grin tugged at the corners of his mouth as he thought of Colton and the impish way his left eyebrow arched up when he was concentrating on something. He was his own flesh and blood. His own second chance.

He'd failed with Chris. Susan was correct about that. She'd said once that money and gifts couldn't take the place of a loving parent. He hadn't liked hearing it at the time, but she was right. It seemed as if she was right more and more often these days. He needed her balancing force in his life.

WAVING TO MRS. J., who, as usual, was puttering in her yard, Andrew slammed the door of his car, bounded around the back of the house and up the steps to Susan's house. He couldn't wait to see her. In the final minutes before reaching town, he'd reached a conclusion. He wanted Susan Montgomery in his life. Permanently.

But he didn't know how she felt about him. She'd never said. She'd been warm and passionate, but that didn't really mean anything. She could just be interested in a physical relationship. She'd never made any move to suggest that she was interested in him beyond him being Colton's grandfather or her lover.

Still, if he was going to get anywhere with her, he would have to take it slowly. And that wouldn't be easy, he thought as he banged on the back door with his fist. He was an impatient man by nature, and when he discovered what he wanted, he did everything in his power to get it. And he wanted Susan Montgomery. No. It was more than that. He needed her. Now. Tonight. And always.

CHAPTER THIRTEEN

SUSAN RAN THROUGH the spotless kitchen to throw open the back door. "Hi, stranger." Without a second thought she opened her arms and invited him to hug her. "It seems like an eternity since I've seen you."

"Umm...thirteen days *is* an eternity," he said. Accepting her invitation, he buried his face in the softness of her brown curls and pressed her curves against his body. "It's been too long for me, too."

She felt his warm breath ruffle her hair and smelled the intoxicating fragrance of his after-shave and musky maleness as she snuggled closer to him. "I've missed you."

Keeping her lower body pressed into his, he leaned his head back to look into her eyes. His own were warm with passion, desire and something more. "I'm sorry again for the way I acted about the turtles the last time I was here. I shouldn't have tried to prejudice you." This time, Susan thought, he looked as if he meant it.

"You're forgiven." She smiled up at him. "The turtle watch turned out to be fun and it gave me a chance to talk to Billy's dad, Nick, about his problems at school. I think it may be a real turning point for them and for my class."

"Tell me about it."

She took his hand and led him to the dimly lit living room while she explained, "I went Saturday before the sun came up. Mrs. J. kept Colton. I could hardly believe my eyes when I saw the toy-size boat that was to take us out. I've never ridden a boat in the ocean, but it was okay. It took about an hour to get out to the abandoned well . . . then, when we . . ."

Andrew smiled.

"What are you grinning at?"

"You." He ran his finger along her cheek before pulling her down beside him on the sofa. "You're cute when you get excited. Do you realize you haven't stopped for a breath?"

She snuggled against him and finally caught her breath. She had looked forward to this moment all day. She had paced the floor, wrestling with her dilemma until finally she'd come to a decision. It was time. She had to tell him the truth—tonight, before things went any further.

In preparation for the evening she had soaked in a skin-softening perfumed bath, lit the fireplace, put on soft music and chilled a bottle of wine. She'd planned to remain cool, to be sophisticated, but when she'd seen Andrew at the door, she'd opened her arms to him without a thought. Resting her head against his shoulder, she breathed deeply.

"That's better. Now, what happened next?"

"We cruised around all day looking for turtles."

"And?"

"We didn't see any." She circled his ear with her fingertip, then replaced it with moist lips and hot breath as she whispered, "And don't you say I told you so."

"I wouldn't dream of it," he murmured turning his head so that their lips were almost touching, teasing her, tempting her with the promise of a kiss.

Time slowed. The flicking fire paled and the carefully chosen music faded as she parted her lips in anticipation. Moaning with desire, she lost herself in his embrace, feeling safe and secure. Secure enough to tell him, "Andrew, I have to—"

"All you have to do right now is kiss me." His warm breath brushed her moist lips for a second before he tightened his grip and hauled her harder against him. When they touched hers, his lips were warm and hungry, gently persuading her to respond.

The week of frustration and wanting came out in his probing kisses and in his searching fingers roaming her willing body. She kissed him as she had never kissed another man, kisses that left her weak and dizzy.

Catching her breath, she shifted onto her knees, facing him, and cupped his chin between her hands as she covered his face with little kisses. She started with his forehead, then skimmed his eyebrows with the softest of touches. She planted kisses down the bridge of his nose, across his cheekbones, memorizing the taste, the feel, the smell of him.

He clasped the curve of her waist, then caressed her sides before gently releasing his grip on her. Without a word, he began to unbutton, one by one, the tiny pearl buttons that graced her white angora sweater.

"You're beautiful." He bent to kiss the swell of her breasts.

Pushing toward him, Susan threw her head back and arched her back as his wet mouth played havoc with the flesh barely hidden by the skimpy lace of her bra. As his lips continued to work their magic, she sighed with pleasure and buried her hands in his hair.

In the valley between her breasts his trembling hands groped at the fastener of her bra.

"Let me," she whispered, covering his hands with her own. She could feel her heart racing as she released her swollen breasts for his touch. The flickering fire illuminated his face as he worshiped her with his eyes.

She, too, watched him with wonder, fire and desire running through her veins. When he slid his hand up her leg, she moaned and reached for him, finding his lips with her own. "Make love to me...now... upstairs," she pleaded between kisses. She would tell him everything later.

"Yes." He mouthed the words against her lips. "Yes, I want to love you." He stood and offered her his hand. His warm fingers closed around hers, then he gently pulled her to her unsteady feet. When he started to lead the way to the stairs, she stopped him.

"Wait. I've got something." She floated to the kitchen and returned with two of her best crystal wineglasses in one hand and a bottle of white wine in the other. "For later," she said, starting up the steps and looking over her shoulder with smoldering eyes veiled by long dark lashes.

He stood silhouetted against the dying fire, his lean body tense with anticipation, his eyes blazing with desire. When he took the first step toward her, she turned to lead the way to her bedroom.

On the third step, he reached forward and took hold of her ankle. Catching her breath, she stopped as he slid his hand under her skirt and up the silky skin inside of her calf. To keep from falling, she leaned against the wall, letting his hand roam freely up and down one leg and then the other. She surrendered to his touch. Her legs grew weaker and weaker until they wouldn't hold her upright.

When his hand moved between her thighs, she sank on one knee and rolled over until she lay on the soft carpeted stairway, offering herself to him. The glasses and bottle of wine were still tightly clutched in her hands.

Now she could see him. He knelt below her on the stairs and slowly removed her shoes. He kissed and nibbled at her toes, working upward until she was lost in a mindless fog of aching need.

She wasn't sure at what point her skirt ended up around her waist and her lacy panties came off. She only knew the feel of his mouth and hands as they caressed her burning skin. Her senses spiraled, reveling in his touch. She was his to do with as he pleased.

And he did. He teased her with his tongue and fingers again and again while the pleasure inside her grew sharper. The wine bottle rolled from her grasp onto the step as her mounting longing crested in a final explosion.

"Oh...Andrew...oh..." she moaned, tossing her head from side to side. His name rolled from her lips, over and over.

When at last she caught her breath, Andrew sat back on his haunches and grinned. "That's just the beginning of a long wonderful night, a night we'll always remember," he promised, picking up the wine bottle she had dropped and getting to his feet. Before she could protest, he scooped her into his arms and carried her to the bedroom, wineglasses forgotten.

She wanted to please him as he had her. Slowly and with trembling fingers, she began to undress him. His shirt fell to the floor, exposing hard muscles covered by brown hair. A scar snaked across his left shoulder. "What happened?" she asked tracing it with her fingertip.

"Another reminder of Asia," he explained, catching her hand with his and bringing it to his lips. "I don't want to remember that tonight. Tonight I want to think of us."

She lowered her head to kiss his chest, splaying her fingers through the curly mat of hair sheltering his small hardened nipples. As her lips nuzzled his flesh, her hands glided lower, searching for his belt buckle.

Fumbling with the button of his jeans, she looked up to his eyes, which had darkened to a navy blue maelstrom. When she popped the button open, he caught his breath and held it as she slid his zipper downward.

Receding denim exposed the muscled thighs that had teased her memory. The reality of his tight buttocks and firm stomach was better than anything she had been able to recall. He kicked the jeans loose, then buried his fingers in her hair as she knelt before him.

When he could bear her loving attention no longer, he urged her gently onto the bed.

Later, as she lay half-asleep beside him, with one leg thrown over his hairy thigh, she felt his muscles tense. "Is something wrong?" she asked, turning to look at him beneath half-closed eyes.

He sat up a little straighter against the headboard and cleared his throat. "Susan, I've got something to tell you, and I've been putting it off."

A bolt of fear ran through her, chasing away the pleasant fuzziness in her mind. What was he going to tell her? She swallowed and closed her eyes, preparing herself for some unknown pain she knew was coming.

"I got a letter from our kids."

Instantly alert, Susan sat up on her knees and faced him. "A letter? Why didn't you tell me before?" she accused, running her fingers through her matted curls. "Where are they? Are they all right?"

"I didn't tell you about it because I knew that you weren't going to like what it said." He tried to pull her back in his arms.

"What did it say?" she prompted.

He got right to the point. "Chris and Lisa want Colton and are coming to get him.... They could be here anytime."

Susan stared at him in disbelief, letting his words sink in. "They want to uproot him again, just when he's got some stability in his life. But I won't let them play with him like that—not a chance in hell!"

She jumped out of bed and grabbed a floral robe hanging on the bedpost. Cramming her arms into the sleeves she snapped, "That makes me so angry I could..." Sputtering, she couldn't think of decent words to finish the sentence. "We can't let them get away with it. What are we going to do, Andrew?"

"I really don't know. I've thought about it and... well, we don't have a lot of options." He sat on the side of the bed and rested his bare feet on the fluffy rug by the bed.

"Let me think." She got up suddenly and started pacing around the room. "We need to go see a lawyer, and—"

Andrew reached out, caught her hand as she passed and pulled her into the V between his legs. "No judge is going to award you or me custody when the kid has two parents." He ran his hand absentmindedly over her buttocks.

"But they abandoned him. They're in California. Involved in a strange religion. They don't have any money. They're not even married." Susan gave him a pleading look. "They can't do this to us and to Colton. How can you just sit there and accept it so calmly?"

Andrew took a deep breath. "I'm not accepting it calmly, Susan. It's just that we've got to be pragmatic. One thing I haven't told you is that they've got a plus in their column now. They got married."

Susan threw her hands up. "You think that's a plus?"

Andrew opened his mouth, but before he got a chance to answer, Susan jumped up and attacked him verbally. "It's what you want, isn't it? It's what you've been waiting for. You're tired of coming here and taking care of him!"

"No!" Standing up, Andrew grasped her shoulders and forced her to look at the pain in his eyes. "How can you say that after all we've been through? You know what that little boy means to me. You knew it before I did."

Susan wilted against him. She buried her face in the hair adorning his bare chest, where moments before she'd felt passion, and tried to retrieve her words. "I know. I shouldn't have said that. It's just that I'm so upset."

"We'll think of something. I just need a little more time." Andrew caressed her hair with gentle fingers as if he were comforting a child, then tucked a stray curl behind her ear as he looked into her tear-filled eyes. "If you want, I'll go see a lawyer and get some advice."

"Please," Susan said. "You really don't think a judge would let us have Colton, do you?"

"I don't know," he admitted.

She wrapped her arms around his waist and felt his heartbeat beneath her cheek, his warm breath across her forehead. He was thinking. He would help her. This time she wasn't alone.

For several silent moments they stood beside the rumpled bed, bare skin pressed together, each one gaining sustenance from the other until he finally spoke. "We'd have more legal bargaining power," he proposed, "if we were married."

Susan's heart skipped a beat. "What did you say?"

"Marry me," Andrew repeated against her hair.

Susan pulled away and stared disbelievingly at the man whose arms had just encircled her. "I thought you didn't want to get married again."

"I didn't think I did...but if we get married, we would have a better chance of keeping Colton."

"Marriage isn't something to joke about, Andrew."

"I'm not joking. It just might work." Eyes on the floor, he began to pace as he continued to speak in a more animated tone. "Don't you see the logic? Colton needs a mother and father. This shuttling back and forth won't work forever, and if we were married, we might have an even chance of the courts awarding us custody of Colton."

"You know, Andrew, in a strange way, I do see your logic." In a softer tone, she added, "But that's beside the point. I can't marry you."

An almost palpable silence filled the cozy bedroom when Andrew halted and stared at her. "Why not?"

"Why not? You act as though you were asking me to dinner. Right out of the blue, you say 'Marry me.' White bread or wheat bread? No big deal."

"What *is* the big deal, Susan?"

"It's contrived."

"It's our grandson. Besides, it's not just for Colton." Andrew ran his fingers through his disordered hair before he began a search for his clothing. Finding them twined with Susan's in a pile, he dug out his jeans and tugged them on. He didn't zip or button them before he turned to face her. "There are other reasons to marry. I love you and I guess I was foolish enough to think you loved me. And you can't deny that we're attracted to each other. Not after the way you just made love to me."

She couldn't. He was right about that. But attraction wasn't enough.

"Marriage is more than logic, Andrew, and it's more than passion. It has to be a mating of souls, of..." As if to protect herself against the tension that crackled between them, Susan picked up a feather pillow and hugged it to her breasts. "I'm not sure exactly what all it should be, but I've always dreamed of..."

Abruptly cramming his shirttail into his open jeans, Andrew growled, "That's the problem, Susan. You're always dreaming and waiting." While buttoning the last button on his sleeve and fastening his belt, he stared at her upturned face, as if refusing to believe he had just been rejected. "Hell, Susan! If someone dropped hundred-dollar bills at your feet, they'd blow away before you decided to bend over and pick them up."

He searched for his socks. After digging one from under the bed, he sat on her dainty dressing stool and pulled them on and jammed his feet into his shoes. "Life doesn't come to those who wait. You've got to take life into your own hands, or else it'll pass you by before you know it."

Under his unwelcome onslaught, Susan wilted onto the bed. Tears ran down her cheeks before she dropped her gaze to the floor. He was right in some ways. She had been drifting through life instead of taking control. She should have done something long ago... about George, about Lisa.

Coming to sit beside her, Andrew gave her a half-hearted smile. "Hey, I'm sorry." He tilted her chin upward with his finger. "Look at me, Susan. Please. I didn't mean to make you cry. You made a start by moving to Corpus to find Lisa. That was a hard decision. Now's not the time to stop. We have a responsibility to Colton, and I don't think we've done too badly. Can't you put aside your fears, or whatever it is, for him? For us?"

Susan studied him for several seconds. There was an intensity about his voice and his movements that she had not seen before. He was being honest with her, exposing himself to rejection. "Andrew..." She drew a deep breath and slowly exhaled, leaving not only a void of air but also of courage. This was the time to tell him. She had been dreading this moment since Thanksgiving—since she'd become aware of how much she cared for him. But she had to tell him. Now. "Andrew," she repeated as he stepped back from her, "I couldn't marry you right now, even if I wanted to."

"Why not?"

To keep from seeing the censure she was sure would be in his eyes, she looked down at the lace-trimmed pillow she was still clutching and whispered, "Because I'm still married."

A look of incredulity flooded Andrew's eyes. "I think I didn't hear what you said."

Hesitantly Susan repeated her words. "I said that I'm still married. To Lisa's father."

All color drained from Andrew's face before he stood and faced her. "You can't be. I thought that was over a couple of years ago. When Lisa left."

"It was. It is. We're separated." Susan stood up. "It's just that I haven't gotten a divorce yet."

A look of pain crossed Andrew's face before he turned away from her and addressed the door frame. "I can't believe I'm hearing this."

Susan watched Andrew with his shoulders slouched in dejection. It hurt her to see him—what was it? Angry? Hurt? Disgusted? She walked up behind him, stopping only inches from where he was leaning against the jamb. She had never known him to be without words. He had always been in charge. "Andrew, I'm sorry I didn't tell you before. I wanted to but the time never seemed right."

"Save it."

"Don't be so upset with me, please." She wanted to touch him but was afraid he would rebuff her. "Down deep, you know our getting married wouldn't help us keep Colton, so my marriage really shouldn't affect you one way or the other."

"The hell it shouldn't. I love you." He stopped.

Susan studied the back of his head, the proud way he shrugged his shoulders and straightened his back. "I'm sorry. You're right, of course."

"It doesn't matter." The words thrown at her were laced with bitterness.

"Yes it does, Andrew," Susan said softly.

He wheeled around to face her. "I just made love to you with everything I've got. I just proposed to you. Doesn't that mean anything?"

Her fear of commitment had led them to this moment. Taking a step closer, she touched his arm. "Would it make it any easier if I said that I do love you?"

Andrew pulled away from her touch. "No, it wouldn't. In fact, it would make it worse." He searched her face with blue eyes now dull with pain. "How could you—" he indicated the bed "—make love to me like that? How could you stay married to him?"

"It's a long, complicated story with many reasons, none of them good enough on their own, but..." Susan stepped back, took a deep breath and leaned against the door frame opposing him. "In the conservative small town where I grew up, divorce was unthinkable. While Daddy was alive it was easier to stay married than to cause trouble in the family."

The muscles in Andrew's face remained taut as she continued to explain.

"After Daddy died and Lisa left, I asked George to move out. He wasn't very agreeable. Our marriage had been miserable for years, and I couldn't tolerate how unconcerned he was about Lisa leaving. We've just drifted along since then. I thought that what little money I had would be better spent moving here and finding Lisa than on a divorce."

Andrew's face remained expressionless.

"Anyway, every time the subject of divorce has come up, George just goes nuts. He doesn't want me, but can't live without being attached to me in some way. I'm his anchor, and I don't have the courage to destroy his last bastion of stability. I don't love him, but I'm afraid of what will happen to him if I take that final step.''

She reached out to touch Andrew's arm. ''You ask how I could make love to you? Oh, Andrew, I can't remember the last time I made love. I can hardly remember the last time I had sex. George had other women for that.''

''Sure.'' He shrugged her fingers off. ''Face it, Susan, it was just another one of those decisions you didn't want to make. How can you be such a Milquetoast? Don't you want to be in charge of your life?''

When she didn't respond, Andrew picked up his watch and wallet from the nightstand and headed for the hallway. ''Look, we aren't getting anywhere, so I'll be going.''

She followed him down the stairs. ''Wait, Andrew, just because I'm not divorced doesn't mean we can't—''

''Can't what, Susan? Share a bed?''

''That's not fair.''

With his free hand, he grasped her chin and turned it toward him so he could claim her lips. There was no gentleness, only frustration and disappointment. Releasing her as quickly as he had embraced her, he asked, ''Tell me this. Would you have married me if you were free?''

''That's not a fair question. It started out as what would be best for Colton, but this doesn't really have much to do with Colton, does it? I guess I...''

Seeing the confusion in her eyes and the hesitation in her voice, he commanded, ''Don't answer. I don't think I want to know.''

As ANDREW stalked down the darkened path and climbed into his car, his barely controlled anger boiled up inside, quickening his pulse. How could he have been so stupid as to fall in love with Susan to begin with? He had known from the first day that she was trouble. She was everything in a woman he didn't want, but she was also everything he did want. She was funny, affectionate and unaffected. She made him feel comfortable. Like cornflakes for supper. The other women he had known would have tried to put on a show... flowers, candlelight and the whole bit. But Susan's actions said, This is how I am. Real. Ordinary.

No, no, not ordinary. Susan was anything but ordinary. The memory of her smiles, her gibes and her messes spoke only of her. Her moans as he made love to her came flooding back. He banged the palm of his hand against the steering wheel. Damn it all!

Andrew remembered Susan telling him that her husband was an easygoing fellow who had never taken marriage seriously. He'd drifted in and out of Susan's and Lisa's lives, letting Susan support them much of the time. Searching his memory of their conversations, Andrew couldn't recall that she'd ever said "ex-husband." Always, it was either "husband" or "Lisa's father." He had just assumed that she was divorced. Perhaps because that was the way he'd wanted it.

Silently he called her a pushover. But no sooner than the thought had formed in his mind, he recalled his own marriage. For years, he and his wife had been married in name more than in spirit. It was his wife who had initiated the divorce after she became interested in another man. Maybe his situation wasn't so different from Susan's, he admitted to himself. Still, he had not misled her. There was no getting around the fact that she *had* misled him.

CHAPTER FOURTEEN

For Susan, if a day began wrong, it usually stayed wrong. That had been the case today. Her students, sensing that her mind was elsewhere, had given her a harder time than usual. The day had stretched interminably. At least she could count on Colton's affection, she reminded herself as she nudged the back door open and dumped her books on the kitchen table before starting for the stairs.

She wouldn't have blamed Andrew if he hadn't shown up to keep Colton that morning. To say they hadn't parted amicably the night before was a gross understatement. She had lain awake for hours remembering the pleasure of their lovemaking. In her wildest fantasy, she'd never imagined such abandon.

The memory of their conversation cut through her. It wasn't every day she received a marriage proposal. She should have been pleased, but the circumstances weren't right. If only she had gotten a divorce. If only, if only, if only... She pressed her hand to her forehead as though she could physically stop the litany of what ifs.

Andrew had been so brusque when he arrived this morning that he'd barely uttered "Hello" before helping himself to a cup of coffee and disappearing upstairs. It had been obvious he wanted nothing to do with her. That hurt. She didn't feel that what she had done or neglected to do was all that horrible. It might have been stupid, but it wasn't horrible. Who was she kidding? For whatever reason, she'd misled Andrew.

Hearing happy gurgles coming from Colton's room gave her hope. It sounded as if Andrew's mood had improved during the day. She tiptoed up the stairs and watched silently as he played peek-a-boo, to Colton's absolute delight.

The growing baby must be feeling better. He had run a little fever the night before, but finally, this morning, a second tooth had broken through. She wondered if Andrew had noticed it. Unable to put off the confrontation any longer, Susan went over to stand beside the bed. "Hello. How's Colton feeling?"

Andrew glanced in her direction. "He's been drooling and gnawing on everything he could get his hands on all day, but he seems to be feeling fine now. Did you notice that he has a new tooth?"

Susan nodded. "He was real fussy with it last night after you left. We sat up into the morning hours until he fell asleep from exhaustion."

"I guess you were tired all day, then. Did you have a good day or was it a regular Monday?" Andrew asked without really looking at her. The tone of his voice indicated that he really didn't care but would listen if she wanted to talk. It was as close to an olive branch as she was going to get.

Susan took it. "It was pretty exhausting, to tell the truth. The kids decided to be monsters. Ironically enough, Billy was the only one who behaved himself.''

''Maybe things will work out with him.'' Andrew didn't sound as if he really thought so or cared one way or another.

''I hope so. I think Billy and his dad have rediscovered each other. Billy said he was going back to live with his dad.''

Andrew rolled over onto his back and held Colton above him.

Visions of their lovemaking flooded her mind when she saw his body stretched across the bed. She imagined lying in those arms with her head nestled in the hollow of his shoulder.

Susan willed away those thoughts, knowing they needed to deal with the issues at hand. She wanted to tell him that problems could be solved if people tried hard enough, but, afraid of how he might react, opted for a more neutral opening. ''You're in a better mood than you were this morning.''

''Not really. I just decided not to be an A double S,'' he explained.

Susan grinned at Andrew's spelling. ''I don't think Colton knows what you're saying.'' She shifted her weight from one foot to the other, then leaned against one of the bedposts. ''Andrew, about last night...I don't want you angry with me. It's important that you understand my position.''

''You've already explained, Susan. I won't lie and say that I understand because I don't.'' Andrew thrust Colton into her arms and rose from the bed in one fluid movement. ''But I've gotten over most of my anger." Pulling a diaper out of the box, he pitched it on the bed. "He probably needs this."

As she changed Colton, she saw Andrew open his mouth several times to say something, each time stopping as though he was uncertain about what to say. "There you go." Susan patted the baby. Turning toward Andrew, Susan crossed her arms over her chest. "Well?"

"Susan, I've been thinking all day. It's been like one of those open-ended questions in school that we all used to hate. I decided that I'm going to California to find Chris and Lisa. I've got to talk to them. I can't stand the limbo those two irresponsible, unstable, fickle, unreliable, immature nincompoops have put us in."

A wave of relief spread over Susan as she listened to Andrew carry on about their children rather than her. She knew his words were a smoke screen hiding his concern for their well-being. "That's quite an impressive list of negative attributes you're attributing to our children," she said, not quite stifling a smile.

"What's so funny?"

"Andrew, I don't think it's a good idea for you to talk with the kids. There's no way you would keep from saying what you're saying right now. And name-calling and preaching will get you nowhere except cut off from Colton entirely. Neither one of us wants that. Maybe I'd better handle it."

"*You* handle it? If you did, it would be the first thing I've ever seen you take charge of."

Susan flinched at the attack on her. "There's no need to be an A double S about it. I still think you're too angry right now to talk reasonably with them about the situation.''

"Okay, then—let's see what you can do.''

"I DON'T WANT Andrew to leave tonight, not while he's still angry with me," Susan explained to Betsy during their midweek conference period.

Anger was an emotion that Susan avoided. She always put a buffer between herself and her true emotions. Thus, she initially found Andrew's intense reaction to her married state baffling.

Betsy put aside the report she had been working on. "What difference does it make, Susan? I thought you didn't even like him.''

"At first I didn't, but things have, well . . . changed during the past few weeks.''

"They must have. It was just a short time ago you didn't have anything good to say about him. You were calling him bossy, among many other less repeatable adjectives.''

"I did, didn't I? We're all entitled to change our minds." Susan stacked her papers and books together as she confessed, "He and I are so different. He's such a perfectionist that I feel I can never quite meet his standards. But in spite of it all, I think I've fallen in love with him.''

Betsy stared at Susan. "You think you love him and don't know?''

"How does one really know if they love someone? I thought I loved George and that didn't work out. I thought Lisa and I made a great mother-daughter team and that didn't work out. I just don't trust my own judgment anymore.'' When Betsy didn't reply, Susan continued, ''Andrew's a wonderful man. He's fun to be with. And you're right. Three months ago I didn't think I'd ever say that. What will I say a month from now?''

''He's not like your first husband, is he?''

''Not at all. George was likable, particularily by the opposite sex, but didn't have a reliable bone in his body. I was responsible for everything. The house, the finances, everything. I had to continually prop him up. It got to the point that I just didn't have the energy to keep it going any longer.'' Susan closed her eyes for a few seconds, then opened them and leaned toward her friend. ''With Andrew it's different. I can rely on him. But the best part is I can talk to him—really talk to him about how I feel.'' She stopped. ''Or I could, until the past few days. Now he won't even listen to me.''

''Sounds like a lovers' spat to me. Why won't he listen to you?''

''It started when he asked me to marry him.''

Betsy dropped her pen on the chipped Formica-top table. It clattered several times before rolling off the edge. ''I can't believe you didn't tell me what was going on, Susan. That's wonderful.'' She jumped up to hug her friend.

''No, it isn't.''

''It isn't? I'm totally confused.'' Betsy sat back down in the straight-backed plastic chair. ''You love him, he loves you, and he asked you to marry him. He's upset with you. What's the deal?''

''I can't marry him because I'm still married to George.''

Betsy shook her head. "I won't even ask you to explain why you're still married, but, for Pete's sake, do something about it. You can't let a man like Andrew just slip out of your life."

"You make it sound so easy. Andrew got so irate Sunday night that he stormed out of the house when I told him. Monday and yesterday were pretty chilly and it hasn't warmed up even one degree this morning. He only nodded curtly when I said hello."

"Susan, it sounds like he has a right to be upset. How would you have felt if he'd been the one who was married?"

Susan bit her lip. "I'd feel betrayed," she admitted.

"So?" Betsy asked.

"I didn't mean to hurt Andrew." Susan's voice took on a beseeching tone. "I honestly didn't."

"Look, you don't have to justify anything to me. I believe you. I know you'd never purposely try to hurt anyone. Andrew knows that too, I'm sure."

"If he does, he's hidden it pretty well so far."

"Feelings are fragile, Susan. My grandmother said he was getting awfully attached to the baby."

"He is. He's so upset by it all that he wants to confront Chris and Lisa and demand that they leave Colton alone. An ultimatum, he said. I'm a fine one to talk, but he just doesn't understand that family relations don't operate like a business."

"Yeah, I've learned that working in the office. Students aren't all alike, and they each have to be handled differently," Betsy agreed.

"He thinks there's only one way to handle things, and that's head-on. Make a plan and attack. His way." Susan leaned back in her chair. "That's not being completely fair to him because he's mellowed a lot in the past few months. I think he's really afraid. Anyway, I told him I'd handle this one."

"What are you going to do?"

"For starters, I'm going to call Jack Green, Chris's friend in Houston, and find out how to get in touch with Lisa and Chris."

ANDREW WAS SITTING in the porch swing when Susan arrived home. "Hi," she called as she walked across the damp grass toward him, ready to tell him what she had learned. "It's kind of cold to be outside, isn't it?"

"Brisk." He said it as if daring her to disagree. "I like it."

She watched his breath condense in the freezing air. "Uh-huh, brisk. Where's Colton?"

"Asleep."

To protect her skirt, Susan laid a purple scarf over the wet slats of the porch swing and sat down beside Andrew. "Guess what I did during my conference period today at school."

"What?"

"I called Jack, Chris's friend in Houston."

Andrew's distant expression changed to one of tentative interest. "Why?"

"To find out where Chris and Lisa are living in California." Susan pulled her coat more tightly around her neck.

"And?" Andrew prompted.

"And what?" Two could play caveman language, she thought. Sometimes he could be so frustrating.

"For God's sake. Where are they in California?"

"They're not." Susan had begun to enjoy herself. She'd sworn she wasn't going to antagonize him, but darned if he didn't ask for it.

Andrew swiveled in the swing until he was face to face with her. "What do you mean, they're not?"

"They've left already. I don't know when they'll be here. Jack didn't know how they planned to get back here since they didn't have much money. Apparently they got disenchanted with their new religion."

"That's about par for the course. Chris has never stuck with anything for very long. And money—he'd beg it from a sick person if he had to. Oh, I shouldn't say that. As far as I know, he's only begged it from me. Didn't have to beg hard either." Andrew got up from the swing. "He probably got it from his mother. She always came through if I didn't."

"Then maybe the kids will go to North Carolina to see her," Susan said hopefully.

Andrew turned to face her. "Not likely, if they're coming to get Colton."

"But they may go to North Carolina first, then come back. That gives us a little time."

"They're going to show up in Houston first. That's where they left Colton. Susan, are you sure . . ." Andrew sought her eyes as his unspoken words hung heavily between them.

Susan sensed what he wanted to say but knew that his hurt, his anger were too fresh to touch. Her arms, longing to comfort him, lay still at her side. She ached from the memory of their lovemaking. She ached for the easiness that had developed between them before she told Andrew that she was still married to George. She moistened her lips. "Am I sure of what?"

Averting his eyes as though he'd changed his mind, he muttered, "It doesn't matter."

"Oh, Andrew, it does matter." Susan slowly rose from the swing, afraid he would reject her. She pressed her hands flat against his chest as she spoke. "I was wrong in not telling you everything earlier. I was probably wrong in half of everything I've ever done, but I'm not wrong in loving you. You matter to me."

"I want to believe that, but then I tell myself if you really loved me we wouldn't be in this mess."

"What ever else you might think...don't doubt my love for you."

Andrew encircled her coat-covered arms with his hands, tenderly sliding them downward until he reached her shivering hands. "Sometimes, when I get off work, I pretend that you're waiting for me on the docks. I even catch myself looking for you. I imagine your face lighting up when you spot me getting out of the helicopter. Did you know that your smile floods your face?"

Susan shook her head.

"It starts in your eyes. They twinkle first. Then the smile moves down to your lips." He lifted her chilled fingers to his waiting lips, turning the cold into warmth as he fanned them with his hot breath. Looking at her, he felt a current of desire. Finally, in view of all the neighbors, he wrapped his arms around her and pulled her body close. Her face rose eagerly to meet his.

He kissed her hungrily, exploring the fullness of her willing lips. "Lord, I love you, Susan. Too much for my own good, I sometimes think," he whispered against the soft skin of her neck before he claimed her lips again. "I can't leave you alone."

Susan smiled as she traced his tender lips with her fingertip. She was still in a daze at the beautiful words that had come from those lips. After the past three days of feeling empty, stripped, as if something was missing from her life, she now felt whole again. Andrew still loved her. "I don't want you to leave me alone."

"As long as you're married, I don't have much choice, do I?" When she didn't respond, Andrew released her and stepped back.

Her mind still foggy from his kisses, Susan reached out to stop him. "Don't go," she pleaded.

He ignored her outstretched hand and took a step off the porch. "I think I've already outstayed my welcome."

"No. You don't understand."

"Then why haven't you done anything about it before now? Why don't you do something now? Are you sure you aren't staying married because deep down you still love George?"

"No! I don't love George, Andrew. Try to understand at least part of my reason. The only savings I have is in my teacher's pension. In this state, if I filed for divorce he'd most likely get half. I haven't wanted to give him that satisfaction."

"A few months ago I would have said that if you married me you wouldn't have to worry about supporting yourself. Right now my job isn't too secure, but I do have some sav—"

Susan cut him off. "Andrew, I wouldn't marry you for Colton or for money."

"I see."

"No, you don't. The only reason I'd ever marry you was because I loved you and wanted to spend the rest of my life with you...not so I wouldn't have to work."

"I guess that's academic, considering the situation."

"I guess it is." He wasn't even trying to understand, she thought.

"Whatever the circumstances, Susan, I won't share you with another man, even for a little while. Get a divorce or it's over." His words lay heavily in the air as he turned and without a backward glance marched to his car.

CHAPTER FIFTEEN

AFTER ATTENDING the early-morning meeting with some of the management, Andrew was glad to get back to the platform and go to work. The brief but straightforward meeting had both confirmed and abated his fears. He was still employed—at least for the time being—but the company planned to combine the operations of several platforms, cutting personnel in the process. That meant more work and longer hours for him, too.

Although he wouldn't push the point, he didn't want longer hours now. Colton was still his responsibility. He didn't really figure that Chris and Lisa would make good on their threat if they gave it a second thought. And if they did, they'd soon tire of the responsibility and leave him God knew where while they went off on their next search for meaning. Andrew was determined not to let them do that. Colton needed security. The security of a family like he and Susan could offer.

"Hey, Bradley, how goes it?" Dan, the balding, potbellied Cajun operator propped an elbow on a mound of paperwork and stifled a yawn. "Good flight?"

"Any flight you walk away from is a good one," Andrew said, ignoring the first question since he seldom shared his personal life with the crew, not even with Dan.

"Oh, there's been a kid trying to reach you all morning. Says he's your son. There's a piece of paper on your desk with a number where you can reach him."

"Aw, hell! That's all I need." Andrew glanced at the number. Though it wasn't his home number, he recognized the Houston prefix. "Guess I'd better take care of it," he muttered as he strode away from the startled Dan.

As soon as he entered his office the phone started ringing. He grabbed the receiver and held it against his chest for a moment, waiting to calm down. Finally he brought the receiver to his ear. "Brazos 576, Bradley."

"Dad? Is that you?"

Chris. Andrew didn't want to talk right now. Susan didn't trust him to say the right thing while he was upset, and he was afraid she was right.

"There aren't that many Bradleys out here. What do you want?" he barked in a tone that matched his mood.

"Uh...Dad...we're back."

"That's obvious. What the hell do you want this time? Spit it out. I don't have much time."

Chris's voice grew firmer. "We want to know where Colton is."

Andrew threw the hard roll he'd been eating toward the trash can. "Well, you can just continue to want. You left him once, and you're not getting an opportunity to do it again. He doesn't need to be bounced around."

"I thought our letter made it clear that we realize we were wrong. We'd like to make it up to you."

"You seem to be having a hard time understanding me, Chris. Let me word it another way. No!"

"Legally, his mother and—"

Andrew's back jerked upright. "I don't give a tinker's damn about what's legal," he shouted into the receiver. "But if that's the tack you want to take, we'll find out what's legal!"

"Look, Dad, take it easy. Things really have changed. Lisa and I are married now."

Take it easy, he says. Take it easy. Smart mouth, no-good...

He managed to get some control over his emotions before he growled, "Your letter said all kinds of things, but none of it changes the fact that I'll have another person to support if things continue the way they have in the past. So you just might as well know up front that I'm through. No more money!"

"I understand that, Dad. You shouldn't have to take care of us, and we don't want you to. We're determined to make a living on our own so we can provide for our son and maybe make things up to him."

"Yeah, sure you are." Chris's comments destroyed the thrust of Andrew's attack, but still, he was skeptical. He'd heard the same type of malarkey from Chris for years. "And how do you propose to do that?"

A moment passed before Chris responded. "I saw Joe Whittenburg this morning and asked him about a

job offshore as a BR man on a drilling rig. He said
that competition for jobs was fierce but he might be
able to help." He paused for a moment, then asked
cautiously, "How's the work going for you, Dad?"

"I think I've got at least another year on the pay-
roll, but the industry's hemorrhaging, Chris, and no
one gives a damn." Andrew sat down, sucking in a
deep breath. Was Chris actually concerned about
someone other than himself? Andrew felt himself
soften.

"Chris, while you're hunting for a job, try to find
one so you'll be home at night. From experience, I can
tell you that being gone for days or weeks at a time
isn't good if you want to have a family."

"Yeah, I thought of that and how it was with you
and me. We never saw each other much."

Andrew fidgeted. He'd had the same thoughts, but
having Chris say them made him defensive. Talking
about feelings made him uncomfortable, though Susan was teaching him to be more open. Stifling his urge
to explain his actions as a father, he realized if there
was any chance for him to help his grandson, it must
begin here. "No, Chris, I guess we didn't."

"I did a lot of thinking in California, Dad. I could
have done it just as well here, but, there, I was—well,
stranded, I guess. Had plenty time to think. I realized
I want roots. I want to do things with my son." Chris's
voice was barely audible as he continued. "I really
thought about you and me a lot...things like how I
always pestered you for money, or how you were never
sitting in the stands yelling for me at my Little League

games like the other kids' dads were. I don't want it to be like that with me and my son."

Andrew closed his eyes before he responded, defenses building again. "I was making a living for you, Chris. Did it really matter to you so much that I wasn't there? You always acted like it was okay with you."

"What did you want me to do? Cry? I was trying to please you by acting like a man. 'Be tough. Don't let people see your weaknesses,' you always said. I was afraid I'd disappoint you if you saw how much I wanted you to be there."

The line was silent for several seconds while Andrew struggled with guilt and defensiveness. Finally he whispered, as much to himself as to his son, "I was a fool."

"Let's just say we've both made mistakes. I haven't exactly been an ideal son, and now I've nearly blown being a father. I want an opportunity to change some of that. I want to raise my son. And I'll look around for a job where I'll be home. But right now, Lisa and I just want to see Colton. Please, Dad, tell us where he is."

Andrew thought for a minute. What would he accomplish by keeping Colton from his parents if they truly had changed? But this wasn't the first time Chris had said he was going to change. Every time he'd messed up, he'd sworn up and down that he'd learned his lesson, then turned right around and pulled yet another stunt. Why should this time be different?

"Colton's in Corpus Christi with Lisa's mom," he blurted out before he could change his mind. "But don't expect her to just hand him over to you like a sack of groceries. She loves him a lot."

"Thanks, Dad."

"One more thing, Chris. If you screw this up and hurt Colton in any way, you'll have me to answer to this time." Andrew's words were crisp and emphatic, leaving little doubt that he was dead serious.

"I understand."

"And be easy on Susan. She's already suffered enough, taking on your responsibilities while you were off lollygagging in sunny California. I'll call and let her know you're coming."

"Okay, Dad, I get the picture. All I can say for now is that I'm sorry."

"Yeah, sure."

Easy for him to say, Andrew thought, dreading the prospect of breaking the news to Susan. He had a feeling she wouldn't take it very well.

SUSAN, sprawled on the living room floor with its floral rug hidden beneath red construction paper, glanced over at Colton who was sleeping soundly on his pallet. "One of these days, kiddo, a teacher will be doing this for you." The thought brought a smile to her lips while she cut out the pattern of her twenty-second valentine. Tomorrow her students would decorate them for their mothers for Valentine's Day.

Tears unexpectedly misted her eyes. Valentine's was for lovers—for love. She thought of all the people she had ever loved. Except for Colton they were all gone— her parents, her husband, Lisa and now Andrew. It's just not fair, she thought, picking up the remnants of red paper. She couldn't bear to lose Colton now.

The ringing phone interrupted her thoughts. Crawling on all fours, she lunged to grab the receiver before the second ring. "Hello."

Andrew's business voice rolled through the lines. "I hope I didn't catch you at a bad time."

She caught her breath and stifled her self-pity before answering, "No. I already have Colton asleep and was doing a little to help Cupid along."

"Cupid?"

"Valentine's Day."

"Oh. I forgot about that coming up. How're you helping Cupid?"

Susan briefly explained the art project before asking, "What's up? You don't usually call on Thursday nights." In truth, she was surprised that he'd called at all after the way they'd parted.

"Our kids, or rather Chris, phoned me this afternoon. They want to see Colton."

Susan felt as if someone had kicked her in the stomach and stuffed cotton in her mouth. "I've been expecting it," she admitted, licking her suddenly dry lips. "What did you tell them?"

"I told them he was with you."

"What do you want me to do?" she asked.

"What *do* you want to do?" He avoided answering.

"I don't know. I want to keep him, but I've done a lot of thinking. Every day I see children who are shuttled from one relative's house to another's. Like Billy Lupton, for example. His grandparents couldn't take the place of his dad no matter how hard they tried or how much they loved him. I don't want that for Colton. I want him to have a stable home life. Maybe Chris and Lisa can be good parents. But I love him so much, I don't know if I can let him go." This was what she had been dreading. "I don't know if I'm strong enough to let him go," she repeated softly.

"There doesn't seem to be an easy solution. How do we know how things will turn out?" Andrew's previously officious voice now reflected his own pain. "I feel like I'm playing God with Colton's life."

"We may not have a choice. Do you think they're sincere about wanting to settle down?"

"Who knows? Chris gave me this spiel about how he and Lisa have changed. It was all I could do to keep from saying I've heard that song before."

"Well, if they can be half-decent parents, it would probably be better for Colton to be with them. Grandparents should be the frosting for kids, not the cake."

"I guess you're right."

Susan switched the phone to her other ear. "But what if they haven't changed?"

"I threatened Chris, for whatever good it might do. Susan, you don't have to turn Colton over to them. You do what you think is best, and I'll back you up. Even if we do have to go to court."

"Thank you, Andrew."

"For what?"

"For supporting me." When he didn't respond, Susan continued, "Andrew, I can't live with the way things are between you and me. I'm sorry. I lov—"

"Don't," he stopped her flow of words. "Don't say it until you are willing to back it up with some action."

THE NEXT AFTERNOON Susan studied her estranged daughter, surprised at the raw anger welling up inside her. She had always been patient with Lisa—disappointed sometimes, but never angry. Now, she felt her facial muscles tighten and her head start to ache dully.

"Mother, uh, may we come in?" Lisa, long brown hair pulled back with a floral bow at the nape of her neck, bit her bottom lip.

Susan stepped back from the doorway to allow Lisa and the tall slender boy with her to come in. She watched as Chris put his hand on Lisa's back and guided her into the room. His gait was that of his father's, only faster. His hair was lighter, and he was slightly taller. He turned suddenly, causing Susan to wince at the resemblance.

"Mrs. Montgomery, I'm Christopher Bradley."

She remained motionless, her dark eyes averted.

The young man shifted his feet on the carpet beneath him and crammed his hands into his pockets. "This is pretty hard."

She didn't intend to make it any easier.

Lisa stepped in front of Chris to protect him from her mother's silent anger. "Mom, we want to start over and do things right this time."

With those words, the invisible dam burst in Susan's mind. "Well, young lady, you can't just waltz in here like everything is normal. It isn't. You ran away from *me*, which is one thing, but you ran from your infant son, which is another thing entirely. Want to do things right, you say. What do you know about what's right?''

"Maybe not much yet. But I do know what is wrong." Lisa slumped onto the sofa and ran her hands up the side of her nose, catching tears as they slid down her cheeks. "Chris is right. This is hard. All I can do is say we were foolish, selfish and probably all those other things you're thinking right now. But we know that now, and we want a fresh start. With Colton and with you.''

Susan was unmoved by Lisa's tears. She'd seen them too many times before. "You want a fresh start with Colton? You abandoned him when he needed you the most. How do I know you won't do the same thing in six months?''

"I understand where you're coming from, Mom. But we're sorry, and we *do* want to be good parents to Colton. We want another chance.''

Chris slipped his arm around Lisa's shoulders as she began to cry harder. "Mrs. Montgomery, we're not asking for your understanding. We know you can't forgive us yet.''

"No, I can't. I love Colton so much. You have no idea how much. And I can't stand the thought of that little boy getting hurt by you or anyone else." Susan's eyes filled with tears.

"Oh, Mom, I'm sorry." Lisa crossed to her mother and tentatively embraced her. "I'm so sorry for hurting you.''

Susan stepped back and ran the palms of her hands over her daughter's wet cheeks. "It's good to see you again, Lisa. I hunted all over for you."

"I know, Mom. I was such a smart-aleck kid that I thought I knew how to handle life better than you. Didn't you ever once feel that way about your mother?"

Susan nodded. "Lots of times. But it didn't cause me to run away. Or abandon you." She smiled faintly. "I'm sorry—I had to say it at least once. I'll try not to mention it again."

Changing the subject, Lisa asked, "Can we just see him?"

Susan studied her daughter and new son-in-law. They looked humble, sincere, unsure of their welcome. How could she deny them the chance to get to know their own child? "I guess so. His room is at the top of the stairs. You two go up alone to get him."

An agonizing half hour later, three figures emerged from the doorway, the tallest carrying a wide-eyed little boy with one arm while his other arm encircled the petite woman at his side. A family. They looked like a family.

Even though Colton didn't cry while his daddy carried him, he reached toward Susan when he saw her, whimpering until she took him. Once he was safe in her arms, he turned his gaze back toward Chris and Lisa.

"Don't worry, he'll get used to you. Maybe you should stay here for a few days and let him get to know you." Susan could have bitten her tongue. She certainly hadn't planned to make that offer.

"You don't mind?" Lisa asked tentatively.

"Of course I mind, but stay, anyway." Susan managed a half smile. She was prepared to fight them for Colton if they didn't show a lot of promise in a short time. But for her own peace of mind she had to give them a chance.

"Thanks, Mom."

Chris and Lisa whiled away an hour playing with Colton until he began to get cranky. "What's wrong, honey? Are you wet?" Lisa cooed.

Susan watched as the two young parents changed their baby's diaper as though it were the grandest pleasure they had ever experienced. They seemed to be truly glad to see their son.

As SHE TWIRLED her hair on top of her head, Susan stared at the single red rose on her dressing table. It had arrived Valentine's Day with a card signed simply—Andrew. He hadn't forgotten.

Turning, she saw Lisa standing at her open bedroom door. "How long have you been there?"

"Not long. You were deep in concentration, so I thought I'd just stand here until you finished getting ready."

"Is Colton asleep?"

"Uh-huh. Putting him on the drier works wonders, just like you said."

"You can thank Andrew for that little trick. It was one of the suggestions in Andrew's infernal child-rearing book. The vibration helps soothe a cranky baby, like going for a ride in a car." More than once, she'd wanted to set Andrew on that drier.

"I'll remember to do that." Lisa walked over to the bed and folded herself into one of its plump pillows. "Colton looks so precious. I didn't know you could see a baby's eyes moving behind its eyelids when it's sleeping. It makes me wonder if he's dreaming." A wistful expression crossed her face. "I've already missed so much."

Susan sat beside Lisa, hoping she was ready to talk. Many issues had been broached the past week, but some had been avoided. "Yes. You missed a lot of firsts . . . times you can never make up."

"You haven't chewed me out the way I thought you would," Lisa said.

"It wouldn't do any good at this point. But I'd like to know why you didn't bring Colton to me instead of leaving him with Andrew."

"There were several reasons. The decision to go to California was a sudden one and we didn't have the time or the money to bring Colton to you."

"West Texas is between here and California."

Lisa lowered her head. "I was still hurt. I didn't know you'd left my father and I didn't want Colton brought up in the same situation I was. I also knew you'd be disappointed if you knew I'd left my baby so . . ." Her voice broke.

"I would have been . . . I am . . . but we have to put that behind us and go forward."

"I'm just so scared, of the future sometimes."

"We're all afraid of the unknown."

Lisa hugged her knees to her chest. "Mom, can I ask you something?"

"You can ask. I may or may not answer, though."

"What happened between you and my father?"

Susan shrugged. "I suppose we got married too young, Lisa. People change dramatically in early adulthood, and we ended up not liking the same things. I only pray that doesn't happen to you and Chris." Susan remembered how George had never paid attention to the infant Lisa, whereas Chris had doted on Colton for the three days he'd been at her house.

"I hope not. I miss Chris so much, and he's only been gone a few days."

"Maybe he'll find a job in Houston and you and Colton can join him fairly soon." Susan forced herself to say the words even though she found the thought of Colton leaving with his parents almost unbearable.

"Then you'll be by yourself. Don't you ever get lonely?"

"Sometimes."

"Mom, I wasn't blind when we were living together. I saw how irresponsible Daddy was. He left you alone a lot. How come you stayed with him?" Lisa asked.

Susan had never discussed her marriage with her daughter, so she was surprised that Lisa had even been aware that there were problems. She decided not to offer a denial. "I guess I thought it was the best thing to do."

"Best or easiest?"

"I've been asked that before, Lisa, and..." Susan began before she stopped and stared out the window.

"From whom?"

Turning back to her daughter, Susan sighed, "It doesn't matter."

"It does." Lisa demanded, "Who?"

"Andrew."

"Why should it matter to him?"

Susan didn't answer. She still wasn't sure how much of her personal life she wanted to share with her daughter. It made her uncomfortable.

Lisa's eyes widened in understanding. "Aha. That's where the rose came from! Mom, do the two of you have something going?"

"Not now."

"But you did, huh?"

"Lisa, this conversation is getting sidetracked," Susan said in answer.

"No, it isn't. I told you about me and Chris. Now you tell me about you and Andrew. Hey, wouldn't that be something if you and Andrew got married. You'd be my mother and my mother-in-law." she let out a brief giggle.

"Well, don't hold your breath, young lady, and quit jumping from A to Z. We're entirely different, Andrew and I. When he first came to present me with Colton, I thought he was a terrible stuffed shirt."

Lisa burst out laughing. "That's what Chris says. Well, actually, he uses a single word, but stuffed shirt will work just as well."

"Chris would find out he's wrong, just as I did, if he really got to know his father." Susan's defense of Andrew was immediate. "He's not stuffy. Not at all." She reached out and touched a soft rose petal with trembling fingers. "In fact, he can be very thoughtful and sweet."

CHAPTER SIXTEEN

ONE WEEK faded into two and the first of March rolled around while school and her students shielded Susan from the self-pity that had engulfed her since putting Lisa and Colton on the plane for Houston to be with Chris. He had sent for his family after his second paycheck provided them with enough to rent an apartment. Colton had warmed to Lisa as though they'd never been apart. Though she was pleased they were a family again, Susan found herself constantly aching for her grandson.

The nights had been the hardest. She couldn't sleep. She would wake up and listen for Colton's breathing before she remembered with a pang of sadness that he wasn't there.

Even now, sitting in the school library sandwiched between Betsy and Milly Adams, Susan felt the emptiness. Listlessly she turned her head when Mr. Garcia walked into the room. He was escorting a tall blond man.

Betsy whispered, "Who's that?"

Susan smiled briefly at the newcomer, then turned to explain to the others at her table. "That's Nick Lupton, Billy's dad from the aquarium."

"Wow." Betsy and Milly said at the same time, leaning forward and giving the newcomer welcoming smiles.

Mr. Garcia looked around the room, unconsciously rubbing his paunch, then opened the meeting. "Thank you all for being here...."

Susan's mind began to wander. After visiting Lisa and Chris last weekend, she was certain that Colton was getting lots of love. Which was more than she could say about herself. Andrew's physical and emotional absence had created a vacuum she was sure nothing else could fill.

"We are lucky to have such dedicated people on our staff...." The speaker's voice droned on somewhere in the background.

She knew nothing about Andrew's present life. Was he as miserable as she? Lisa never mentioned him. It was as though he had ceased to exist, except in her persistent erotic dreams, which often left her sleepless.

Mr. Garcia's voice barely penetrated her mind. "Our beaches are a priority. They must be kept safe for wildlife and for our pleasure...."

For wildlife and pleasure. That, she heard. Susan closed her eyes briefly and leaned back in her chair, remembering the afternoon she and Andrew had visited the winter's deserted beach. Hand in hand, they strolled over the rolling dunes, two images moving on the silent landscape of her memory. There on the beach the whispering wind played with her hair while the loving man played with her heart. Andrew turned her toward him, their mouths hungry for each other.

His warm hands caressed her damp skin as they sank onto the sand....

"Mrs. Montgomery?" Mr. Garcia's booming voice and Betsy's sharp elbow in the ribs brought Susan back to reality.

Again Mr. Garcia called her name. "Do you have anything to report, Mrs. Montgomery?"

A blush spread up Susan's face as she remembered where she was. She was sure those around her knew what she had been daydreaming. How could she? At a committee meeting? Not knowing what she'd been asked, Susan tried to fumble her way through. "No, Mr. Garcia. Not just yet."

Milly stared at her with a puzzled frown on her face. Billy's dad smiled and turned his attention back to Mr. Garcia. She squirmed in her molded plastic chair, trying to get more comfortable. Betsy raised her eyebrows and whispered, "Something wrong?"

Mr. Garcia seemed confused, so he continued. "Mrs. Montgomery's class turned over a Kemp's ridley turtle to the state aquarium. Her students learned about the restrictions concerning the possession of the endangered species. One of those students' fathers is the director of animal husbandry there." Mr. Garcia nodded toward their guest. "Mr. Nick Lupton has graciously agreed to speak to us this afternoon."

Nick took his place behind the makeshift podium. "Mrs. Montgomery, I appreciate that you didn't steal my program." He pointed to the slides projected onto the library wall. "I was asked to tell you some of the characteristics of the Kemp's ridley turtle. If you'll notice, it won't win any beauty contests. It's fairly large, with the approximately two-foot-by-two-foot adult weighing between eighty-five and ninety pounds...."

Trying to clear the erotic daydream from her mind, Susan squirmed in her seat again, disconcerted at the dampness she could feel between her legs.

"You've all probably heard the old wives' tale that if a turtle bites your toe, it won't let go until it thunders? Well, that's not too farfetched. The ridley bites and is as stubborn as a bulldog...."

She had to collect herself. *Breathe slowly and listen,* she told herself, shaking her head at Betsy's questioning look.

"The turtles eat shrimp, jellyfish and squid. These are plentiful under offshore production platforms which become artificial reefs in a short time. In captivity we feed them a special gel made from carrots, spinach and vitamins as well as squid. Most of the turtles at the aquarium come to us because they were injured. We have one that's missing a hind leg...."

Billy's dad was preparing his summation when Susan willed herself to tune in. "Remember that much of what happens around us appears to be largely outside of our control, but the way we choose to react to it is within our control. If you really care, why don't you show it by getting out there and doing something?"

After the meeting was dismissed Nick stopped her before she could get out the door. "I wanted you to know that I'm grateful for what you've done for Billy and me. It seems that I was so wrapped up in my work and grief I didn't realize that my parents couldn't substitute for me. Billy seems more settled now."

Susan didn't remind Mr. Lupton about his initial resistance to her meddling. But because she'd seen what could have happened to Colton, she fought for Billy. "You're welcome. In class, he quotes you all the time."

"At home, he quotes you all the time. Say, I'm going out on another turtle watch this weekend. Would you like to come?"

"I don't..." She started to decline his invitation, then, remembering the long, lonely weekend ahead, she stopped in midsentence and reconsidered. Besides, it wasn't a date. "I don't have other plans. Sure, I'd love to go."

"Good. About six o'clock Saturday morning. I'll come by and pick you up."

"You don't have to do that." She noticed Betsy standing expectantly at her elbow.

"It's no problem. Besides, we'll have to drive up the coast a ways to meet up with the others," Nick assured her as he looked at the tall dark woman to Susan's left. "Who is this? I don't believe we've met."

Betsy smiled. "That can be remedied."

Susan made the introductions, wondering if this might be the beginning of Betsy's promise to her grandmother. Leaving them flirting with each other, she slipped away unnoticed toward the half-empty parking lot. She couldn't go home just yet. "I'll go stir-crazy. I've got to work off some of this frustration," she said to no one as she climbed into her hot car. "I'm already talking to myself."

She took the circular drive around Corpus Christi, past mansions overlooking the water, through the less affluent neighborhoods, and down the palm-lined highway stretching out over the gulf. She found a deserted spot along the beach and pulled over.

Blue-gray water stretched to the horizon until it blended with a turquoise sky. It was a beautiful afternoon. If only she could enjoy it. She had never felt so lonely, and it was her own fault. For the past few years, she had been building walls around herself instead of bridges. Now she was paying the price.

She removed her low-heeled pumps and panty hose before stepping onto the cool sand. The sand felt good, squishing between her toes as she strolled along the beach savoring the salt air, letting the wind toss her hair into unmanageable tangles and thinking of Andrew.

Finding a nice flat rock, she tried skipping it across the undulating water. It sank. Andrew would have done it right, she thought, brushing away a tear.

"This is ridiculous! This fantasizing has got to stop." Her mind made up, Susan strode back across the beach to her waiting car with a renewed purpose. Lying directly beneath her car door was a perfect sand dollar. She knelt down, picked it up and laid it on the dash of her car. In some elusive way it symbolized the decision she had just made.

"Control," Billy's dad had said. We control our reactions. Determined that it was now or never, she wheeled into her driveway, stormed into her house and grabbed the phone.

"Hello, Mr. Garcia," she said breathlessly as soon as he came on the line. "I'm sorry to bother you at home, but something's come up. I need to take a day off tomorrow. I've got some personal business to take care of."

Then, picking up the phone book, she turned to the yellow pages and located Attorneys, divorce. She was going to take control of her life.

"HOW MUCH FARTHER?" Susan yelled to Nick over the roar of the boat motor. Her stomach was beginning to get queasy from riding the choppy seas.

Nick consulted his watch. "We left Port Aransas about two and half hours ago, so we should be at the platform in twenty, thirty minutes at the most."

Nick indicated a pinpoint on the horizon. "That's where we're headed. We'll join up there with two men from Parks and Wildlife who've been doing a boat surveillance."

Susan nodded and held her stomach as the bottom dropped out of a wave and they plunged ten feet, then rose back to the top of the crest. The same up-and-down pattern had been repeated over and over until she wasn't sure she could keep her breakfast down much longer. Why she'd bothered with a motion patch, she'd never know. The looming platform looked like a haven.

Loosening her seat belt, she closed her eyes and rested her head against the boat wall. Silently she sang, "The Lord's My Shepherd."

"We're almost there," Nick promised.

The platform looked monstrous up close. As they edged up to one of the steel cylindrical legs, Susan, clutching the side of the boat as though to hold it still, asked how they were going to get off a boat that was bobbing up and down.

"They'll lower a basket by crane onto the deck of the boat," Nick explained. "You time the pitch of the sea, then step on. The guys up there will lift us up. Come on, I'll show you."

Boarding the basket looked simple enough when Nick did it. When it was her turn, Susan was far from confident as she stepped onto the ring and held on to the nylon webbing.

She heard Nick's encouragement beside her as she rode the sixty feet from the churning water to the bottom platform deck. She wondered how often cables were replaced. What if they were weak and rusted?

Two hands reached out to steady the basket as it swung over the metal deck and came to a rest with a reassuring thud. Nick helped her off, then introduced her to a short black-haired man. "Susan, this is Dan Hebert. He's arranged for the helicopter."

Susan held out an unsteady hand. "Pleased to meet you, Mr. Hebert."

"I'm sure you'd like to get started. The charges are scheduled for noon," Dan explained, leading the way up a narrow metal gray stairway. "Good you wore sensible shoes." He indicated Susan's sneakers. "Don't have cause for women out here, as a rule, but we've had a few gals come out here thinking they was a fashion show. Trying to impress the guys with their heels, which got all caught up in the holes in the grating." He laughed heartily. "Woowee, they was a sight."

Chauvinist! Susan had to practically jog up the steps to keep up with him. After three more flights of steps, they arrived on the top deck of the platform where a Bell helicopter rested on a painted bull's-eye. Its rotors turned slowly but still put off enough wind and noise to make communication close to impossible.

Taking the seat indicated, Susan buckled her seat belt and put on earphones. She felt her initial excitement mounting again. She was off that boat, and this was her first helicopter ride! Nick gave her a big smile and the thumbs-up signal.

She watched intently as the pilot went through his preflight check. As the engine's roar got louder, her heart beat faster. All of a sudden they were airborne. The helicopter rolled to its side as it made a tight circle of the platform and headed toward deep water. *Oh, my God!* Susan groaned, clutching the edge of her seat in fear she would fall out. *Not again.*

The fifteen minutes it took to reach the caisson that was scheduled for demolition allowed Susan to regroup. Away from the resistance of the beach, the gulf waters appeared much calmer. Beginning in small concentric circles, the pilot began circling, allowing Susan a view of everything below through unobstructed glass. It was perhaps the most awe-inspiring sight she'd ever seen. She knew Andrew did this often and wondered if he ever felt as insignificant as she did at this moment.

The pilot circled the area in ever-larger circles while the four passengers combed the sea for a Kemp's ridley turtle that might have wandered into danger. Once one of the men signaled where he thought he could see a turtle, which upon closer inspection turned out to be a floating car door.

Shortly before noon, the demolition was given the go-ahead. The helicopter retreated a safe distance as the men in the work boats completed preparations after which, they, too, retreated. The charge was set and a large plume of water blew into the air, lifting the caisson from its moorings.

Susan watched as men aboard the work boats worked feverishly to attach cable to the metal caisson. Once it was secured, a crane lifted the caisson from the water and set it on the deck. Susan realized she'd seen competent men who knew their job and did it with no wasted energy. Maybe their breed was becoming an endangered species, too.

The thought brought her back to task, as she and the other watchers began scanning a seemingly endless surface for a turtle or any other marine animals that might have been damaged in the blast. She found her sunglasses did little against the glare of the sun reflecting from the crinkled surface of the water. An hour later, satisfied that for now the ridley turtles in the gulf were safe, one of the men gave the signal to return to the platform.

Dan climbed the stairs and stepped onto the helipad to greet the four turtle watchers and the pilot as they disembarked. "Hungry?" he asked, leading them down the stairs.

"Starved," Nick conceded. The last time Susan could remember being so hungry was when she was a child coming in from school.

"Come on then, the grub's still on."

The dining area was larger than she'd expected. Condiments were strewn down the middle of the one of the two long tables that together would seat twenty men.

"The crew's done been through eating for near on thirty minutes."

Susan realized that Dan's comment was to let them know that they'd been thrown off schedule by the turtle watchers. She considered apologizing, when Nick intervened.

"It's awfully nice of you to keep it hot for us, but you do realize that we packed a lunch for ourselves." Nick laid a friendly hand on Dan's shoulder. "Everything you've done for us is over and beyond our expectations. Not everyone is as cooperative as the guys on this platform."

Dan grumbled that hot food was better than a sandwich any day just as the cook uncovered the food in the serving line that separated his immaculate stainless-steel galley from the dining facility. "'T weren't no problem. Anyways, we got some other outsiders here, too."

"Other environmentalists?" she asked, hoping too much animosity wasn't being created.

"Personnel folks," Dan grunted.

"Oh." Susan heaped her plate with the fried chicken and mashed potatoes and the trimmings, then settled down in one of the steel tubular chairs to enjoy it.

"See," Dan said, "Three Can delivers quite a meal."

Susan's head jerked up when she heard the cook's name. It had to just be a coincidence. Fate couldn't be that cruel. "Three Can Stan?" she asked, fork in midair.

The slender cook bowed low, "At your service, ma'am."

Shock at being on this platform was turning into nervousness when Susan heard the outer door squeak open. A man dressed in red coveralls filled the doorway. "Dan, are those turtles watchers through with our—" He stopped in midsentence when he spotted the guests sitting at the table.

Her fork still paused in midair and her mouth open, Susan stared into Andrew's cold blue eyes.

"Yep. They just finished and are settin' down to some grub," Dan explained. "You done met Dave and Monty. This here's Nick Lupton, and the little lady goes by Susan Montgomery."

Andrew nodded toward Nick, then said, "Susan and I have met."

A light came on in Dan's brown eyes. "Oh! This is the Susan that..." He seemed to think better of continuing, so he looked from Andrew to Susan, then shook his head in wonder.

Everyone else in the room vanished for Susan. Andrew stood a mere eight feet away, looking more handsome than ever. She ached for him to lay his hand on her shoulder, anything, just so she could feel his touch.

"Hello, Andrew," she said, trying not to betray how distraught she was feeling.

"Hello." Turning sideways, he picked up a cup. "I just came in for coffee," he explained after giving Dan a withering look that spoke volumes. The look slid over to Nick. "See any turtles?"

"No," Nick confessed.

Susan would have sworn the edges of Andrew's mouth were working to conceal a look of recrimination.

Acknowledging the confession with a quick nod, Andrew said, "I'll be in my office." After filling his cup, he headed toward the door. He didn't even look at Susan again.

"Don't mind him," Dan offered an explanation. "We all just found out this hitch that some of us are going to be reassigned or laid off. Been eatin' on 'em."

"Reassigned? Where?"

"Don't know yet. Most likely overseas."

She wanted to find Andrew and ask him how the changes would affect him, but was too embarrassed to ask where he was. The fear of his rejecting her again was too great. Humiliation was bad, but humiliation in front of his friends would be more than she could bear.

Finally unable to stand it any longer, Susan motioned toward Dan. "Mr. Hebert, would you mind showing me where Andrew is, please."

"No problem." Dan led the way to Andrew's office.

Electricity crackled across the few feet of air separating Susan from Andrew when Dan closed the door behind him.

"What can I do for you?" Andrew rolled his chair around and leaned back.

"I . . . Dan said that you might be reassigned or laid off."

"Looks that way. They're combining the operations of this platform with several others."

"Do you have any idea where you will go?"

"No." His answer was curt.

Susan was at a loss for words. She shuffled her feet and thrust her hands into the pocket of her windbreaker.

"You must like these turtle watches," Andrew said, getting up and coming to stand by her side.

"No, not really," she said, thinking of the boat trip. "But the weekends are lonely now that Colton is with his parents and you—"

He interrupted, "I'm sure you can find other interesting activities in a city the size of Corpus."

"Andrew, we've been through this before. Turtles aren't our problem."

"No. I guess not. But they're one of mine." Andrew leaned against the opposite wall, crossing his arms over his head. "Diane is back out here."

"Diane?"

"The woman who visited the platform last fall to make layoff recommendations." His right hand emphasized his reminder. "Well, she's back. I thought I was secure for another year. Now I don't know. And you tell me turtle watchers aren't a problem?"

"Oh, Andrew." Susan took a few steps his way. "You've got so much experience. You won't be laid off, will you?"

"I don't know. I don't really want to talk about it, Susan. Okay?"

Susan understood Andrew's dilemma. Andrew thought of himself as the provider, the planner. She knew that Andrew blamed a lot of the oil company's financial concerns on the regulations made by environmentalists—by people like herself. If she ever hoped for a future with him, this day must not become a divisive element standing between them. "Have you seen Colton and the kids?" she asked hesitantly.

Andrew nodded, his demeanor softening at her question. "He's really growing. I miss him."

A knock on the door saved her from having to respond.

"Come in," Andrew said.

A woman's face peered around the door. With brisk strides, she walked up to Susan and offered her hand. "Hi. I'm Diane. It's nice to see another female out here for a change. You with the turtle people?"

"Yes."

Nodding toward the scowling Andrew, Diane continued, "Don't mind him. His bark's a lot worse than his bite."

Susan couldn't help but smile at the pleasant woman. "Thanks for the tip."

Diane turned to Andrew, "Got a minute?"

"Sure."

Susan knew that was her cue to leave. "I, uh, I'll be seeing you."

Andrew held the door for her, then stood and watched her as she descended the steps to join the others. She felt his eyes on her back. Just before she was out of earshot, she was almost positive she heard Diane ask, "How does Russia sound?"

Several minutes later Dan led the way back down to the landing where they were to be lowered by basket into the boat.

Taking a breath, determined not to make herself look like a bigger fool than she felt, Susan climbed onto the basket. As the crane swung them free of the platform, Susan looked up. Andrew stood twenty feet away. He looked sad. He gave her a slight salute before the basket landed with a thud onto the deck of the boat.

LOG

"DID I MISS ANYTHING?" Bertha asked after returning from the rest room.

"No, we waited for you," I explained as she took her seat. "No need in having to repeat everything twice."

"Now, where were we?" Virginia asked.

"Let's see." I adjusted my thimble and went back to work on the quilt. "Chris and Lisa moved to an apartment in Houston with Colton. Susan called an attorney and filed for divorce."

"That must've been hard on you. Them taking the baby, I mean," Bertha commented. "I don't think my weak heart could have taken the shock."

"Yes, I really miss that little boy." I've been through a lot in my life and don't break down easily, but there was something about not seeing that baby that left me close to tears. "Andrew called to tell me goodbye and thank me for all my help."

"With him gone, what do you think Susan will do now?" Era asked.

I dabbed at my eye with the cuff of my sleeve. "I'm not sure. I have a feeling she won't stay here after school's out. Not with Lisa and Colton gone."

Bertha declared, "If I were her, I surely wouldn't stay here. I'd move to Houston."

Virginia and Era concurred. "She'd be near Colton, and maybe she and Andrew could patch things up."

"I don't know. According to what Betsy told me, he was really angry when he left here the last time."

"Oh, that doesn't mean a thing. You know how men are." Bertha attacked the quilt with renewed vigor. "They boil and fume, have their little fit, but when they get the urge for a woman, they come back on bended knee."

"Bertha Clark!" Virginia scolded. "You shouldn't say things like that."

"Why not?" Bertha asked indignantly. "It's the truth. Isn't it, Era?"

"I wouldn't—"

Bertha interrupted. "See, even Era agrees, and she's a prude about sex."

"I am not!" Era retorted. "There are just some things that ladies don't talk about."

"What if Susan gets the urge first?" I asked, playing devil's advocate.

Era rebuked me. "Women don't get the urge."

"Oh, wake up, Era. How long has it been since you've had a man?" Bertha inquired.

"I swan, Bertha! That isn't any of your business," Era sputtered, straightening the buttons on her blouse.

"Come on. Tell us," Bertha urged. "How long has Robert been dead? Since the early sixties?"

Era flushed with color. "Yes, he died in sixty-one, but there are some things that are simply private, Bertha. I—"

"We need to find you a man." Bertha stopped her stitching and waved her needle toward Era. "There's *a widower that lives down the street from me. He's not to my taste at all, but he might suit you."*

"Leave Era alone," Virginia snapped.

Bertha ignored her and continued, *"Anyone who hasn't had a man in thirty years probably wouldn't know what to do anyway."*

"I sure hope Susan and Andrew wake up before that much time passes," I interjected, trying to ease Era's discomfort.

"Somebody needs to do something," Bertha pointed out.

Virginia patiently explained the fallacy in that line of thinking. *"They don't need four old ladies meddling in their business."*

"When has that ever stopped us?"

I got to thinking about what Bertha said and decided to call Lisa. The two of us came up with a plan.

CHAPTER SEVENTEEN

THE CRACKED WOODEN STAIRS leading to the second floor of the apartment complex creaked with each step Susan took. Strolling the length of the walkway, she followed the chrome-plated numbers until she reached 214. A feeling of strangeness came over her as she knocked on the door. She was going to stay overnight in her daughter's apartment.

A jeans-clad Lisa swung open the door as soon as Susan knocked. "Hi, Mom, I've been waiting on you. Come on in. I've been working on the apartment today. What do you think?" Lisa stepped back, allowing Susan to enter.

Susan dumped her armful of packages on the floor of the nearly empty living room. Straw mats and baskets dotted the previously bare walls, personalizing the prefurnished apartment. The afghan Susan's mother had crocheted for Lisa as a child was draped over the back of the sofa. "You've really worked since I was here the last time. You've made it look more comfortable, more like your own." Susan smiled at her daughter, pleased that Lisa had a domestic side. "Is there anything else you need that I might be able to help you with?"

"No, Mom. You've given us a lot to help us get started. Chris said absolutely no more. If we can't afford it ourselves, we'll just wait. Andrew offered to get us a microwave and a..." Lisa stopped in midsentence when she saw her mother's face. "He's already been here this week, checking up on us just like you are."

Susan's heart tightened at the sound of Andrew's name. "Maybe we come to see you because we care about you, not because we're checking up on you."

"I know you care, but I also think you're checking on me." Lisa waved her hand toward the sacks and boxes heaped on the beige carpet. "What's all this?"

"Stuff I got before I heard Chris's decree. It's just a few things for Colton. Some diapers and such. There's a little something for you, too." Susan slid a slender box bearing the name Joske's, an exclusive Houston department store, from the sack. "Here. This one's yours."

Lisa took the gift, gingerly lifted a corner of the lid and peeked inside, glancing back and forth between the box and her mother.

Susan reassured her daughter with a smile. "It won't bite."

Dropping the box lid onto the sofa, Lisa carefully peeled back the crisp white tissue paper that hid soft pink silk.

Susan held her breath. Even though Lisa had a history of detesting any clothing that her mom purchased for her, Susan had bought the teddy and panties on impulse. She seldom went to a store as expensive as Joske's except to browse. Feeling good that she and Lisa had reestablished a relationship, she'd been attracted by the lingerie as a possible gift for her daughter.

Lisa held up the sexy teddy by its tiny straps. "Oh, Mom, it's beautiful." She threw her arms around Susan's neck. "Thank you. Thank you." Tears glistened on her lashes as she released Susan and folded the tissue back around her gift.

Susan swallowed before she spoke. "I knew that you probably didn't get to buy anything special for your wedding night. When I saw this, it reminded me of what you used to say about how when you got married you were going to wear sexy underwear to keep your husband's interest."

"Boy, was I naive. There's not enough money for those kinds of things, or enough time to shop, or enough energy. Being responsible for a family is a lot harder than I thought it would be. Taking care of two guys and their clothes wears me out, and Colton is a supercharged energy machine. Now that he's crawling, he's into everything. I never get finished before it's time to start over." Lisa paused to catch her breath. "I feel like I'm stringing beads and there's no knot in the end of the string."

Susan laughed. "I know that feeling well."

"How did you manage to take care of Colton and teach school, too?"

"Necessity, plus a little experience under my belt. And I had Mrs. J. and Andrew to help out. You'll be going full swing in no time. You've done very well so far."

"Chris helps out some, but he's always so tired when he comes in from work."

"How's his job at the machine shop coming along?" Susan asked, taking a seat on the simple, old-fashioned sofa that would be her bed for the night.

"Since he's the new kid on the block, he gets to do all the dirty work and all the gofer jobs, but he says that's okay. It's shift work, but at least he's home some of every day. Colton gets to see him and he gets to see Colton, which is a lot better than if he were offshore." Lisa set the box containing her gift on the table. "Colton thinks his dad is just about the greatest thing ever."

"That's wonderful." Susan's lingering doubts about her decision to return Colton to his parents evaporated each time she talked to Lisa. Glancing at her watch, she said, "It's almost four o'clock. Will Colton wake up from his nap any time soon?"

"It's about time for him to wake up now. It's rare for his nap to last much over an hour. It seems I get him down, do one thing, and he's awake again. But since you're here, I guess it's okay for you to speed the process along."

Susan went to the small alcove that she had helped Lisa and Chris turn into a nursery and returned minutes later carrying Colton. "I didn't have to speed anything up. He was awake and fingering the designs on his bumper pad. I must say, you never woke up the way he does. You used to wake up crying." Susan bounced the baby up and down. "Just look at him. I can't believe how much he's grown since I saw him last."

"It's only been a couple of weeks, Mom," Lisa reminded Susan.

"Well, it seems like a lot longer. I really miss the little fellow, except while I'm sleeping, which is also a lot longer. Waking up at night is the only part I don't miss." Susan nuzzled Colton's neck.

"I think his grandpa misses him, too."

The room got quiet. Susan stared at Colton's hand as it curled around the finger she offered.

"You can't avoid him forever," Lisa said.

"Avoid who?"

"You know who. Andrew, that's who. Don't you think we've noticed that you won't talk about him? He's just as bad. He cuts us off cold if your name comes up in a conversation. He wouldn't come to see us that weekend when you came."

Hearing that Andrew didn't want to be reminded of her stung Susan more deeply than she cared to admit. "Some people are just incompatible, Lisa."

"I don't believe you for a minute," Lisa retorted. "Incompatibility isn't the problem between you and Andrew. Chris and I may be stupid about some things, but this isn't one of them."

"I didn't realize it was that obvious." Susan looked up at her daughter.

"Well, it is, Mom. So what happened between you two?"

"It's a long story."

"I've got plenty of time to listen and you've got all weekend to tell it. Shoot."

Susan looked down at her hands. "It really just sneaked up on us."

"Well, what's the problem?"

"The problem is that legally, I'm still a married woman." Susan set Colton down on the floor to play.

"You know what, Mom? For an intelligent woman, you're . . . I don't even know the word. How long has it been since you've seen my father?"

"Lisa, you shouldn't use that tone when you ask about George. Show him some respect."

"I'm sorry, Mom, but he doesn't exactly deserve my respect—or yours, I might add."

"I asked him to leave the month after you ran away. I haven't seen him since." Susan didn't like the critical look she was getting from her daughter. Neither of them had made the wisest of choices, but Lisa had been a teenager. She had her youth as an excuse, something Susan no longer had. "He's called me a couple of times after I moved to Corpus Christi. He wondered if there was any chance of a reconciliation."

"And you said no, I hope."

"Of course." Susan nodded, then added as an afterthought, "He got Andrew once when he called while I was at work."

"Oooh... what happened?"

"Nothing really, but it didn't help. Andrew figured out who it was."

"The fact that you wouldn't take my father back is a beginning, Mom. You had the courage to do the hard part." Lisa crossed the living room to stand beside her mother. "Now what?"

Susan cleared her throat and announced, "I filed for a divorce last month."

"Good. Does Andrew know that you've filed?"

"No. And please don't tell him," Susan replied. "I want to be the one to do that."

"I won't say a word. Promise."

"That isn't particularly reassuring. You were never very good at keeping secrets." Susan smiled. She felt better. It was nice to be able to talk to Lisa again, even though she was discomfited by Lisa's assessment of her parents.

"Well," Lisa said, slapping her knees, "now that your problem's solved, how about some spaghetti and meat sauce for supper?"

"Sounds tempting."

"Sounds easy. It's one of the few things I can cook without making a total mess. Chris will be home pretty soon with a hollow stomach."

"Can I do anything to help? Grate cheese or something?"

"Just watch Colton. It seems like he's always eager to play when he wakes up from his nap." Lisa started toward the tiny kitchen.

"Count your blessings that he wakes up in good spirits. Like I told you, most babies are a lot fussier." Susan pulled Colton out from under the coffee table where he was fingering carpet fuzz. He promptly crawled to the edge of the kitchen and back to the living room, delight spreading across his face as Susan played chase on her hands and knees. "I'm going to get you," Susan was threatening when the doorbell interrupted their play.

"Would you get the door?" Lisa called from the kitchen. "My hands are wet."

"Sure." Susan scooped up Colton and hurried to the door. Deciding against opening the door before looking, she tiptoed and peered through the peephole. At first she couldn't see anything, then a man's shoulder came into view. The figure shifted slightly. Andrew!

What was he doing here? She wasn't ready to see him. Susan glared at her daughter. How could Lisa purposely invite Andrew for supper knowing how awkward they would be around each other? With her heart fluttering, she took a deep breath, flicked the chain and opened the door. "What are you doing here? You're supposed to be offshore."

Andrew stared back at Susan, the woman who'd occupied all his spare thoughts and then some. The woman who'd made it hard for him to keep his mind on his business. In a weak moment, he'd told Dan about Susan. Dan had just shaken his head and accused Andrew of "rutting."

Now she was standing before him with unassuming elegance in her pink slacks and white sweater, the same one she had worn the last night they'd made love. He liked her in pink. He liked her regardless of what she wore. She had a grace and radiance that made everyone around her feel good. But their relationship was no longer his decision. Hiding his anxiety, he willed neutrality into his voice. "I could ask you the same question."

"I don't have to go to school Monday. Besides, I have every right to be here," she added defensively.

"So do I . . . have a right to be here."

"Yes, I suppose you do." After a moment of awkward silence, Susan suddenly pointed to the folded newspaper. "I read the morning headlines about layoffs. I was concerned. Are you, I mean . . . was your schedule changed?"

"This is vacation time." Andrew responded, not bothering to tell her that he faced a probable transfer halfway around the globe. Not that it would matter to her, since they no longer had a relationship.

Lisa stepped through the doorway of the tiny kitchen. "Hi, Andrew," she greeted him, drying her hands on a small terry towel.

Andrew shot her a quick reproving glance before greeting her with a curt "Hello."

"I hope you're not hungry yet. It'll be at least an hour before it's ready. We're having spaghetti, and I left the onions out of the sauce."

"That's a relief." Looking at Susan from the corner of his eye, Andrew knew the night would be difficult. There was no way he could be civil without wanting to take Susan in his arms. But that was not an option, he reminded himself. Wanting to run, he said to Lisa, "I didn't realize that there would be other *guests* for supper. Maybe I should leave and come back another time."

"Oh, nonsense. You and Mom aren't guests. You're family. You two guys watch Colton, okay? It'll make him happy." Lisa grinned and shrugged before disappearing into the tiny corridor kitchen, leaving her reluctant guests to fend for themselves.

In the uncomfortable silence that followed, Susan shoved Colton toward Andrew. "Say hello to Grandpa," she commanded.

The coolness in Andrew's eyes warmed visibly when he took Colton into his arms and cuddled him to his chest. "How've you been, fella?"

Susan studied Andrew as he played with Colton. Laugh lines crinkled at the corners of his eyes and his mouth turned up in that lopsided smile she knew so well. He sure didn't look as if he was missing her. He probably didn't love her anymore, probably never had and was just now realizing it. Shaking the unwelcome thoughts from her head, she watched him ride Colton horsey on his foot, saying the rhyme over and over to the baby's giggles.

> "Ride 'em horsey, down to town.
> Goin' to buy this baby some candy.
> Watch out, Colton, don't fall down."

Andrew lifted Colton onto his lap. The little boy, propped on his knees, peered into Andrew's eyes while his pudgy hand prowled through his grandpa's shirt pocket. He pulled out a pen and chewed on the cap before throwing it on the floor and returning to the pocket in search of more things to toss around.

"Are you trying to be like your grandmother?" Andrew dryly admonished Colton. To Susan he said, "No school Monday, huh? I guess you're glad. I'm surprised you aren't on the floor making cutouts."

Susan gave Andrew an overly polite smile as she retrieved the pen Colton had thrown on the floor. "Actually, I took the day off." She handed the pen back to Andrew, being careful not to let their fingers touch.

"I see." Crossing his ankle over his knee, Andrew formed an effective corral around Colton who stood tiptoeing on the floor and clutched his grandpa's pant leg with slobbery fingers.

Susan sat down. "What do you plan to do on your vacation?"

"Not much," Andrew replied, allowing Colton to wriggle down onto the floor and crawl out from his barricade.

"Going anywhere?" Susan addressed Andrew as she stood up and went over to where Colton was exploring the trash can.

"No."

Susan retrieved a piece of paper from his mouth. "Paper isn't good to eat, Colton. You'll have a nice meal in just a little while." Even though she had to pry the remaining paper from his hands, she felt she got more of a response from talking to the baby than talking to the man sitting six feet away from her.

"You told me you'd like to go see the Smithsonian someday. This would be a perfect time, wouldn't it? Cherry trees in bloom and all?" Too late, she remembered that they had once discussed going there together.

Andrew's blue eyes clouded over. "I'll just hang around here." He reached over and picked up an advertising flyer and buried his head in it. She'd suggested going to Washington, D.C. He'd like that, but not without her. There wasn't anything he could do until she got a divorce. Apparently she did not feel about him as strongly as he did her or she would have done something by now.

"I'm sorry. I didn't mean to suggest..." Susan wanted to reach out and bridge the ridiculous gap that two egos refused to cross.

He mumbled something from behind the paper shield before lapsing back into silence.

Just as she decided to escape by going to the tiny kitchen to offer Lisa some help whether she wanted it or not, Susan heard a key click in the door lock.

Chris, his clothes covered with grease, stepped into the apartment carrying his work boots. Seeing Andrew and Susan, he held his arms with boots dangling and made a complete turn like a model. "Look at this, folks. Proof positive that the kid has a job."

Lisa stepped out of the kitchen and flashed a smile toward her parents. "Doesn't he look cute?" She puckered up and received a quick kiss from Chris, who was careful not to touch her with his clothes. She took his boots and carried them to the kitchen.

"Excuse me while I go shower and change. Something smells good, so I'll be quick."

Susan smiled at this. Chris had barely started shaving. Yet she knew he had a man-size job. She was grateful to him for breaking some of the tension between her and Andrew. "Let me set the table for you, Lisa."

When they gathered around the table, Susan put Colton in his bear-adorned vinyl high chair and secured the tray in position. She didn't say anything when Andrew asked if the tray was pushed in too close. Taking the tiny blue bib Lisa handed her, she tied it around Colton's neck. He promptly started fretting. With persistent fingers, he tugged at the bib in an effort to get it off.

"He hates to wear one," Lisa explained, pulling up a chair next to Colton.

Susan tried to ignore Andrew, but the table and tiny alcove made it impossible to keep much distance. With the tines of her fork, she moved some of her spaghetti and sauce to the side of her plate where she began mashing it. "This will take his mind off it." Filling the tiny spoon, she leaned toward the baby. "Here, Colton. Take a bite-bite."

Colton opened his mouth and leaned into the spoon. He worked the food around with his tongue, spitting some of it out on his chin. Then he grinned.

"Is that good for him?" asked Andrew.

"I don't know why not," she answered, giving the eager Colton another bite. "You can buy little jars of it in the store."

"Then buy him some in the store."

"It costs more," Susan said, aware of the dig.

"That's hardly the point. The book said that a baby should never eat food from someone else's plate. It isn't sanitary."

"For Pete's sake, Andrew. This is perfectly all right. I haven't contaminated the food." Andrew's presence already had her nerves taut, so his contentiousness stretched her to near-breaking point. You and your damn book, she felt like saying, remembering his promise not to mention it again.

"So you're an authority now?" Andrew pointed his fork at her.

"No more than you're trying to be," she said evenly.

"It amazes me that Gerber has spent so much money in salaries and benefits for chemists and nutritionists when all they had to do was—"

Susan threw her fork on the table, her eyes shooting fire at him as she pushed herself back from the table. "I've had it with your insults and know-it-all attitude... and... and that stupid book of yours."

A chalk-faced Chris interrupted. "Lisa, I think our guests would like some more to eat."

Lisa, trying to stifle a smile, took her cue. "Oh, excuse me. Would either of you like some more spaghetti?"

"No."

"Not for me, thanks," Andrew answered at the same time. Why had he allowed Susan to goad him into losing his cool? He had always tried to be in control. That was what he wanted Chris to see—control—but just now what he saw was his dad being childish. Chris and Lisa must have thought their parents had taken leave of their senses.

Lisa continued the theatrics. "Let me get you some more garlic toast."

"No, really. I've had plenty." Andrew folded his napkin and pushed his plate aside. "You're a good cook, Lisa. Thanks for the meal."

"You're welcome."

"I think I'll go outside for some fresh air and have a smoke. If you'll excuse me...." He left with her chocolate eyes crackling behind him.

The four people at the table watched him disappear out the door before Susan commented, "He doesn't smoke."

Chris and Lisa burst out laughing at the same time. "Oh, Mom," Lisa said between giggles, "you should have heard the way you two were going at each other."

"Yeah, Mrs. Montgomery. I've never seen Daddy lose his cool like that before."

Lisa continued, "You've even made him forget he doesn't smoke anymore."

"Oh, I think he's smoking, all right," Chris added, "but not cigarettes."

"Steam was coming out the top of his head," Lisa added, drawing little circles over her head. "You were percolating pretty good, too, Mom."

"It's not funny." Susan wiped the red sauce from around Colton's mouth. "I'm going to bathe Colton and put him to bed. Looks like he's getting sleepy."

"Don't change the subject, Mom. We didn't mean anything. It's just funny to watch two people who obviously love each other being so pigheaded."

ANDREW STOOD on the plank walkway outside the apartment and listened to the sounds of Houston's traffic and insects. He reached into his pocket to get a cigarette before he remembered that he hadn't smoked in five years. The woman was causing him to lose his mind. He couldn't remember his own name half the time.

He wanted her for his wife more than he had ever wanted anything in his forty-two years. He had always gone after whatever he wanted, but this time his hands were tied. He felt helpless. He wanted to rant and rave at her and demand that she do something. But he couldn't. It had to be her decision. It wouldn't work otherwise. She had to want him badly enough to make a move. She had to want him as badly as he did her.

CHAPTER EIGHTEEN

MARCH HAD BLOSSOMED into April. Wrapped up in her pale pink windbreaker, Susan turned her face to the cool ocean breeze. It was soothing in its relentless caress of her skin and at the same time irritating as it tangled her hair into a mass of mocha curls. For several minutes, she watched the gray sea gulls scavenge for scraps along the murky water's edge before she went back to pacing the endless shell docks. She was like Andrew. They both hated waiting.

Waiting made her nervous. Today, she didn't need anything else to make her nervous. Just the thought of seeing Andrew again after that fiasco at Lisa's had her stomach in knots. He had slunk out that evening when she was putting Colton to bed, and she hadn't heard a word from him since then.

Not that she'd expected to. He had made it pretty plain that it was up to her to make the first move. And she had. Now she needed to tell him. She wasn't sure how he would respond. Would he be glad? Did he still love her, or had he decided that he didn't want her?

He had said once that he fantasized about her waiting for him on a Thursday morning when he flew into Freeport. Well, here she was pacing the docks at seven-fifteen. The sun had been up for only a short time. The helicopter wasn't allowed to fly until after sunup.

She'd watched it leave an hour ago, ferrying a new crew out to the platform, so it should be returning soon.

She couldn't have missed him unless he wasn't returning home today. That was a chance she'd had to take. Lisa had assured her that he had gone to work offshore this week. Surely his hitch hadn't been extended. If he didn't come soon, she feared she was going to change her mind and drive back to Corpus Christi.

No. No, she wasn't. Not yet.

She had come this far. She loved him too much to back out now. Andrew Bradley was the man she wanted above all else. The man she wanted for a husband. He brought stability and excitement into her life. What a strange combination, she thought, excitement and stability.

The buglelike call of the gulls almost drowned out the hum of the approaching helicopter. It was within a hundred yards of her before Susan noticed it. She bit her lip, hoping Andrew would be on it. The helicopter would have to make a couple of trips to complete the hitch change. Andrew could be on either of them.

She shielded her eyes from the reflecting glare of the sun. As the copter landed within the restricted chain-link fence, she could make out the men inside, though they were too far away for her to determine if one of them was Andrew.

While walking slowly toward the fence, she studied each man carefully as he alighted. The first one was too short. The second too fat. The third one had black hair. Her heart sank. She couldn't bear the tension any longer.

Threading her fingers through the holes of the chain-link fence, she held her breath as the remaining man jumped to the helipad. Even though his back was to her, he was the right height, the right build and his hair was a golden brown. It had to be him!

The man turned and saw her. He stopped, then started toward the gate, at first in a steady stroll. As she headed for the gate, he picked up his pace until he was almost running. So was she.

It was Andrew. She could make out every detail. The way his jeans fit. His red oil-company jacket. The offshore bag he clutched in one hand and the briefcase in the other. It was her love. He was close enough that she could see his smile as he sprinted the remaining few feet to her. He was smiling!

He dropped his bags at his feet and gathered her into his arms. "What are you doing here?"

"Can't you guess?"

"I'm afraid to."

"My divorce was final yesterday." Susan reluctantly pulled back so she could look into his eyes. They were a warm blue. Loving. She hadn't made a mistake. "I'm free to accept that proposal—if it's not too late, that is."

She watched the laugh lines gather around eyes that shone as he lowered his lips to hers. The kiss was all the answer she needed.

He whispered against her ear, "Let's go somewhere so we can be alone."

"Is that a proposition, Mr. Bradley?"

"You bet." He led her to his car.

The sun played peek-a-boo behind heavy gray spring clouds. With the exception of the occasional piercing shaft of light that shone like a spotlight on the beach, the overcast sky melted into the dark sand creating a monochrome backdrop for the two figures. Andrew and Susan walked hand in hand, content for a while to simply be together.

After a while, he turned her to face him and grinned. "Before you ask me to marry you I have to—"

"*Me* ask *you?*" Susan feigned horror.

"Sure. I asked you last time and you turned me down, so now it's your turn," he joked. "But I have to tell you that my job has changed. Starting the first of September, I'll be sent to Russia for up to three months at a time. It wouldn't be fair to—"

Susan held a finger to his lips as she looked into his eyes. "Andrew Bradley. Will you do me the honor of becoming my husband? I would like to be with you every minute of every day. But being with you some of the time is better than none at all. And just think of the fun we'll have during the months you're home."

"Yes, I'll marry you." He tilted her face upward to punctuate his words with kisses. "With all my heart . . . forever and ever."

"Oh, Andrew, my world has been turned upside down by you. I can't tell you how much I've missed you and . . . your quotes from the dumb book and all those other irritating things you do."

"Irritating, huh?" Andrew leaned back so he could see her face. "What irritates you the most?"

"Waiting, Andrew. Waiting."

He smiled into her eyes and took up her challenge. "No more waiting. Let's cut over this sand dune. It might be a little warmer out of the wind." He pulled her after him as they danced around clumps of grass and driftwood. They skirted marooned jellyfish and strands of seaweed in their mad dash for cover.

After clambering over the dune, Susan sank to her knees in its sheltering hollow. "Andrew, wait. I've got sand in my shoes."

"Wait? No way. Not after what you told me."

Susan scooped up a handful of cool sand and eyed Andrew threateningly. "You like sand?"

"You wouldn't dare," he warned, backing up when she rose and stalked him with the dirt. Suddenly he leaped toward her, grabbed her weapon-filled hand and twirled her into his arms. With her body firmly clamped against his, he looked down at her helpless expression. "You're just no match for me, Suzy-Q."

Giggling, Susan begged, "Let me go, Andrew," while sliding one leg between his to try to trip him. Something sharp pierced the sole of her foot. "Wait, Andrew. I've stepped on something." Reaching down she fingered the pieces of a fractured sand dollar. "Oh, look, I've broken a shell."

Andrew knelt beside her and picked up the pieces. "Have you heard the legend about the sand dollar?"

She shook her head as she looked at the fragile etchings on the delicate white shell.

Andrew fitted the edges of the broken halves on the ivory shell together. "See, these little slits on the side represent the wounds of Christ." He turned it upright and shook out the fragile cells hidden within. As he cupped the tiny pieces in the palm of his hand, his voice caught as he explained. "They look like doves, the doves of goodwill and peace and all that stuff."

Susan smiled into his eyes. "How wonderful. That's what we'll have, Andrew. Goodwill and peace. And love."

Andrew's expression clouded as he dropped the remnants of the shell onto the sand before pulling her body against his again. "I don't ever want to let you go, Susan. Never again, for the rest of our lives."

Her heart seemed to stop beating during the eternity it took for his mouth to find hers. Willing and yielding, she pressed herself against his body, eager to feel his warmth against her. He slid his hands down to the curves of her buttocks and brought her even closer. Feeling his need, she settled against him, wanting him more than she ever had.

Andrew slid a hand up her back, steadying her trembling body while he searched for the zipper of her pink sweat suit. As he slid it downward, he exposed her flesh to the cool ocean mist and to his warm lips. Susan leaned back against the firm hand implanted in the small of her back and arched toward his kisses. Threading her fingers through his hair, she moaned as his mouth sought her breasts.

Grasping the elastic waistband of her sweatpants, he tugged them over the satin-smooth skin of her thighs. She shivered from the cold and from desire as the cotton puddled around her ankles, leaving her legs and buttocks exposed to his firm, exploring hands.

"Kick 'em off," Andrew commanded before rising to claim her mouth again.

Stepping out of her pants, Susan grappled with the front of his shirt. Her fingers were clumsy with anticipation as they fumbled with the buttons. When the shirt was finally free, she slid it off his shoulders, wanting to savor every inch of him as it came into view. She traced the jagged line of the faint scar snaking across his chest and through the dark mat of hair that disappeared into his jeans. The taut skin burned under her fingertips as she raised her eyes to meet his.

"I love you... I love you... I love you," she whispered. Pressed against his hot flesh, she drank in his scent. He smelled faintly of after-shave and soap. She wound her fingers through the hairs on his chest. Ridges of muscle rippled beneath the palm of her hand.

Andrew pressed her naked body hard against him as he sought her lips once more. It wasn't enough. She wanted more. As the shaft of sunlight skimmed over the sand toward them, Susan reached upward, opening her arms in welcome. Andrew kneeled down in the cool sand beside her, their eyes consummating their love even before Susan pulled him to her. His body sheltered hers from the increasing wind. As the ocean waves crashed only yards from them, she became lost in the eddy of passion. Just as she thought she'd die from her need, Andrew covered her body with his. The world consisted of them.

Together.

Forever.

EPILOGUE

"WELL, HOW WAS THE WEDDING?" Bertha asked, still slightly miffed that she hadn't been invited.

Seeing as how it had been at my house, I had to soothe her feelings. "Only their immediate family, me and my Betsy were there. Andrew didn't want a big to-do. Still, it was the best little wedding you ever saw," I explained to my quilting club. "I was the matron of honor, you know."

"What kind of ring did he give her?" Bertha asked.

"They exchanged identical gold bands. Susan didn't want a diamond."

"Why, I never," muttered Bertha. "Whoever doesn't want a diamond?"

Virginia raised an eyebrow. "I, too, wanted a simple gold band."

Bertha didn't say anything else, knowing that Virginia could have afforded a diamond ring for every finger.

"He also gave her a gold sand-dollar pendant. Supposedly it has some special significance for them."

Virginia smiled and whispered, "Peace and goodwill."

We all nodded our heads in agreement.

"Are they living across from you?" asked Era.

"Until school's out. Then they're going to move to Andrew's house in Houston. He thought he was being assigned overseas, but another man took early retirement or something. So Andrew's now in charge of a multiproduction unit here in the gulf." I was so proud of him, but I couldn't help sighing, knowing how much I'd miss them.

"Thank goodness. A newly married couple needs to be together," Virginia offered.

"That's what I always told you," Bertha assured us, as if the whole thing had been her idea. "It's going to be boring around here for a while. I guess we'll have to go back to watching the soap operas to spark up our lives, unless... Say, Era, you still hunting for a man?"

My Valentine 1994

Celebrate the most romantic day of the year with
MY VALENTINE 1994
a collection of original stories, written by
four of Harlequin's most popular authors...

**MARGOT DALTON
MURIEL JENSEN
MARISA CARROLL
KAREN YOUNG**

*Available in February, wherever
Harlequin Books are sold.*

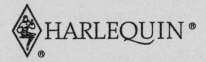

HARLEQUIN ®

VAL94

Relive the romance...
Harlequin® is proud to bring you

by Request™

A new collection of three complete novels every
month. By the most requested authors, featuring
the most requested themes.

Available in January:

WESTERN
LOVING

They're ranchers, horse trainers, cowboys...
They're willing to risk their lives.
But are they willing to risk their hearts?

Three complete novels in one special collection:

RISKY PLEASURE by JoAnn Ross
VOWS OF THE HEART by Susan Fox
BY SPECIAL REQUEST by Barbara Kaye

Available wherever Harlequin books are sold.

**Where do you find hot Texas nights, smooth Texas charm
and dangerously sexy cowboys?**

NEW WAY TO FLY
by Margot Dalton

New Look—Texas Style!

Rancher Brock Munroe is smitten with Amanda Walker. But he hates
what she does for a living. Amanda is a personal shopper. To Brock it's
a ridiculous career—dressing people who have more money than sense.
Still, Brock can't quite figure this lady out. It seems that with Amanda
what you see is much less than what you get.

CRYSTAL CREEK reverberates with the exciting rhythm of Texas.
Each story features the rugged individuals who live and love in the
Lone Star state. And each one ends with the same invitation...

Y'ALL COME BACK...REAL SOON!

Don't miss *NEW WAY TO FLY* by Margot Dalton
Available in January wherever Harlequin Books are sold.

When the only time you have for yourself is…

STOLEN moments ™

Christmas is such a busy time—with shopping, decorating, writing cards, trimming trees, wrapping gifts....

When you do have a few *stolen moments* to call your own, treat yourself to a brand-new *short* novel. Relax with one of our Stocking Stuffers— or with all six!

Each STOLEN MOMENTS title is a complete and original contemporary romance that's the perfect length for the busy woman of the nineties! Especially at Christmas…

And they make perfect **stocking stuffers,** too! (For your mother, grandmother, daughters, friends, co-workers, neighbors, aunts, cousins—all the other women in your life!)

Look for the STOLEN MOMENTS display in December

STOCKING STUFFERS:

HIS MISTRESS Carrie Alexander
DANIEL'S DECEPTION Marie DeWitt
SNOW ANGEL Isolde Evans
THE FAMILY MAN Danielle Kelly
THE LONE WOLF Ellen Rogers
MONTANA CHRISTMAS Lynn Russell

HSM2

 **WORLDWIDE LIBRARY**

HARLEQUIN SUPERROMANCE ®

Women Who Dare will continue with more exciting stories,
beginning in May 1994 with

THE PRINCESS AND THE PAUPER by Tracy Hughes.

And if you missed any titles in 1993
here's your chance to order them:

Harlequin Superromance®—Women Who Dare

(limited quantities available on certain titles)

| TOTAL AMOUNT | $ |
| POSTAGE & HANDLING | $ |

($1.00 for one book, 50¢ for each additional)

| APPLICABLE TAXES* | $ _____ |
| TOTAL PAYABLE | $ _____ |

(check or money order—please do not send cash)

To order, complete this form and send it, along with a check or money order for the
total above, payable to Harlequin Books, to: *In the U.S.*: 3010 Walden Avenue,
P.O. Box 9047, Buffalo, NY 14269-9047; *In Canada*: P.O. Box 613, Fort Erie, Ontario,
L2A 5X3.

Name: _____

Address: _____ City: _____

State/Prov.: _____ Zip/Postal Code: _____

*New York residents remit applicable sales taxes.
Canadian residents remit applicable GST and provincial taxes.

WWD-FINR